Luke Cassidy

IRON ANNIE

Luke Cassidy is a writer from Dundalk, Ireland.
Iron Annie is his first novel.

IRON ANNIE

IRON ANNIE

LUKE CASSIDY

VINTAGE CRIME / BLACK LIZARD

VINTAGE BOOKS

A DIVISION OF PENGUIN RANDOM HOUSE LLC

NEW YORK

FIRST VINTAGE CRIME / BLACK LIZARD EDITION, JANUARY 2022

Copyright © 2021 by Luke Cassidy

The Cataloging-in-Publication Data is on file at the Library of Congress.

Vintage Crime / Black Lizard Trade Paperback ISBN: 978-0-593-31481-4
eBook ISBN: 978-0-593-31482-1

www.vintagebooks.com

Printed in the United States of America
1st Printing

Yeah, I'm not doing that.

CONTENTS

IRON ANNIE

WAIT TIL I TELL YE

THE SWELL'A THE NIGHT

Bakin deep in the swell'a the night she was, sat there sittin through the barrels'a shite comin spewin out'a yon lad's mouth. Tryinta impress her he was. T'impress *her*. Can y'imagine yon? Ar Annie n'all? The fuckin Iron Ann.

See, she'd been in the Town three months by then—chompin at the bit, rarinta do a job by herself. I wantedta give her somethin simpleta start with. Easy prey, the teeth on her sure.

Yon buck. So sure'a his own charm he didn see it comin, the slap on the side'a the head. Ach no, she didn hit him like. Much smarter than that, ar Annie, much smoother. *As if.* An her out collectin pennies for the poor an marchin agin the war, an it not even happenin round here anymore.

Naw, she juss lifted his bag an him in the toilet. Had his fancy computer an a bunch'a other kit, his wallet n'all. Sure the bag was near worth more than anythin he had in it.

Yon fuckin peacock prick, down from Dublin, big fuckin smoke. I caught up with him down by Defenders', me an big Shamey Hughes. We were only watchin out for her, see. Said

I wouldn interfere, I promised her. But it was her first solo flight, I wasn gonna leave her all on her own either.

"I hear you've still got the accent," he saysta me when I call him out, an him only two years out'a the Town, but now he's talkin like a proper D4 dub. Cunt.

See, this lad thought himself the big man now that he'd gone an made a name for himself below in the big smoke. Out makin a big noise in all the street an givin people grief, askin after Annie.

She shouldn'a tauld him her real name. The fuck was she thinkin? Anythin would'a done. Calypso. The fuck. Whatever.

After that Annie disappeared for a while, went on one'a her wee turns. She'd wantedta handle it soft she said, to talk her way out'a it. An with her it might'a worked haigh.

But fuck it sure. We don't pardon pigs round here, we cut their throats.

THIS'LL SOUND
FUNNY, BUT

JELENA

That was deadly that time when Annie's pal Jelena cameta visit. Polish. Cept I don't think she was Polish, cause she was from Serbia an that might be someplace else. But sure it's all the same anyway. Usedta be the same fuckin country a few years back didn it?

That was some craic I'll tell ye, the three'a us in bed together. Now, it wasn like that, not exactly, juss like . . . Almost that, cause we all wanted it, but Annie kinda didn want it. She wanted it too but she said it'd be weird an yer wan Jelena bein an auld friend an that. Still n'all, she didn do nathin when ar Jelena reached her hand acrossta me, which wasn even hard, cause the bed's not big. An I knew Annie was only pretendinta be asleep, cause her breathin changed cause she liked it too, she liked that it was happenin, an she liked that she was there. I liked that she was there too. Some craic. That Jelena had some way with her hands. Juss dove in an wriggled bowt like her fingers were a spoon lookinta worry out the best bit'a the tub'a ice cream, juss that one special bit y'know, all fudge or somethin tasty. Fuckin deadly.

———

The mornin after, she brought us up a pot'a coffee, Jelena did. Well, it wasn a pot actually, it was somethin called a *džezva*, a funny-shaped yoke that was wide at the bottom an narrow at the top, made'a copper, with all designs an that on the side. She got it in Bosnia, she said. Brought it as a present for Annie. Looked dead nice. Annie seemedta really like it too, reminded her'a th'auld times. *Džezva*. Took me all morninta learn that one. The coffee was shite n'all, cause it had the bits still in it, an they got caught in yer teeth. She could'a juss used instant sure, but naw, she wanted t'use this special coffee. *Shite*. She said that's how people drank it in Serbia, an Bosnia too, an I didn say nathin cause I thought if I did she wouldn do that thing again, th'ice-cream thing. Cause I know Polish people are pretty poor, I mean why else would they come to a shithole like this an do shite jobs, an why would they drink shite coffee? So I didn tell her the coffee was shite. But she didn do th'ice-cream thing again, even though I was nice an learnedta say *džezva*, so I guess it was juss a one-time thing.

Still, it was deadly havin her there an that, cause she was dead sound an Annie was dead happy cause they kept talkin bowt th'auld times, college times, in Glasgow n'all. Must'a been good times, which made me a bit sad cause she didn know me in th'auld times an she'd never even beenta Dundalk back then. But still, I was happy cause she was happy.

CHIP

Dundalk. The fuckin Town. Round here, that's what ye call it, cause yer either part'a the Town, or yer not. Ye don't needta be born here or nathin, ye juss needta be there long enough that the place knows ye. I'm a good example'a that, cause I'm from Mullaghbawn. Now, Mullaghbawn's juss over the road, across the border like. But we've another way'a talkin there, so I don't even sound so much like I'm *from* the Town, but now I don't sound like I'm from Mullaghbawn either for bein so long gone. There's loads'a people like that, ye wouldn believe it, cause the Town's a bitofa hole—but there's people from everywhere. Not juss Polish an Chinese like, but French an Australians an even folk from Sligo n'all sorts'a places. Now, most'a them only came in the last couple'a years, for the work an that, but still, it's dead funny when ye hear a Frenchie or a Connaughtman talkin with a bitofa Dundalk accent.

The Town's not like other places though. Dundalk's alive. The Town remembers. Knows howta hauld a grudge.

Like this one feen, I remember from way back, when

I'd juss movedta the Town, bowt ten year ago now. Chip we called him, cause he had a big fuckin chip on his shoulder, an he wore it like a badge'a honour. Now, most folk don't really like it when ye point out the chips on their shoulders, even when they know rightly that they have one. But Chip, he was a proud fucker, an a real nasty bit'a work. The kind who spent his summers tearin wings off flies an shite like that when we was a wee lad. Pure vicious like.

He usedta bully all the smalltimers, too. I was juss startin out like, dealin hash out'a a schoolbag an that—back when there was hash, before cheap weed flooded the country. There was this lad, Fahey, from over in Monaghan somewhere. Had one'a them big broad mucksavage accents they have over there, but he was dead sound. Usedta sell speed, mostly to kids for their exams—to help them study an that. Daecent skin like. Definitely didn deserve havin his dog done in, a lovely wee dog it was, some kindofa mongrel, but dead cute. Chip set it on fire—we all knew it was him. An that jussta scare the lad out the game. But in fairness, no space for soft hearts like him so there's not. With me it was different, me bein a woman an that—he'd never have hit me say, but he did other things. Took liberties, cause the cunt was big, an nasty, an I wasn well set up in the Town yet. I mean, like, me purse wasn th'only thing he shoved his paw inta. Most'a the lads bowt're daecent enough that way, but this cunt juss took things too far, throwin his weight around. He had *notions*. Actin all big time an that. They say *fake it til ye make it*, but that's juss bollix sure. Round here if ye fake it yer found out in bowt two seconds flat, the small size'a the place.

He had some contact or other—a lad in Athlone, a big

coke man, supplied all the midlands. Fuckin Athlone'a all places. Chip, the fuckin thick, he flooded the Town with coke, real cheap like, tryinta drive other suppliers out'a business. Like Ryanair or some shite. But juss like Ryanair, he ended up pissin everyone off. It wasn juss the dealers, this shite from Athlone was toxic. I mean real bad, cut with all kinds'a crap.

One weekend four kids got tookta hospital. Two'a them died. Sixteen an seventeen. Bad craic that. An everyone knew it was Chip—teenagers can't afford proper coke sure. The Rat King paid him a visit, tauld himta cut it out. An when the Rat King turns up with his crew, ye fuckin listen. Man's royalty after all.

Prick should'a listened, but naw. Mulpin. Two weeks later, two more kids got draggedta hospital, an sure Dundalk hospital is pure cat, hopeless like.

There was a meetin at Smokey Quigley's. Smokey's was sacred—safe ground. Everyone could get together there an have a civil word see, be they a gard or a gouger, on the run or juss tryinta do business. All the main players in the Town would get together there now an then, jussta keep things runnin smooth, a tradition that went way back. It was also juss a great spot for a pint, or for a session th'odd time.

I wasn usually at them meetins yet, me bein a smalltimer back then, but they invited me, y'know, cause'a what happened. I was readyta brush it under the carpet like, try an forget bowt it but Smokey said it was serious. I was surprised like, that they'd listenta me, them all bein men, besides Smokey. But I think it was *cause'a* her that they did, cause'a the sway she had in the place. She was pure bawdy, I'd never seen her like that before, nor after, the jowls on her quiverin with rage—on

account'a them teenagers. Like a judge, full'a some righteous
anger, an yeah, she was right to have it. Everyone knew, everyone listened. See, Smokey's normally so cool, so calm, seein
her like that was a shock. She's a fair sizeofa woman, y'know,
an with that shock'a red hair on her, she looked pure terrifyin
so she did, like a war-queen, like she'd'a murdered the wee
cunt then an there if she could'a, juss plain ripped his head off.

"I'm not having this. Not in Dundalk. Not in my Town
hey. The humpy wee bastard!"

Finally, Paddy, *the Commander* as he likesta be called even
though no-one calls him that, he stood up. Big heavy-set
awkward-lookin baldie lad, he knocked over his pint on the
way up—spa. Kinda ruined the whole soldierly effect he was
goin for. Cleared his throat an starts off on some fuckin spiel
bowt *the cause*. That's where I tuned out. But th'upshot was the
RA were finally gonna do their job.

Now, Paddy, the local ringleader'a the fake RA-heads—
the "*Real*" IRA or whatever they liketa call themselves, he's a
dealer himself so it's pretty funny him actin like a vigilante an
that. Half'a them ones're at it. They deal what *they* say is clean,
an come down hard on all the honest drug dealers when they
feel like it. I juss can't stomach all that *for the cause* shite-talkin
that does go on. Still, it was good someone took care'a yon
cunt Chip an his toxic coke. Dead teenagers is bad craic so it
is. Dead scumbag dealers? Not so much.

That's how the Town works. Makes its own kinda balance,
keeps things tickin along without attractin too much attention. A'course people know we're a bit mad—but they need
that. The Town's like a safety valve for the rest'a the country.
We're a bit wired so they can act proper, like Ireland's finally a

normal country or somethin, an then still get fucked on yokes
at the weekend. It's good for them sure. But ye wouldn believe
the things that do be goin on round here. I don't know if Annie
ever fully appreciated the Town in that way, its importance in
the big picture like.

THE CHICKEN AN THE MOTH

Gettinta know Annie was like, well, y'know yon buck, the poor feen who pushes the big rock up the hill again an again gettin nowhere every time he got somewhere. Spillin over th'edge inta nathin.

Like a chicken scratchin at that same patch'a dirt, all bewildered by the mere fact'a *bein* a chicken, juss scratch-scratch-scratch until th'urge comes over ye to lay a fuckin egg an even *that* ye don't know a fuck why yer doin it, like the moth goin round an round the lamp that's left on, juss smashin inta it brushin an burnin all night until it dies.

For a full year me mind was juss a stupid scratchy chicken, a kamikaze moth, scratchin an bumpin an burnin round Annie. An I still think'a her every day, several times a day. Usedta consume me, usedta be all I thought bowt, sittin there scratchin me hands far past blood an feelin sorry for meself. Pure waste'a time though. Annie, she wasted everyone's time, but in a way where ye were mostly happyta have it wasted. Mostly.

Like that time I sent her upstairs at the Store. Jussta drop off a bag'a yokesta some feen who was sellin them that night upstairs where they play the music an that. I had Shamey Hughes an his pal Johnny in the car too, but I didn wanna send them in sure, cause they're both musicians, they practically live in Spirit Store. Best pub in Town for the music, the gigs n'all. Still, I didn wanna waste time so I tauld them not to go. I sent Annie.

Ten minutes later, we're still there. She's not answerin her phone so I send Johnny up, tellin him *strictly* jussta grab her an get out. I'm not worried or nathin, juss startinta get pisst off.

Yon buck's ten minutes gone, an I start stewin when Shamey leans forward inta the gap between meself an the passenger seat.

"Here, Aoife," he saysta me, "don't be worried, they're probably juss havin the craic with someone so th'are."

I look back an he's givin me one'a them big smiles he does, the big Shamey smiles that only he can do. Dunno what it is, but there's juss some strange softness bowt him, his dirty blond hair, baby blue eyes—looks like he couldn hurt a fly, an him a massive fucker. Straight away it was like the pot's been took off the boil. The nasty chest tightness's loosened a bit, not gone like, juss looser an warmer. I feel a little further away from the light.

Anyway, he doesn move back but juss stays there, jussta cheer me up. I really appreciated that, cause that's the way it is with Shamey. I think it's cause he's dead good at music—he juss feels ye.

"Here, what's the craic with Annie an yerself anyway?" he saysta me.

I really wasn expectin that one. Now, I've known Shamey longer than anyone in the Town, I know him from back home even. He's like a brother or somethin. He usedta be dead good friends with my brother too, before. Shamey's kinda like what

I think Liam would'a turned out to be, proper sound. Cept even a sound brother can probably be a pain in the hole sometimes. Still, I trust him, I mean I love the fucker.

Anyway, I saysta him that it's not like himta be such a spa but he keeps at it.

"Is it cause we're both women that ye think I can't be serious bowt her is that it? Ye think there's needsta be a dick knockin round somewhere for it to be real? Ye ham child."

"C'mon now, y'know that's not it. In a way, I'm dead happy for ye. Really. I'm juss sayin."

I ask him what he means by that.

"Look, yer the smartest person I know. Surely ye see that she's juss out for herself like."

The tight starts wrappin back around me chest an I ask him what he's on bowt.

"Well, I mean, I like Annie an that, really. I do. I don't agree with the Rat King bowt her. Y'know all that *Iron Annie* craic he's always bangin on bowt. Lad's overthinkin things. I don't think there's anythin wrong with her, not really, I juss think she's out for herself in a normal kindofa way. Fair enough like, loads'a folk are."

I tauld himta gimme an example. Scratchin away at me hands I was, I could feel them startinta bleed there where the fingers meet the nails, like the chicken I was, juss scratch-scratch-scratch.

"That time, the Mick Moore job. Ye think she really juss forgot to tell ye? She juss didn want ye to know, an *you* were th'one introduced herta Mick. An don't forget bowt what went down at Smokey's . . ."

"No-one fuckin knows what went down at Smokey's!"

Like I said, even sound brothers can be a pain in the hole. It's pure ignorance like, assumin the worst'a someone cause they're from elsewhere.

"No-one knows for sure, fair enough. But all the same, it's a bit rich, imaginin that it was juss an accident, the gards gettin evidence like that so fuckin brazen that even they couldn look th'other way cause sure wasn it the PSNI pushin themta raid the joint from up Narth. How d'ye think *they* could'a known bowt it? Don't forget that Annie's from East Belfast."

"I fuckin know where she's from!"

"Alright. Grand. I'm juss sayin. Ye juss gotta tryta look at things with a clear head. All I'm sayin."

By then the tight'a me chest was like barbed wire all wrapped round me an gettin tighter with each word. Me mind, juss a thousand flappy moths all pressed up agin the filament, sizzlin so they were, but refusinta budge, an no light gettin out t'all, not a bit, juss dusty shiftin shadows. The shapes moths scream when they're hurlin themselves all kamikaze at the light, so drunk on the bright'a it they don't even feel the burn.

I can't answer. I mean I can't argue, I don't know what to say. So I juss send Shamey upta see what the fuck's goin on in there.

I'm alone then, an I open the door cause it feels dead hot in the car. But that doesn help. I'm lookin out on the water down at the dock, an there's swans an the moon n'all that shite an I should be thinkin it's dead nice an that but I juss feel sick. A gaggle'a teenage girls stumble out'a a taxi squealin like so many *piglets*. They look like piglets too, all pink an plump. Piglets with lipstick. Me mind's pure vicious juss then.

Me phone buzzes. It's Shamey.

Shamey: U gotta see this. C'mon up.
Me: Right. Comin.

The fuck else am I meant to do sure?

Upstairs I see Annie up onstage. Singin. The fuck like? An she's a beautiful singer, but I never heard her sing before, never. Didn know she was really inta music. I feel kinda scared, cause it's like I don't know her but I'm also juss totally stilled by the beauty'a it. I think I knew then that I loved her, I mean I admitted it, an I didn even care that there was loads I didn know bowt her.

Shamey comes upta me an puts his arm round me, real warm like, an I lean inta it. It's real nice when Shamey hugs ye, ye feel dead safe an that so ye do.

"I'm sorry bowt before. Bowt what I said. I dunno how Smokey got stung. No-one does, sure. I'm sorry."

"I'd say Smokey knows, somehow," I reply, noddin so he knows we're good. He skulls half his pint an shoots me a creamy stout smile before shovin me the glass to take a gouge out'a.

Shamey's different from other men in that way. He's ableta say sorry. It's like a superpower so it is, that an his smile.

Juss then Annie sees me an she smiles at me too, a lovely big smile, juss for me. An I start to feel OK, the moths, they drop off. They don't fly away, they're still circlin but at least they're not gettin burnt anymore. I still don't know a fuck how she ended up on stage. But I don't need to.

HERE'S THE CRAIC

THE BIG JOB

Rovin round the same three streets'a the Town, sorta stuck in a rut I was round then. I was havin a bitofa hard time in me head, not cause'a anythin particular that happened or that, juss loads'a these little things like. Like when Annie'd say somethinta me first thing in the mornin or whenever we'd get up, somethin like *you look really cute just after you've been cryin*, with a sortofa smile like I should do it more often or somethin. Usually I'd juss take out me phone an make like I was on Tinder or somethin, jussta keep meself from scratchin at me hands. I was pretty shite at Tinder, cause I never knew what to say. The guys on Tinder are pigs, anyway, an the women ye find on it round here tendta be too serious or juss tryinta tee up threesomes for their fellas. Fuckin see-through, that craic.

With Annie I had the feelin'a havin her an not havin her too, like she was there an that, like I knew we were together but I didn always have the feelin'a bein together. Probably juss cause'a the whole open an free craic. It was mostly her that used it, an mostly I didn care that much. I mean when things were good, they were really, really good, but when they were bad . . . Fuck me. I know that couples that fight tendta have stronger relationships, I mean that's what she'd say after we'd have a row, cause I usually got dead upset. I think she was tryinta make me feel better. It was always these mad highs an lows. It's like with sex or chemistry or that. Like th'engine'a yer car, cept instead'a diesel an air, it's burnin yer body, an yer time. An it's always burnin away, juss that when it's goin well ye don't hardly notice it t'all but when it's goin bad yer chokin on the fumes'a yer own frustration.

It was around then that I got the call from the Rat King. Somethin was up.

Now, the Rat King an me, we go way back. Some lad so he is. Rat King is like the king'a the gypsies, cept he's not. I'm not even sure how that works like, if there even *is* a king'a the gypsies or if that's juss some bollix settled people made up for the movies. Most travellers I know, I can't imagine them bendin their knees. Naw, the Rat, he's pretty upfront bowt bein a pretender but the lad still gets royal respect. He says sometimes pretenders like him end up makin somethin'a themselves, but mostly they're pure sloppy an get smothered in their sleep, an sure, no-one cares cause settled folk don't care bowt travellers, they'd love them all to be smothered in their sleep, they'd love themta juss go away cept they won't. So most settled folk are dead frustrated cause they haveta call them *the Travelling Community* even though they're juss thinkin *scum*.

I like travellers though. Specially the Rat King. Funny fucker. Got a great sense'a humour bowt bein smothered in his sleep, too. Says they'll never get him cause he's an insomniac.

I go roundta see him, an he shows me this big secret'a his. The buck is drinkin tea. Tea if ye don't mind. Pours me a cup, biscuits n'all. He even feeds oneta his rat. Yeah. The fucker's got a pet rat, cept it's no pet-shop rat, it's a proper rat, off the streets like. The feen takes it round with him everywhere, in his coat pocket an that. He's makin small talk, strokin yon disgustin thing an drinkin tea. I've no patience for it but.

"So what's the craic? Y'ask me round here, it sounded dead important n'all. Spit it out like."

"Can we not enjoy a civil cup'a tea, ha?"

"Naw, it's not that. I'm juss. Like, it sounded important on the phone."

"It fuckin is," he saysta me, this dead flat look on his face, but I can tell that's juss his control.

Turns out the fucker's gone an swiped ten kilos'a coke. Ten fuckin kilos! Robbed it from some other crowd he had a boneta pick with below in Meath. But still, he said he didn want them knowin it was him did it, cause if they found out they wouldn care bowt bein discreet an that, he'd turn the Town inta a battlefield.

The stuff was pretty much pure—we tried a bit on top'a the tea an bickies. Sweet Jaysis, I never had anythin like it. *Uncut.* He fixes this gaze on me, dead serious like.

"Now, see for talkin's sake, if you shift this for me, I'd let ye keep half the cash."

"Fuck away off. Yer not serious. Are ye? That's . . . I dunno how much money that is. Fuckin loads. More wedge than either'a us've ever seen. Much more."

"Aye, an that's why I'm askin *you* to shift it. I need this moved, an real quiet like. No-one can know it came from me. So say nathin, specially not to Annie, right?"

I look at him for a second. Sometimes it's hardta keep a straight face talkinta the Rat King, cause he's always jokin or makin some weird face or playin with his nasty rat. But this time he's dead serious. An I don't really needta think bowt it much. See, the Rat King an me, we've seen what's inside each other's bones. Still, I didn like him singlin out Annie like that.

I said I'll do it, I'll shift it, but I needed time. I neededta think. Gettin rid'a ten kilos'a pure driven snow without makin any noise? Easier said than done.

THE FIRST NIGHT

Swayin through a thousand thoughts like swimmin in some kinda soup, like when yer drunk an things are all jaggin an that. Folk say yer head spins, but it doesn, does it? Juss clips away in a jagged kindofa way, like yer sight was an auld scratched CD, skippin but always on the same spot. Well, this was like that, but different, cause it wasn me sight that was jaggin, but me thoughts. From the sheer shock'a what I saw.

I'm talkin bowt the first night I spent with Annie. Cept there's somethin I forgot to say. Well, lots actually. Like bowt that bein the first time I slept with a beor. Cept I didn know she was a woman when we started. Yeah. Now, I know this sounds weird, but she was dressed like a man, see, an she'd introduced herself as *Andrew*, not Annie. I tell ye, she really looked like a man, too, a fuckin gorgeous man. Had this wee moustache n'all, but it was a fuckin fake. Remember thinkin it looked weird, that moustache, but sure moustaches always look weird. In fairness, I'd been on the drink, but not that bad like. Not like how I get sometimes. Could happen t'anyone.

Where was I anyway? Aye, Annie's pussy—I wasn ready

for that. She dropped her pants, an I was expectin, well, dick. I did feel a bit weird. Not angry or that, cause he, I mean *she'd* already gone down on me, an fuck me, I never came like that before in me life. Three times I came. An that was juss her idea'a foreplay, juss with her tongue an two little fingers, sweet slippery magic. Pure class. I thought men weren capable'a doin anythin like that. Then I realised that, yeah, they're not.

She sees me head-swimmin an that, an she sits down beside me. Lookin round, it made a bit more sense. Didn look like a feen's room. Too many bewks for a start. But it didn look like a beor's room neither. Nathin girly bowt it t'all. Now that I think bowt it, that's juss like Annie. Fuckin impossibleta pin her down haigh.

Here she was sittin next t'me on the bed, a gorgeous man without a dick, or rather, with a pussy. I fuckin knew it like, I knew there was somethin weird goin on. I mean I *wish* I knew it. Felt like a right spa then.

I hadn said nathin so she was there tryinta figure me out, to read me. Annie loves readin people, as much as she likes readin bewks. Maybe more.

"I'm sorry," she says, "I've shocked you. I didn't mean that. But I was sure you knew. I thought you were just playing along with me, you know? I would have told you otherwise."

Annie, she has another way'a talkin. Dead proper like, like someone off telly. British telly but. Ye wouldn think she's from the Narth. Ye wouldn know where she's from.

With her sittin beside me, I have her smell all down me spine. In me skin. It was all I could breathe. An it was excitin me, different from how a lad does, though in fairness I hadn really noticed that before even if I wish I could say I had. The smell though. I start to get that warm feelin, all frantic at the bottom'a me belly, an me chest heavin, without me even thinkin much bowt it, cept when she puts her arm round me, which only makes things worse.

"You're really lovely. I didn't mean to shock you. I just feel really, well, I feel really nice with you. I thought you were feeling the same. I thought you knew."

I think I tauld herta shut up, an we went at it again. Felt like the first time but. Cause this time, this time I knew. I knew she was a beor.

An it was fuckin deadly. I'd been with plenty'a lads, but there'd always been somethin lackin. Feens are mostly juss interested in themselves, see. That's when they think sex ends, when *they* finish. With Annie, it was waves'a orgasms I had, one after th'other. Juss like the sea so they were, rhythmic, regular, an strong. Felt like I might drown in them, gaspin for air I was, but in a good way. Scary good. Nathin like bein with a man, but much better, all smooth an sweet an stiff fingers findin exactly the right places like they were in cahoots. An patient. Pure class.

"The official record for the female orgasm is one hundred and thirty-four in an hour. I want to beat that."

"Who the fuck's countin?" I says.

"I'm just saying. No man's ever going to give you that."

"True, but that doesn explain the crossdressin bit, if ye didn mean it, trickin me. Did ye?"

"No! Not at all. No, that's different. It's like, well, research. Learning, I guess. About men. And myself. About what I'm like when I'm a man."

"The fuck're y'on bowt?"

She rolled her eyes at me. Annie loves rollin her eyes.

"It's like this. We're given roles, right? Like actors. Male roles, and female roles. Those are usually the shitty, two dimensional ones—like at the Oscars. But what if we're just people? What if I'm just a person, and there's this big kind of conspiracy, but an unconscious one, telling me that I'm a woman and that's what I need to be and I need to *act* like a woman *all* the time. And I *like* being a woman. I mean I like my body, but I don't always like what being a woman *means*. I wanted to understand this whole thing better. I wanted to understand men, too, and what I'm like when I'm a man, and maybe why they treat women the way they do. Still don't get that bit to be honest. So, sometimes I'm a man. Sometimes I'm a woman. And I like it. It feels good. Right, somehow. It makes me stronger."

Sayin this she rolls over an kisses me nipple. Sent a slice'a electric all through me, I'll tell ye.

"My name's Annie, by the way."

I'm bowt to say somethin thick like *niceta meet ye*, when me head starts goin again, but different this time. Better.

Pure class.

DISCIPLININ THE BUCK

Hoofin all the shite out me sight so I can see through me mind's eye, cause like, if a mind's got an eye it must be ableta see, even if mine's usually all kinda full'a all the stuff happenin all round like some kinda all-seein eye that can't focus on fuck all. Still, when I get mad everythin's hoofed out, an yon eye's all squinty. Real tight, nathin but a line, a laser beam like, from me to the thing annoyin me. A good thing too. The beatin in me chest, different from that nasty nervous rattle I do get them other times. Naw, this was steady. Determined. Boomin. A war drum. Pure ragin I was that time when the Buck Maguire lifted a load'a gear on me.

Yon wee prick felt like he had every right cause his big cuz—*The* Maguire—was a big deal on the scene an that. He did fuck. Cunt was so sure'a himself he didn even care bowt bein subtle n'all. An with a prick like that, there's nathin elseta do but be as subtle as a brick in the face right back at him. An him such a wee smalltime skitterofa shite, but all shrouded in pride, him bein from the Town. Empty pride, but he felt it still seein as to him we was juss blow-ins sure. *His* turf, that's what he thought it was, so he thought he could do whatever he wanted, like the Town itself'd protect him. But Dundalk's not that kinda town, couldn give two shites where yer from really, it's what's at the bottom'a yer bones that counts. Annie once said the Town was like one'a th'auld Greek gods. *Full of spirit and mysterious power but fundamentally unconcerned with human affairs, beyond how they amuse them.* Seems bowt right. Annie had this notion how it was the perfect settin for a Greek tragedy, all brutal an bloody an senseless. Sure it often enough is haigh. In any way, yon prick the Buck Maguire had it comin so he did.

He was th'only one who could'a known we had the pills, cause see his cousin sent him as a delivery boy. Pure case'a base jealousy that, cause *The* Maguire had trusted me with that job an not him. He didn like that. Reminded him he was only a smalltime shite an I wasn. The Buck Maguire didn like that. An a'course he hated losin out to a woman so he did. Most guys do. Fuckin spas.

Anyway, I calls up Shamey Hughes an tells himta get the fuck over an to bring his pal Johnny with him. He's smaller than Shamey but bowt a hundred times more aggressive, which is good, cause Shamey's dead protective when his pals are on the line. So I thought it best to bring the wee jennet. Annie, she got herself dressed up like she was goin on a night out—always does at times like them.

We jumped in Shamey's yoke, a wee souped-up Beamer, auld but flashy an fast as fuck. Kinda didn suit him that car, but suited ar needs at that moment. This shit was *punitive*, as Annie said. Neededta be.

Landed up at his place up in Muirhevnamor. Real quiet

it was, it bein a Sunday afternoon an that. We didn care. Ye
haveta be a bit brazen sometimes. No fuckin bother haigh.

Shamey keeps a sledge in his boot for things like this.
Resourceful fella. I took it to the door. Hadta be me sure. We
were inside in two seconds. The Buck's in the front room with
some young one an one'a his scumbag pals. Wee Johnny jumps
the scumbag pal but the Buck pulls a fuckin *gun* on me. A gun,
can y'imagine? Anyway I get up in his face screamin at him
fuckin shoot me then, ye cunt ye! Go on! Do it! A'course he froze
sure, an Shamey knocks it from his hand an then him from his
feet. I slap him round the head a bit, an I think Annie kicked
him in the bollix, all the while Shamey's standin back kinda
wincin. I took the gun. Kept it. Free-ninety-nine sure.

The young one's hidin behind the door at this point, cryin
or somethin. I hate when women act the way they think men
want themta act, weak an scared an that. Makes me pity them,
an I hate pityin women so I do. Reminds me'a mc ma, an that
reminds me'a me da an he's a prick.

Johnny actually did a pretty good job with The Buck's pal.
Fair fucksta the wee jennet. Gave him a good hidin like, so
he juss sat there moanin like a bitch the rest'a the time. The
young one ran away a'course, an we let her go—we'd no truck
with her.

Shamey props up The Buck on an armchair an I start askin
him where's the pills. Shamey's hauldin onta him good an
tight. The wee prick starts mumblin, somethin bowt his connections. Naught but the blusterofa wee calf with his bollix in
the vice sure. Even spat at me so he did. But all I hadta do is
run me blade along his cheek an out it comes like vomit. Pure
bile like.

"Inthekitcheninthefuckinbreadbin."

"Now that wasn't so very hard, was it, Bucky?" says Annie real sweet like.

I hand her the blade an go get the stuff.

"Keep her lit," I says.

Three hundred pills like, not to be laughed at. I guess, somewhere in the back'a his feeble little mind, The Buck knew what was comin. Meself an The Maguire never talked bowt it mind, but we've worked together loads since. Think he was even grateful I took him down a notch.

Once I've got them I give Annie the nod. The smile on her. Dyinta do it so she was. She shifts up her skirt an sits down on his lap. Sits in real close on him. He can probably smell her—Annie's always turned on by a bit'a action so she is. She's addictedta it. Like foreplay she says. An *aphrodisiac* she calls it. An it turns me on whenever she's turned on.

She starts kissin his neck an ears an that an ye can see the bulge like. Poor bastard has no control over it.

Annie's grindin on him an he's kinda whimperin. Then she says, loud enough so we all can hear: *today, we decided to damage each other*.

She takes me blade, sharp as a razor, an cuts him deep in the cheeks. Two stripes on each cheek. Shamey's lookin away, but can't stop himself from groanin a little too. The poor fucker still has his boner sure, an him screamin like a pig. Annie's still grindin him the whole time, an I'm there thinkin she is juss the sexiest person in the world.

Nobody calls him The Buck Maguire anymore. Now we call him Stripes.

A DAY AT THE BEACH

Closin in on yerself, yer own head an the mind gets smaller somehow, closer an that, like it's bowt to collapse under its own weight, all sway-sway-sway-crash. An ye look round in other people's eyes an ye see the same thing like, this kinda fidgety unease, but with an edge'a pure menace. The heat.

It was June I think, or maybe July, when it was dead hot an that for two weeks on the trot an it didn rain or nathin. The farmers were all bitchin, the same bunch who'd been moanin when it rained too much in March. National emergency they said. Juss lookin for more government money sure. Some people were sayin it was global warmin, other folk said it was somethin the Russians put in th'airta make the clouds stay away for the World Cup. But we're not even near Russia, so yeah, it's probably global warmin in fairness. All the same, farmers love free money so they do.

It was like bein on holidays, but the holidays cominta you. I mean, the bad bits, the heat an the crowds an that. Meself I've only been on foreign holidays th'one time, in Lanzarote. Fuckin load'a bollix. Spent a week wanderin round yon dumb island. Capital'a fake—Spanish islands nowhere near Spain. I have this one memory'a bein on the beer an starin at these three German lads who'd decided t'occupy half the bar. The *noise'a* them. No idea what they were sayin like, but I juss remember this mad vicious feelin comin over me lookin at them all plump an pink an loud juss pourin the beer inta themselves sure. An in a *desert*. It takes loads'a waterta make beer, I know that from a video I saw on Facebewk one time. A desert's a wild place, it's like a place in the pure rejection'a life, all life, but specially human life. Yet there we are on the beer callin it Spain. The fuck is that all bowt? It's brutal, the desert. No forgiveness, an I was there thinkin *somethin should fuckin eat them*.

Now, it wasn *quite* as bad as Lanzarote, but y'know what I mean. Meself I juss wanted t'ignore it an get on with life, but everyone kept goin on usin words like *summer*, an *heatwave*, words that are juss elsewhere from Ireland. It was when they started talkin bowt *the beach* that I knew I was in trouble.

Now, by beach they meant various rocky bits'a seaside out in Cooley, cause ye can't really go swimmin in Dundalk Bay on account'a all the mud. I was hopin it'd blow over, but it didn. I don't have good experiences'a beaches, an I hate the look'a meself in a bikini, never mind them granny swimsuits. Thick thighs no matter which way I looked. Annie said I looked grand, but sure that's easy for herta say—she actually has a figure see, an she loves gettin noticed for it, which is all the time. But at the beach that time she was like a friggin lighthouse.

She got round me, outflanked me. Talked Shamey Hughes an me pal Tommy inta takin the spin out. So I could hardly be th'one dry shite an stay behind. Th'only one good thing was that what with Tommy comin we wouldn juss sit there talkin work. Tommy didn like that, didn wanna know, him bein on the straight an narrow n'all. An fair playta him like. People are usually dead nosey bowt the stuff we get upta. Dead annoyin that.

Tommy an Shamey spun round in Shamey's yoke. Fuckin packed it was, an with all the shite Annie had with her we were like a tin'a sardines so we were, stunk near as bad as that too by the time we got out there. The driveta Gyles's Quay felt like a trek, an it only out the road sure.

When we got there I saw why it was that we hadta drive like a tin'a fish. The lads had a full feckin kitchen with them. Gas barbecue, beer cooler, peck that would'a kept us fed for a week, the works. Mad craic altogether. A'course, Shamey had his guitar which was good actually, probably th'one really good thing we packed.

We hadta park a half mile from the beach. Massive line'a cars, an then a column'a troglodytes all squirmin their way down the beach with all their truck an that, like a band'a weary soldiers who'd deserted the war an taken half the gear with them. The real shock though, was when we got over the wee humpty bit before *the beach*.

Like a colony'a walruses it was. Juss as fat an loud an maybe narkier. Walruses are the narky ones, aren they? Big mad tusks like elephants on them sure, they must be. What need d'ye have'a tusks if yer friendly? An the smell'a the place, the slow rot'a seaweed an whatnot. Mingin.

As we get closer, the scene gets uglier. Now, Annie accuses me'a bein somethin she calls a *misanthrope*, which means some cunt who hates all th'other cunts. But that's not quite right. I actually like people, mostly. It's juss when they do stupid shit an won't let up that it pisses me off. Like draggin me to Lanza-fuckin-rote an callin that a good idea. Or worse, to Gyles's Quay. Who the fuck was this Gyles fella anyway? Can't'a been from round here, not with a name like that.

The worst thing bowt bad ideas is that people usually refuseta admit they were ever bad. Even when they post pictures bowt it online as if they were somewhere good an then get dead depressed cause they don't get any likes cause everyone actually knows deep down that both Lanzarote an Gyles's Quay are shite. No amount'a filters can change that. If only they could admit their mistakes they'd save themselves a lot'a misery. At least Tommy had the senseta leave his dog at home thank god. Fuckin dog selfies. What's even wrong with us like?

Carryin all that kit through the vulgar press'a humanity in that heat—pure humiliation. A full fuckin kitchen. Could'a juss brought a few sambos an some cans, be grand sure. But oh no. The boys an their friggin toys. Nonsense. They're worse than birds the way they show off sure, squalkin an everythin.

Fuckin everythin they had there, the folk on the beach. Wee tents, mini swing sets an a thousand toys for kids who were too spaced out starin at screens in any way. An then there's the middle-aged men with a centre'a gravity bowt a foot away from where they remember it bein, haulin themselves up on some stupid stand-up surfboard ye paddle with this look on yer face somewhere between pride an confusion cause ye've no idea what to do an yer wobblin too muchta go anywhere anyway, an then ye realise ye don't know nathin bowt tides an currents an stuff cept that they kill people *all* the time an ye don't wanna be one'a them but yer teenage son's filmin ye on some stupid whirly noisy drone, pissin everyone off like, but it's very very important to make that video so no-one can ever watch it *ever*, but everyone on the beach'll know ye've got a fuckin drone. Fuckin deadly, or pure bollix—who can tell?

Now, I'm no misanthrope. I juss wish people wouldn be so thick like. I like people, but they can be awful stupid, specially when it's sunny. Annie calls this sorta carry-on with drones an shite like that *commodity fetishism*. Meself I juss call it actin the prick.

Too hot in the sun, too cold in the sea. Nathinta do but drink til Tommy has the cookin done. Men love burnin meat an callin that cookin, but in fairness Tommy's pure daecent at cookin so he is. An in any way, Shamey was playin the guitar an singin ballads. Crowd-pleasers like, an soon there was a hape'a people round us, like at a festival it was, an sure everyone was passin drink round an chattin. The craic like, it pure dissolved all that commodity bollix so it did, everyone was juss singin along, not even takin pictures an doin all that shite that makes us feel further away from each other even though we're in the same place.

A'course, Annie loved this cause then she had loads'a attention from feens. She loves that. I triedta ignore it so I did.

Night fell. There's a dumb expression for ye. It creeps in, specially in the summer. Real slow. Which is good. I don't like surprises.

It gets dark an folk starts peelin off. We stayed but, an made a fire, which I liked even better cause then I could juss pull a big jumper over me, somethin soasta not have the feelin'a flesh all over me, *my* flesh like, everywhere an unstoppable. Juss that way soasta be in the dark, to feel at home in meself. Shamey was pretty drunk by then, surprise, sur-fuckin-prise. But sure he kept on singin. Didn even realise he was lobster-burnt t'fuck so he didn. Poor fella.

That was a bit weird though, that night. I think it's cause I was less drunk than th'others that I noticed. But I noticed Annie got all edgy an that after all the randomers fucked off an no-one was payin her special attention anymore. See, Shamey kept his distance so he did. An Tommy was one'a the few feens more interested in me than her, though I try not t'encourage him. Still, I like him, he's good craic an it's nice havin a normal friend, I mean someone who's not a wheeler-dealer.

Anyway, Annie went from bein the centre'a attentionta juss bein part'a the group, which was all she really ever was. But she didn like that. So she starts makin these nasty comments bowt me, me size an that. Real bitchy like. Now I know she can get like that, specially when she's been on the gin. Bad stuff gin. But this time she was proper mean like, an flirtin with Tommy like mad—or at least tryinta.

Anyway at some point, Tom juss turnsta me, ignorin her an says out loud, "Who the fuck does yer wan think she is?"

I triedta calm her down, but Annie started cursin the fuck out'a Tom an storms off, still juss wearin her bikini like, an a wee skimpy blanket yoke. Big scarf really. I wantedta go after her but Tommy made me stay. Didn see her for three days after that.

THE BEST CHIPS IN TOWN

Slouchin over in the cockpit or whatever ye call it, the wee box where she sits, the beor in the chippy, sayin *saltanvinegar* with her eyes glazed over. See, it's not even a question, moreofa statement, an the troglodyte next to her juss starts pourin salt an vinegar over me chips. It's juss mechanics, all repetition an muscle memory.

At the same time though, who doesn like salt an vinegar on their chips?

The Rat King cocks his head at me an smiles as ifta share in a joke.

We go an sit in one'a them wee booths in at the back'a th'Europa t'ate ar chips. Rat King has a batter burger too. Th'Europa does a great take-out trade, but usually there's no-one sittin in the back, cept a few hopeless auld lads whose lives got away from them somewhere along the line. Juss sittin there starin at peas or egg an chips, proddin them from timeta time, wonderin what happened through the mist in their eyes. So it's a good placeta talk, cause them ones don't notice nathin. Nathin t'all.

This time though, there are all these fuckin kids, screamin an runnin round the place. All the same I don't mind like, cause that way no-one can hear nathin anyway, not even them auld misty men. They're dead annoyin, them kids, but still, I can't help feelin a bit sorry for them, havin their birthday party in the back'a the fuckin Europa. Class chips though.

Rat King looks at me an says, "Ye thought bowt the job did ye?"

I sit back a bit. I tells him I did, an that I found a wayta get it done without makin any much noise. He doesn say nathin, juss shoves half the batter burger in his gob. Pulls off a bit an brings it to his jacket pocket. I watch, an the flap starts bulgin. It's that fuckin rat, his nasty pet rat. It juss peeks its head out, lookin somewhere between scared an vicious an grabs the meat an disappears back in. He brought the dirty fuckin rat with himta the restaurant.

For fuck's sake.

I saysta him anyway, ten kilos'a the pure driven snow, that's too muchta be gettin rid'a in Ireland without folk askin questions. Well, ye could get ridofit, say a hundred grammes a go, but that'd take too long. Pain in the hole. So I saysta him that I'll take it to England. Now, I'd never beenta England actually, but he didn know that. I didn much like th'idea'a gointa England, but I reckoned ten kilos over there'd only be a drop in th'ocean sure. I tell him I'll go on a wee road trip. We'll pack the stuff inta the sides'a the car, the doors an that, an sure then I'd juss roll overta Liverpool an downta London offloadin a bit here an there as I go. Best wayta avoid attention back home.

The Rat King sets a real serious look on me.

"I didn't know you had a substantial network of contacts in the UK."

It always sets me head a'spin when the Rat King does that. He switches from talkin normalta talkin like he was presentin the nine a'clock news. See, the Rat King's an educated chap, he has a degree in French an economics so he does. Fuckin clever bastard too. Still, it's madta see him switch things up like that, specially with the pocket bulgin away on him an a dirty auld rat in it sure.

I tell him I don't but that Annie has loads'a contacts over in England. She's been there loads, she went to some posh boardin school there see, an she's been clubbin in all the cities round England. So she'll love an excuseta go back. An she's pals with loads'a dealers an coke heads over there, fairly small-time, but we can still get rid'a half a kilo at'a time I reckon. I tell him this an his brow goes all mad knotty on me.

"I tauld ye not to be tellin anyone bowt this, specially not Annie!"

"I didn say a word. I'm juss sayin that's *my* idea. I'll get rid'a it in England, an she'll help me. An she won't know nathin til we're over there, right? Juss trust me."

He calms down, thinks bowt it. That's his thing, see, the Rat King's not like other people, he can actually think. I tell him all I need is for himta give the go-ahead. Juss then, a gaggle'a them kids bursts out'a their booth squealin an chasin each other. They run inta ar table, knockin over the Rat King's drink. One'a the wee girls falls over on the ground an sure the Rat King leans overta lift her up cause sure she's all cryin an that. The mother, or auntie or sister or whoever is in charge'a all them kids comes over all sorry sorry an thanks an sorry an that. The Rat King lifts the wee beor up an hands her over an sure ye should'a seen the look on her face, the mother-auntie-sister one when she sees his nasty auld ear half chewed off. An then the rat pokes its head out'a the pocket. Pure horror-show in her eyes like. They all clear off, the lot'a them. An half'a the chips still on the plates sure.

Then we're left there in near silence, the scrapin'a some auld fella's fork off his plate th'only sound in the place. The Rat King looks at me proper serious again.

"Juss do what ye think will work, but for fuck's sake do it quiet. Don't let Annie know where the stuff comes from OK? That stays between you an me. Annie, I wouldn have her sell Smarties for me."

He stuffs the last few chips in his gob. I'm not really happyta have him talkin bowt Annie like that, but I agree anyway. Fuck it sure.

Job on, I saysta him.

C'MON THE TOWN

GARDA KELLEHER

Annie's not too good with the quiet. Makes her nervous in this weird kindofa way, itchy I s'pose ye might say. Not like the way I itch, but itchinta get awayta where th'action is. Or make action where there is none. Meself though, I need a break now an then, get me head together sure. When things are too hectic, I get the feelin I'm swimmin upside down, an drunk, an I get all edgy an that cause I don't know howta swim—never learned—never mind doin it when I'm drunk. Sure sometimes I can hardly walk when I'm drunk an like I'm pretty good at that usually.

I didn wanna get in a row cause actually I hated rowin with Annie. I'm pretty good in a row with most anyone like, it's juss her that I have a hard time with, cause when she'd be flingin me stuff bowt the place I'd be there wonderin *yeah, but who actually said that we lived together?* I don't remember. An she'd be complainin bowt *this place*, but I mean it was *my* place really, she juss moved in an made it ars, we never talked bowt it an I think that *is* the kinda thing ye really should talk bowt. A'course I wanted her there, but y'know what I mean. Dead annoyin, cause I'd be thinkin all this an scratchin me head an wonderin what to say an next minute she'd be makin tea or massagin me shoulders. There were loads'a lovely things bowt livin together, really lovely things. Like wakin up next to her. That was the nicest bit, probably, juss wakin up an reachin across an her bein there, y'know, juss bein there. I liked best when we hadn gone home together, but she came back all the same. Back to *me*. Times like those I'd lie there an kinda smell her hair, run me hands through it an that. Not in a creepy kindofa way, jussta talkta her hair. Cause Annie hated me askin questions bowt where she'd been. So I could ask other things, like her clothes, or her bag. But her hair was the best. I could get all the news that way, whether she'd been with a smoker, or with some pot head chap, or at a club. I could smell her perfume, or how tired she was or if she had fucked him or what. Which was good like, cause then I didn haveta ask her an I hated rowin with her so I did but I *was* curious.

This time I figured I'd better juss fuck off up the Town by meself. Texted Shamey Hughes for a pint. He couldn come. Fuck it sure. I went on inta Smokey Quigley's alone. Ran inta Garda Kelleher. She's good craic so she is. For a gard like.

Now, ye might think it strange that I know a gard an that, but I reckon that I know half the gards in the Town by name. An they *all* know me. It's better that way, an in any way they're not so bad unless ye get some young buck out to prove himself. Most Gardaí are juss lookin for a quiet life an early retirement. Why else would ye become a gard sure? Th'only ones that are a real pain are the Special Branch, bunch'a trigger-happy hillbilly mucksavages raised on a diet'a Dirty Harry an brown sauce so th'are. Kelleher's different from yer average gard. Brainy, an dead sound too.

I sat down next to her an ordered a pint. Smokey's was neutral ground see, sacred like. No arrests, no messin. A place where everyone could do business.

Good-lookin beor, Garda Kelleher, class tits on her, an she wears her hair in this sexy wee bun. Blonde hair n'all. With the wee snub nose on her an them bright eyes'a hers, she always has a look'a mischief. I wonder if those looks are moreofa help or a hindrance in her line'a work. Can't be easy haigh.

"Well, Gard, what's the craic?"

"Sure it's yourself. Not much now."

"So yer in for a sneaky pint?"

"Well, you know how it is. Quiet night, so I took off early. But they have me on call. This is the only safe place for me. I can always say I'm working."

"An *are* ye workin, Gard?"

"Trying not to. Been pretty hectic recently."

"That craic out Lisdoo way?"

"Oh, you heard about that?"

"Ah now, Gard, c'mon, there's not a lot gets past me in this town. Surely y'know that."

"I've heard something about it alright."

Garda Kelleher gives me this sorta sideways look with a kindofa smirky half-smile. She has a lovely smile so she does, lovely smile for a gard. Usually when a cop gives ye a smile it's cause they think they've got ye. But Kelleher? Naw, she was juss bein sound.

She turns round an looks at me, in th'eyes like.

"How are things in your line of work, anyway?" she saysta me.

"Ah now quiet enough at the minuteta be fair, but I kinda like it like that sometimes. A chanceta breathe like. Though I should say, I don't have a line'a work in particular. I'm more like a Jane'a all trades if y'know that kindofa way?"

"I do surely," she says, an takes a drink.

I don't think she does, not really. But that's so much the better. Not good the pigs knowin too much'a yer business, even the sound ones.

"You know, I'm going for detective."

"Is that right?" I saysta her. "That's class."

"Yeah. Hard for women to make detective though. You have to work twice as hard as a man to get it. They're all worried that you're going to get emotional or pregnant or something like that that they can't get their heads around."

"Pricks."

"Yeah. But I'm really going to go for it."

"Fair play. I hope ye get it."

An I really did mean that. It's good knowin gards ye can talkta, an havin a detective I could talkta would be fuckin deadly. Besides, ye do always haveta work harder than the men in this business, no matter which side'a the court yer playin. So fair playta her like.

She slides a piece'a paper acrossta me, real discreet, under a bottle'a beer. Only Smokey could'a seen sure, an Smokey never says nathin. One'a the rules'a Smokey's.

"Sure look," she says t'me, "probably not best for the two of us to be seen to be too pally, even in here. But let's keep the lines of communication open."

I take the paper an she goesta leave, but before she does she gives me this smile, real suggestive like. Lovely an warm. I startedta wonder a little bowt Garda Kelleher, but in any way, best to keep things professional I thought to meself.

Had another drink juss so it wouldn look too weird. But I

was actually dead happy so I was. In me pocket I was turnin the paper over an over. I wasn juss happy cause she's dead sexy an that, but cause I figured it'd be good if we could help each other out. I'm all bowt women helpin each other out. After all, we're juss tryinta get on, aren we?

HOW ANNIE BECAME IRON

I remember this one time round with the Rat King, juss for the craic. Few cans an the cheer like. He has a good way'a seein things, he sees a lot that other folk juss can't. Though sometimes he gets these notions. Like he follows an idea or a feelin a bit far. Lets it cloud things, lets it shape them.

Like bowt Annie. He had this funny sortofa feelin bowt Annie, since the beginnin like. This time, the time I'm talkin bowt now, that wasn long after Annie'd arrived in the Town.

I like workin with the Rat King cause we don't need each other. So when we're workin on somethin, it's half for the craic an half for the care'a each other. An it's good too, cause by workin together there's a right good balance bowt the Town. Stops Paddy's army or The Maguire gettin too bigofa notion'a themselves sure.

Where was I? Aye, the Rat King an Annie. Well, he got it inta his head that Annie wasnta be trusted. A gut thing I s'pose, an sure I get that. A'course I do. But yer gut can be wrong—I should know.

"Terrible," he saysta me.

"Ha?"

"How you lot see the travellin folk."

"*You* lot?"

"Country folk. Settled people."

"Ah, here, don't go lumpin us all in together. Sure I'm here, aren't I? Besides I don't actually see yis doin too much travellin. Never more than ten mile from the Town sure yer not."

"Would ye look. Discrimination. From you. An you me best settled friend."

"Awah, d'ye mean that?"

"Well, yeah. But I don't have many settled friends."

"Why?"

"I dunno. Stayin in one place too much. Not healthy. An before you start agin, one'a these days, you'll see, we'll juss up the stakes an travel on. Like the fuckin wind we are."

"Yer more like a stale fart so y'are, hangin round here this years gone," I says.

Immediately I regret it. He juss stares at me, dead flat like. Says nathin. I tryta climb out'a the hole I juss dug. "Where would ye go?"

"Dunno. France maybe."

"The fuck? France?"

"Aye. There's great friendship with the French. *Les Gitans*. An great trade in scrap down there. Meself an Squeaks've already been down on the sly see—several times."

"*Gitans?*"

"Ah yeh. French travellers. *Les Gitans*. Beautiful folk. Musical folk."

"But how do yis get on down there? That's another country sure. Different language n'all."

"Sure don't y'know I speak French. Fluent I am."

"Y'are fuck."

"I am. *Je te jure.*"

"Ha?"

"Never mind. Juss trust me. I speak French. Sure didn I study it three year in college?"

"I still can't get over the fact'a ye havin a college degree."

"That's pure prejudice."

"Awah here, would ye stop. Naw, it's not cause'a ye bein a traveller or nathin. Juss cause'a ye bein ye, bein the way ye be."

"Right," he says, takin a big gouge'a his beer. Quiet night in the haltin site that night. Th'only sound ye could hear t'all was yon nasty rat'a his, scratchin away in its box. Weird, this man's connection with that animal. Most people get a cat or some shit, not a wild rat. I never understood how he tamed it, either, how he got it to stop bitin him. But pretty soon it was like a part'a him.

"What were ye gettin at, anyway, bowt the settled folk an that?"

"Ah yeh. Fuckers."

"Why but?"

"Cause'a lots'a things. The way they treat folk who are different. Who don't have a little house, an a little car, an a little family, a little fuckin belly an a partner who fucks ye once a year n'all."

"Man, that's juss one kinda settled folk."

"Maybe, aye, but it's the most common kind. An fair enough, things are grand at the moment. Everyone's got their rights. The gays, the travellers. Even the women now. But fuck me, it could turn on the headofa pin. I think that's the part people underestimate. It's pure emotion like."

"I think ye think too much. Yer worse than Annie so y'ar."

"Annie. She's a good example."

"Ha?"

"Yeh. She's a good example'a what I'm talkin bowt."

"Ah, c'mere, leave it would ye."

"Naw, naw. Listen. It's nathin bad or that. It's the most normal thing in the world, the way she is. She has all these wild ideas for now. She's livin this crazy life, hangin out with us n'all. Sure she even has a girlfriend."

"What're ye sayin?"

"I'm sayin it's only temporary. Sorry, love, I know that's hard to hear. But mark my words. In a couple'a year, she'll join the ranks'a the lumpen-bourgeoisie. Could happen sooner than ye think."

"Ha? The wha?"

"Never mind. I juss mean she'll end up as one'a them people, them settled people who like everythin normal. Predictable. Controllable. Right down to the kinda cancer they'll die of. That's why they hate us, people like you an me. It's why they specially hate the travellers."

"Ye can't be sayin that bowt Annie, for fuck's sake. Sure ye hardly know her. Ye juss made yer judgement bowt her the first time ye clapped eyes on her, cause she looks proper. Cause she looks *good*. For fuck's sake. She's opened me mind. Not like ye to be such a spa for Christ's sake. Ye don't even know her sure, not really."

The Rat King took another big gouge'a beer, then cleared his throat.

"Maybe. But what I'm trying to say is that her views, such as I intuit them, are merely indicative of the perception of the

Travelling Community amongst society at large. The perception is still one of prejudicial stereotypes, which are very much to the detriment of our material and social wellbeing. I'm talking about discrimination. She sees us as scum. Convenient to her for now, but scum nonetheless."

As he was talkin, usin his educated voice n'all, he took yon nasty rat out'a its box, an let it crawl up onta his shoulder. It was fat got, an juss sat there wobblin a bit, but I could'a sworn it was tryinta stare me out'a it. Nasty yoke, probably full'a all kinds'a diseases so it was.

"I'm tellin ye," he goes on, relaxin a bit, "before there were any blacks or Roma or anythin, we were th'original underclass, an we'll always be, not cause'a how we look or who we are but cause'a how we live an that's that. We'll always be here though, much as they might wish we'd go away, th'uncomfortable fact'a Irish society."

"I thought ye were gointa France haigh."

"Yer fierce funny. Y'know rightly what I mean. To them, we're dirt. Like hemroids. It's only when we cause problems that we get any attention sure. They don't see anythin good bowt us. No appreciation. Degenerates an criminals, that's what they think we are."

"But . . . y'are a criminal."

He looks at me then as if I'd offended him like. Even his fuckin rat looked annoyed. The Rat King took a gouge out'a his can an shook his head.

"You're one to talk! You realise that it's society that pushed us inta this? Travellers I mean—not the like'a you. You've no excuse. Us? We're tinkers. Y'know what a tinker is? A tradesman. Crafters. People who tinker."

"Ha?"

He took another gouge'a beer. "Tinkerin's findin a wayta fix somethin. No matter what's wrong, no matter how bad it looks, there's always a wayta fix it. You juss haveta try. But with all this disposable shite we have, sure who needs a tinker? Somethin's broke, juss feck it away. Get a new one. Fuck it. Cheaper in any way. Who wants an auld kettle or pot when ye can get a shiny new one, made in China or whatever. So they threw us away at the same time."

"I don't get it."

"For fuck's sake. I'm a tinker I tell ye. I fix things. I'll always be a tinker. Juss the things I fix, well they're jobs an things. Deals. People. No kettlesta fix anymore, what choice have I sure? Not like anyone'd give a jobta a traveller sure."

"Well, now, I think ye'd get by anyone in fairness."

"You expect me to fuck offta work in a shop is it? In insurance maybe?"

"Fair enough, fair enough."

An y'know wha? It *is* fair enough. All the same, I don't give too much thinkinta this craic though, it's not good for yer head so it's not. Like, the Rat King was right, but if I go tryinta justify meself I know I'm in trouble. I'm a wheeler-dealer an I know it. I'm fine with it. Juss tryinta get by sure.

It was bowt then that Sammy Squeaks knocked on the door'a the Rat King's caravan. We call him Sammy Squeaks cause he does, he squeaks when he talks. Big, big lad, looks like he should be a rugby player maybe. Pure gouger so he is, hardly what ye'd call a looker—his face is all pockmarked—but he's got a heart'a gold. Fuckin genius with metalwork too. He's a welder, see. No-one makes fun'a him bowt his voice cause he looks like he could take yer head off with one swipe. Probably could, too. Dead funnyta hear a big feen like that talkin with a wee squeaky voice all the same.

"Right b'y. Found this one tryinta get inta the site. She alright is she? She says she knows ye."

The two'a us were juss tryin not to break ar shite laughin sure. Big serious head on him. Didn wanna offend the fella like. Dead sound ar Squeaks. But Annie wasn helpin, there stood behind him, already sniggerin, hand in front of her mouth. Sammy turns around, dead thick look on his face so he had. But the Rat King pipes up an tells himta let her in. Says she's grand. Sammy doesn seemta get the joke, goes off in a huff.

In comes Annie in any way, with a big black bag slung over her shoulder. Annie's dead skinny so she is, so the bag looks real heavy, bulgin in the sides an makin a rattly noise an that. She has her dancey eyes then, real shiny, soasta make the green'a them even bolder than usual. Like magic how she does that. I've seen her do it hundreds'a times I s'pose, an 99 per cent'a the time the result is the same, specially on fellas like. They juss slack their jaws an go along with whatever she says. I swear, a lot'a feens'd juss jump off a bridge in that state so they would, if only she said they should. I'd say it was thick carry-on, actin like that juss cause'a someone's eyes, but it worked on me often enough too.

It didn work on the Rat King though mind you. At first I wondered if he was maybe blind or that, but I figured that he's got some magic'a his own. Must do, to've been ableta resist hers.

Anyway, Annie throws the bag down at his feet.

"Well, *Rat King*. What'll you give me for all this?"

Leanin over t'open the bag, she gave him a good chanceta

take a look at her tits. Kindofa pre-sales teaseta up the price. In fairness, she didn know him too well at the time.

"Take a look at that. Real craftsmanship. Take a look at the precision."

The bag is full'a these mad-lookin metal bars. Hardta describe them really, bowt a foot long, with different things etched on the sides'a them, some kinda symbols or somethin. Looked like they were meant to slot together in a certain order. But fuck knows what for. Real heavy duty too, they didn look made cheap.

"The fuck're these, Annie?"

"They're clearly for some highly specialised purpose. A craftsman like yourself must surely appreciate that."

Rat King smiles this big smile at her. Pure badness in it.

"You're a funny fucker, Annie, I'll give ye that."

"Now, come on. Be reasonable."

"Oh, I'm always reasonable. Go on."

"Well, these are high-quality goods, Rat King. Precision tools are worth a lot, you know that. And I'm sure that once you figure out what they're for, you'll be able to make a neat little profit on them. No better man!"

Rat King's rubbin the stubble on his chin, a big grin on him.

"Specialised did ye say?"

"I mean, I'm no expert. But you hardly have to be. Take a look."

"Specialised goods, sure they're worth somethin. But knowin what they're for is usually important, to be fair. Take yerself, Annie. *You* know yer purpose. Y'know it real well. That's what gives ye so much value. But purpose is specificta th'user."

He gives me this kindofa look like I'm meant to know what the fuck he's on bowt, then keeps goin.

"However, specialised goods also carry a significant risk. Small market see, word has a way'a gettin round. I guess you'd juss rather the buckta get backta the travellers than you, ha?"

Now, this was somethin I hadn seen before. Annie thrown off balance.

"What? No. It's not like that at all. I just don't know what they are, for fuck's sake. I figured you might is all."

"Yeah yeah. Well, I tell ye what, I'll take them. But I'll haveta sit on them for a while. Juss so as whoever ye swiped them from forgets they were ever theirs. So ye see, they're not really worth very muchta me, these specialised goods. Ye need the right punter, I tell ye, an that ain't me."

Annie's tryin not to look annoyed so she is, tryinta act like she thinks this is all dead funny. Wee half-closed eyes on her, n'all the dancin stopped sure.

"Right. And what do I get?"

"Well, now, as I say, they're not worth a whole lot t'me, Annie. But since yer a friend an that, I'll give ye a few tins'a Harp or a nice long suck on me knob. You choose."

Laughin in this *ha ha ha that's not very funny ha ha ha* kindofa way, Annie reaches over an grabs a can an sittin in beside me, starin him down the whole time, an him starin right back at her, still with that same crooked smile on her. Triedta do her best t'act like she didn care bowt bein beat.

"You can suck your own dick," she says, crackin her tin.

"Where'd ye get them anyway, Ann?" I ask her, tryin jussta ease the feelin.

"Oh, I was walking through Seatown with one of the Kelly boys. You know, on the way to the Spirit Store."

"Which Kelly?"

"Patrick. The eldest one."

"That prick," says the Rat King, "he owes me two tonne so he does."

"Well, you can consider yourself paid in full then, Rat King."

"Ha? How's that?"

"I spotted this Audi. Cork reg. Beautiful car. Brand new. And I saw this big bag in it. By the look of the car, I thought it'd be worth something. So I got Patrick to open the car for me."

"How?" I asked.

"With a rock."

"Yer jokin," says the Rat King.

"Dead serious. This was all that was inside though. He wasn't in a very good mood after we figured that out though, just because he fucked up such a lovely car for no reason. Still, he'll be happy to hear that he has no more debt with you."

"You're very funny," he says.

"I'm not trying to be."

"I know y'are. That's the funny bit. Y'see what I mean? Y'know yer purpose. Gettin other peopleta do shit for ye, an even when it turns out to be for naught, wrigglin yer wayta make a profit."

"What profit is it for me? I nearly broke my back hauling that bag over here. The Gardaí could have picked me up at any time."

"Oh, come off it. You'd probably've talked them inta givin y'a lift over if they had. Naw. You don't get nathin cept a few cans'a Harp, but now Patrick Kelly's debt is off, he's in your pocket an sure isn that worth more than havin cash in there?"

"So you'll let him off?"

"A'course. That's juss the kinda fella I am. Called honour, that. Though mind you, I hardly think passin it onta you is really doin him a favour. But sure, what do I wanna be doin a prick like that who can't pay his debts a favour for?"

"What a charitable fella," I saysta him, tryinta make a joke'a it.

The Rat King lifts up one'a them metal bars, still lookin at Annie, right in th'eyes like.

"Iron Annie. That's what we'll call ye from now on haigh."

EXTRAORDINARY GENERAL MEETIN

Like a fuckin pond or a pool or somethin like that. Y'know, like the way it is for fish. They can feel movement round them sure. That's the way the Town is. Ye'd never be long hearin bowt anythin goin down. Weren many real players in the place, really.

There was ar crew, well, me an Shamey Hughes an Annie, an the lads that'd sometimes give us a bitofa dig out. Then there was the Rat King an his people. In a way we're kinda extensions'a each others, cause even if we're independent an that we're always there for each other, the Rat King an me. Then there's big Tadhg Maguire, *The* Maguire, Stripes's cousin. I give yon feen a wide enough berth, not cause'a the Stripes business—naw, I think he even appreciated me castratin that wee calf. But The Maguire's a bitofa thick so he is. Has fierce clout below in Muirhevnamor, but he shoots from his hip cause that's all he's got to go from.

An then there's Paddy. An the fuckin IRA. Real IRA or continuity or whatever the fuck they wanna call themselves.

A bunch'a spas that feel jealous like, jealous they never got to be part'a the stories their daddies an uncles tauld them bowt. Don't have any notion that no-one, an I mean no-one wants the Troubles back. Th'only IRA people actually support is the Proverbial IRA, y'know, the sound lads, they'd never do knee-cappins or bombins or nathin like that. That's who people mean when they say *Up the RA* sure, the Proverbial IRA, an nathin real bowt it. Brexit is the best thing that ever happened for that lot. A new sense'a relevance—almost—there at th'edgeofa historical hangover. Juss wait an see what happens if the British army ever rolls back inta Ulster to man a border. In the meantime they mostly keep themselves mur-murin self-righteous slogans in the ditches round Cooley, all *Tiocfaidh ár lá* an that. That, an dealin drugs they confiscate from smalltime dealers. Mulpins. See, accordinta their logic, the streets should be kept clean, an yet we're juss two daecent big drug deals away from a united Ireland an none'a them care if it's a contradiction so they don't. Probably a message in there somewhere. Still n'all, at least Paddy's got a couple'a brain cells so he does. An he respects me. Knows me cousin Match real well too.

Between us, there's a kindofa balance. We don't step on each other's toes like, at least not too much. An a couple'a times a year we have these meetins. Usedta be at Smokey Quigley's. Jussta clear th'air sure, an keep things runnin smooth an that.

This one time though, it was pure out'a the blue. I get a call from The Maguire sayin we needta meet the next day. *Extraordinary General Meeting* he says, real slow an clear like I'm a dope maybe. Prick. Didn like the sound'a this one so I didn.

Smokey was dead sound, as always. Closed the door an watched it herself, from th'outside. Turned off the cameras n'all. No-one would'a minded if Smokey'd sit in on the meetins or that, I mean she was part'a the Town, the business n'all. Fuck, she *was* the Town in a way.

Paddy was in a shite mood.

"The fuck's this all bowt, Tadhg? I'm meant to be above in Belfast right now, so this better be good."

Now, normally, ye say that kindofa thingta The Maguire an he gets his back up. A proper live wire so he is. But I could practically feel the mulpin hauldin the shite inta his bowels. Control, for once. See, The Maguire needed ar help.

The spa'd gone an brought the divil down on himself. A big crew'a lads from Liverpool. See he'd invited them over on a job he was runnin. Pills. Always fuckin pills with The Maguire. He wantedta get inta supplyin them beyond in England so he did. Even had the logistics sorted, an auld fishin boat owned by an auld hippie pal'a his. Cept he'd lost control'a them, the ham. There were meant to be juss a few'a them, an now there were at least thirteen'a the cunts. That, in me imagination was actually dead funny. Imagine, thirteen Ringo Starrs runnin round the Town. Some craic. Cept this was no craic actually.

The Rat King smiled an said what we'd all been thinkin.

"Sure what's it t'us if ye lose out to somethin ye brought down on yer own head ha?"

Paddy an I exchanged a glance. Aye. Fuckin dead right. What's it t'us?

"Listen, ye thick, them fuckers're animals so they'ar. There'll be no respect, no civil meetins like this here. They'll juss flood the place an take over. Ye should see how they have Liverpool sewn up. Pure monopoly so they'ar. Good for no-one cept them. They're naught but a hape'a cunts."

"A hape'a cunts?" says Paddy, scratchin his chin.

"A class-A hape'a cunts, lad. Like attracts like."

"Fuckin dead right," says the Rat King.

The Maguire didn get it.

I thought bowt givin the feen a bitofa hard time. Would'a deserved it so he would'a, but I held back.

"An foreign cunts. English cunts," he says, graspin at straws.

"Appealin t'ar sense'a patriotism, is it, Maguire?" I saysta him.

"Well, if not for the country, then for the Town."

"For yer own arse ye mean. You lot've never done a tap for the cause," came Paddy.

The cause. Fuck me.

"Besides," says Paddy, "the English aren't so bad."

"Really?" comes the Rat King, eyebrows raised, smilin at me.

"Naw. Sure th'English are grand. It's the Brits ye wanna watch out for."

"Look, a cunt is a cunt is a cunt no matter where they're from," says The Maguire, gettin fair flustered at this stage.

"Let's juss hear him out, lads," I says, smoothin it over.

"Thanks. I'm juss sayin, they're a bad bunch. Much worser than me so they'ar. Stick with the divil yis know sure. An I'll make it worth yiser whiles so I will."

"Now yer talkin," says the Rat King.

"How do we know they won't juss send reinforcements?" says Paddy. Proper military head on him Paddy, ye gotta hand him that. It was a fair point.

"They'll not. They're pure businessmen sure. This is juss an investment for them. They'll not throw good money after bad. Nip this in the bud an that's the message sent, right the way backta Liverpool—fuck off."

Paddy suggested bringin in his whole team, an a bunch'a heavies from above in Belfast. Turn Muirhevnamor inta the Wild West. I know that bunch'a lads would'a loved that, all the more once they'd figured out that English are Brits. Fulfil their childhood fantasy'a drivin them out'a Ireland like, the proper Brian Boru wet dream. But then, we'd have twice the dose'a RA heads we already had in this town. No-no-no. No way. They can go shite, too. A bunch'a muscle heads thinkin they own the place? Fuck that. Sure the Belfast bucks'd be juss as bad as these Liverpool lads. But sure I couldn say that, not in front'a Paddy.

"Fuck that," I says, "ye wanna make it that we can't fuckin move in this town without the Special Branch breathin down ar necks?"

Naw. A'course they didn. I had another idea so I did.

A trap.

"I'll send Annie to sweet-talk them. She could sell iceta th'eskimos sure, the mouth on her. She'll spin a yarn bowt how much I hate The Maguire an sure wouldn I juss love ta see the cunt go down."

"For fuck's sake. She's juss some posh bitch so she is," says The Maguire.

"If I were you, I'd not underestimate Iron Annie, Tadhg. She can talk her way in or out'a most anythin she wants. I've seen it," says the Rat King.

I'll be honest, I remember bein dead proudta hear him say so. An him not jokin, not a bit.

"An yer in no positionta choose, so hauld yer whist an juss listenta her," says Paddy.

"Thanks, Paddy," I says. "In any way, enemy'a me enemy n'all that. We'll set them up with some gearta plant on ye, ye thick cunt. Proper nasty shit. Paddy, can ye get us a few kilos'a heroin?"

"Aye, no bother. We've loads'a that shite confiscated above in Belfast an we don't know what to do with it sure. Can't fuckin sell shite like that. Pure death like. Were thinkin maybeta dump it real cheap on the streets in London jussta fuck them up a bit, but I s'pose this could work too, if Tadhg's willinta pay obviously."

"What a knight in shinin armour," says the Rat King.

At least The Maguire is keepin quiet now.

"Good man, Paddy. Anyway, we'll organise it between usta get them lifted with it. Fuckin call in the cavalry an get them put away for a lock'a years."

"Wait, you mean the gards?" says Paddy.

Should'a seen the look on The Maguire's face.

"I do, aye."

"Fuckin too risky," says The Maguire.

"An that's juss why it'll work. They'll never expect it. Not with me there standin beside them."

"Fuck," says Paddy. Feen'a few words haigh.

"How the fuck will ye get away with that?"

"Ach sure don't yous ones be worryin bowt me. I'll be grand haigh. Not a fuckin bother."

The look on their faces. Proper stoney cold. This was serious now, an they knew it.

All me little birdies were linin up in a nice little row now.

We standta leave, me an the Rat King, an I turn back an

say, "Paddy, if it falls through, or they do me, ye can still turn Muirhevnamor inta World War Three."

"Up the RA!" says the Rat King, big sarcy smile on him.

"*Tiocfaidh ár lá*," says Paddy. He doesn't really go in for things like irony, poor fella.

Anyway, we do a wee job with the Liverpool lads, me an Shamey an two'a their bunch. Rat King texts me juss before.

Rat: U got a wee angel guardian. Good luck today.

Me: Wha?

Rat: Squeaks is watchin yiser backs.

Me: No better buachaill.

Indeed there's not. Squeaks is fuckin weapons grade when he gets goin, him an Shamey both.

Real simple wee job, shiftin some gear is all. Let them think we're a bunch'a spas. An a'course since The Maguire is all th'experience they've had in the Town, it's not hardta do sure.

Annie tells them we're keenta have The Maguire gone for good. They love it. Can't do it quick enough.

Now, the gards are real hard on heroin, an in fairness it's nasty auld shite. An what Paddy gets us is enoughta turn half the Town inta fuckin zombies. We let the Liverpool lads know bowt a place The Maguire uses an that we'll plant it there together, the gear. I make sure it's in their hands when the cops roll in. Their whole team is there. It's all bowt coordination, see.

See, the day before I called up Garda Kelleher. Tauld her I'd help her make the biggest haul in history'a the Town if she'd give us immunity. No questions asked. An with that amount'a gear, why would ye sure? I tell her I'm juss doin some public service, that there's some gear an some people I want off the streets. For the sake'a the Town an that. Real bad bucks. Which is true sure. I can practically hear her purrin down the phone at me. No bother sure.

Ye should'a seen the look'a their faces. Surrounded by the Special Branch, an Annie after persuadin themta leave their cannons at home. Not how we do things here, she says, in that lovely posh accent'a hers.

They thought we were walkovers sure. Fuck em.

Garda Kelleher made detective in no time after that. Class.

ON A WEE TURN

Annie loved her wee turns. Goin on wee trips an that. At first it was a bitofa pain in the hole, specially when she did it without me or without tellin me. But I got usedta it soon enough. See, I understood it. I knew how she was feelin, cause I'd been through that kinda thing mcself. I knew it was when somethin had upset her in a way, when somethin had annoyed her an that. See, I'd been there. So I understood why she'd wanna run away from timeta time. An why she comes back. She always comes back.

This one time, years ago now, I went on a wee turn upta Belfast. By meself like, not even for a job or nathin. Naw. See, I was runnin away. I was runnin away from meself, from somethin I'd done. Nathin nasty, I wasn in trouble or that, I'd made a prick'a meself. I got in a row with Shamey Hughes over nathin.

It was me that had a go at him n'all. Fuckin weird. I said he was bein a prick, treatin me like a scumbag at this session he'd invited me to. Went all out unloadin on him. Juss a load'a bollix too, cause he wasn in the wrong. It was juss that I didn know anyone else there an I was smoked out'a it an feelin paranoid as fuck an drunk on poitín, proper old-school shit. So I lashed out at him, cause I was feelin, I dunno, lonely or somethin. Awkward. An he was playin the guitar. Sure I knew he was gonna be doin that. I should'a juss stayed at home.

There was poitín goin round that night. See the lad who organised the session was one'a these folk revivalists—hence invitin Shamey to come an play. The kinda git who thinks crap bread is class juss cause someone baked it at home an all that sorta shite. Grows his own carrots an wears all wool n'all. Poitín must'a been some kindofa wet dream for him.

It wasn bad stuff though, that was the problem with it. I was feelin strange but, all night sorta strange, juss this nasty chest tight an feelin weird bowt talkinta folk an that. See the thing is, there's not all that many folk I really even enjoy talkinta. Most people juss make me feel awkward an weird an that. Round me friends an that I can feel five hundred foot tall, but when it's a bunch'a randomers, fuck me haigh.

So I juss dug inta the poitín, thinkin it might calm me down. Cept it didn. Fuckin set me wild. I'd juss enter people's conversations, say somethin weird, tell them that their breath smelt or somethin. Spoilin for a fight really. But folk juss avoided me.

That's why I had a go a poor auld Shamey, for leavin me alone like a spare prick at a hen's party. I felt like a right arse-hole so I did, even as I was doin it sure. I knew it was wrong, but somehow I couldn stop meself. An a'course Shamey, he knew rightly too. He juss stood there, towerin over me, the drunk sway'a him. He kept tryinta put his arm round me, real gently like, an me cursin him out'a it, an shovin his arm off.

When I was done he said somethin like *I'm sorry. I came hereta play songs. I tauld ye sure. But I'm still sorry.*

That was a bollixofa thing like. I was hopin he'd react an we could get in a row that wouldn be juss *my* fault. But thinkin back on it now, it makes perfect sense. Wouldn be like him.

The next day after that anyway, hungover as fuck, I took offta Belfast. Didn have any clear idea'a why like, it juss felt better than sittin on me arse feelin angry at meself an sorry for meself.

Took the train. Still neededta sleep a bit. I mean I was wrecked so I was. It was a Sunday, comin upta Christmas, an the train was full'a families an that, headin up for a day out or shoppin or whatever. I looked on at them, this sorta bleariness in me, probably the booze still in me system sure. Couldn picture meself in the midst'a all that.

Found a quiet wee spot in a lull between clumps'a people. An entire section, empty. So I slumped in an triedta shut me eyes.

In Newry, this quare feen hops on, an slides in juss in front'a me. Now, see, there's loads'a other seats around, so I'm starin daggers at him, hopin he'll get the message. But naw. He's on another planet like.

This is one annoyin prick, I'm thinkin. Takes out a pen, paper n'all, a newspaper even. Takes off his coat. Rearranges it three times. Scratches his head. Stands up, sits down. Stands up, sits down. Stands up, sits down. Pure demented so he is. The whole time he's mutterinta himself—he doesn even *see* me. Someone calls him, an his ringtone is the soundofa cow bellowin. Fuck me b'y. He looks down at it, shudders. Doesn answer it. Doesn stop it ringin but. Eventually, someone else rings him, it's a normal ringtone this time. He answers, an quickly he's rowin with the person on th'other end. Somethin bowt money.

The whole time, he keeps goin backta his scrap'a paper. Must be dead important, whatever he's tryinta write, but he can't get anythin down. By Portadown, I didn hate him anymore, I was even kinda worried bowt him. By Belfast, I really pray he can get it done, whatever it is he needsta do. By the creases in his frown, I could tell he was in a tight spot, the wee shit. This thing he was tryinta write down seemed like the key, but he couldn get it down right, he kept scribblin it out. I'd'a talkedta him, but I knew I couldn help him. As if I neededta feel worse, an me after cursin him.

So there I am, walkin round Belfast for no reason if ye can imagine that. Feelin like a right spa. An it still early, bowt one a'clock. I went inta George's Market for a feed. The place was buzzin so it was. An I'm juss lookin at these family types, all the normal folk. Usually, I wouldn pay attention much, but they juss seemed everywhere that day, one big happy smiley horde'a shit eaters makin me feel worse bowt bein a cunt. Still. Wasn their fault like.

It was bowt then I get the text off Shamey.

Shamey: How's the head?
Me: Fuckin shite man.
Me: C'mere, I'm dead sorry bowt last night. Don't know what got inta me.
Shamey: I fuckin do.
Me: ?
Shamey: A full fuckin bottle of poitín!
Shamey: Sure look. Yer grand. Will I call over?

Me: I'm in fuckin Belfast man.

Shamey: Job?

Me: No. Tell ye the truth, I don't know what I'm doin here.

Shamey: Fuck.

Shamey: C'mere, I'll come meet ye there. I can drive us home.

Me: Awah, that's dead sound man, but yer grand. I can take the train sure.

Shamey: Fuck that shite. I'll come get ye. We can take a wee turn round Belfast.

Me: But why?

Shamey: For the craic.

An hour later he met me in Kelly's Cellars for a few scoops. Classic Shamey.

So, see, that's how I can understand Annie, when she goes on her wee turns. She juss needsta be by herself sometimes. I accept that like, I don't mind waitin.

THE INSIDE JOB

The hands on me that time, they weren all hot scratchy like they can get. Naw. Naw, that'd even'a been reassurin so it would'a. Sure I'm usedta that. This time they were pure cold. Clammy. Like, not like a dead person's hands. But a dead fish, an you guttin it sure. See, I thought she'd juss pure fucked off, juss gone an vanished like.

Now, normally, when Annie'd go on one'a her turns, downta Dublin say, or backta Galway, she'd always be dead dramatic bowt it n'all. Even a few days out ye could sorta tell it by her, she'd be makin shapes, complainin bowt the Town an that, bowt this place. Even complainin bowt the weather an it the same everywhere. Shite. Either she'd tryta be convincin me to go for a spin—a fuckin spin!—or she'd stage a fight an storm off. An see if she did juss disappear, random-like, that'd be done dramatic too, with a shitty wee note, no real details, juss some guff bowt needin space, or time or somethin. I never asked too many questions bowt it like, not after the first few times. Sometimes it's better juss not to know. Anyway, what's the sense in bein jealous of a man?

But that one time I was worried maybe she wouldn. In the run-upta the big job, that was. I was worried cause I hadn seen it comin, not t'all. Too focused on gettin ready for the trip so I was. I hadta be in touch with the Rat King all the time without Annie askin any questions, cause he was organisin the modificationsta Shamey's yoke, for the job. It was Squeaks who did it. Made these wee pockets in the car where I could hide the stuff. Fuckin genius he is, Squeaks, a bloody artist of a welder, ye'd never know he was there t'all. Problem was, I hadn figured out howta tell Annie bowt the job yet, an the Rat King wouldn let me tell the truth sure.

Her phone didn ring neither, an she didn write or even see anythin I'd writ. But at the same time she hadn blocked me so that was good. Not yet, anyway. Scummy thingta do.

I sat up all night. Hopin she'd come back. I wouldn'a minded who she'd been with, I wouldn'a cared a fuck sure. Juss hopin for some word, waitin, an kinda hatin meself for it, me eyes tired from starin at me screen, starin, juss the bright light starin right back at me, blindin me.

The next mornin I'm woke by the phone ringin beside me. Guess I drifted off at some point after all. I lie there, juss starin at it for a bit, kinda spaced out, y'know? Like woke but not awake. Then I sorta do, I wake up a bit better an answer. Don't recognise the number. Don't usually answerta numbers I don't know. But this time I did.

"Well."

"Hello?"

"Annie?"

"Yes."

"For fuck's sake. Thank Jaysis. Where are ye?"

"I'm up at the garda barracks."

"The fuck're ye doin above at the gards?"

"Just a wee social visit, you know."

"Cop on."

She was quiet for a bit on the line. Thinkin bowt it now, I probably didn needta be so rough, but I was upset too haigh.

"They arrested me."

"They did fuck."

"They did."

"For what? Am I safe like?"

She paused again. I could feel her ragin at me from above in the sty sure, but I still think it was fair enough, askin that.

"I don't know. Are you?"

Now I didn know what the fuckta say. Didn wanna row down the phone at her either, all the same. She continued after a bit.

"As for me, they lifted me on some nonsense. Bullshit like, they've nothing on me."

The rest was a bitofa blur, but the next thing I remember was bein above at the gards. Now, I don't mind meetin gards, bein civilta them an that, but actually *bein* in a cop shop, that always puts me on edge. In foul fuckin form so I was, an sure how else're ye meant to feel an yon gits gawkin at ye, askin all kinda dumb questions bowt me relationship with *the accused*. As if they didn know. Pricks haigh.

Anyway, I got to see Annie. She looked rough, I'll tell ye. Neither'a us had slept, that much was for sure. The rings under her eyes. Pure ragged form, pale menace in her eye. Was a wonder t'me how the gards hadn juss let her go yet from the fear'a her.

"I was with the two Kelly lads. They must have gotten sloppy or something. For some reason they picked *me* up with them. Guilty by fucking association. Fucking ridiculous. Now I'm an accomplice. But I don't think they actually have anything on me. I mean they can't. It's nonsensical. I don't work with the Kellys."

I'm starin at her as she tells me this. I kinda don't believe her, but I also kinda don't care, I mean I don't care if she did a job with them or not. Sure if we're open bowt the sex we can be a bit open bowt that I guess. Not like I tauld her everythin I did, either. Ye need yer own space. An sure what else would she be doin round with them otherwise? It's not as if they're even good craic, y'know? Smalltime thicks. Don't think it was for the ride either. State'a them—fuckin cavemen, the pair'a them. An they're brothers sure.

The gards wouldn let her out on bail or that, they started tellin me bowt this or that act. An sure there's no point in gettin thick with the gards, not when yer above in their wee castle there where they feel all high an mighty god love them.

Down I went to McCormack's. I called ahead an arranged it. Didn wanna get noticed round Smokey's, an Kevin McCormack's dead good at lookin th'other way too. The lad's an institution in his own right, lives upstairs from the pub an he's never away from it. Like Smokey in a way, cept he never gets mixed up in the business. Still, he's dead sound. He wasn openin until later anyway, so he was happyta help. Let Detective Kelleher in the front an stood out on the stoop himself. I came in the back. We could hear him havin the craic with th'odd one as they passed by. Pure daecent skin, Kevin.

"Well, I s'pose that I should say congratulations on the promotion," I saysta her an her with this wee cheeky smile. Suits her, the detective bit. The confidence thing, proper sexy, too. She was juss glowin sure.

"Thanks, thanks," she says, an sits up facin me at the bar.

"What'll ye have?"

She looks like she's thinkin bowt it, then says, "How about a gin tonic? It's early in the day yet."

I go around behind the bar an make two gin tonics.

"I hope you didn't go to all this fuss just to have a drink with me. If it was just that that you were after, we could go any time, you know?"

That last bit. The lift in her voice. A question but not only. Like a statement. Like an invitation. Like a *why don't we?* Kinda stumps me, an I sorta feel a warm, kinda tinglin inside. Fuck me. I know there's somethin there, from before even, but that'd be some quare job, hookin up with a gard. An besides. I was thereta talk with her bowt Annie. Wouldn feel right.

"Awah now, Gard," I say puttin the drinks down in front'a us.

"Detective. But why don't you call me Caroline?"

"Well. Yeah. But y'know, all the same, I don't think it'd really do for the two'a usta be seen—"

She cuts me off, again.

"We could go anywhere. In Dublin, say, we'd just be two friends down to the big smoke for a weekend."

This totally flusters me. She's serious so she is. *Weekend?* Fuck me.

She winks at me, with a big smile, an puts her hand on me knee, lettin it slide down the side, but keepin it real firm an agin me leg as ifta say *sure look, that's on offer any time.*

"What is it, anyway?" she saysta me.

"It's Annie. She got done."

"With the Kellys. I heard."

"Aye. I need her out."

She almost looks disappointed.

"Is that so?"

"Aye. I need her for a job. Big enough now, an trust me, Caroline, it's in the public interest that this job goes ahead."

I'm tryinta seem, well, not cool, juss not desperate an that.

"And why's that?"

"Why's that? You'd think you'd take me at me word by now."

"I'm just curious is all. I'm a detective after all."

"Aye, an who was it helpt ye get there?"

I said that bit a bit rough. There I am scratchin me hands. Tryin not to have her see it, but I see it so I scratch more. Pure cuntofa thing.

She looks at me, a bit hard. Hurt maybe a bit. But maybe hurtin for me, cause maybe she can see me hurtin. She's not bitter like. Me own voice gets thick.

"I'm sorry," I says, "I didn mean it like that. I really juss need her back, y'know, for the job. An besides, she's not wrapped up with the Kellys."

She raised her eyebrows, sorta lookin round liketa make sure we really are alone in there. Leans in a bit. I can smell her. Oh, the smell'a her.

"Now listen, I can't go into details, obviously, but the evidence would suggest otherwise."

"Look, I live with her. I'd know sure."

Sayin this, I'm scratchin real deep. Proper deep. Cause I don't know shite. She doesn't tell me where she does be goin half'a the time, I juss assume it's off for the ride an I don't ask cause I don't wanna know cause I juss really don't wanna know cause sure isn it better that way? It is surely. An in any way, I don't give a fuck if she did some job with the Kellys. Not really.

"Anyway," I says, "here's the craic. I need herta help me with somethin. We're gonna be out'a the Town for a bit. Outside Irish jurisdiction."

The eyes on her.

"Right. So I'd be helping you two go on a romantic getaway."

"No, you'd be helpin the Town. The point is to defuse a time bomb that's juss tickin away."

"Is that so?"

"It is. I can't go inta details either, but if I don't do this, it'll be war, an Dundalk'll be the venue. An I'm talkin total war here. This isn't the kinda thing ye can keep quiet for long, not round here."

Detective Kelleher, Caroline, she kinda sighs, an has a go'a her drink, takes a good auld gouge out'a it.

"I can get her out. But I'm tellin you, just so you know, she is wrapped up with the Kellys. And that's not a good association for you to have. You're discreet. You think of the bigger picture. They don't see three feet in front of themselves."

She's bein sound, but she's also dead right. They are spas. Smalltimers. The fuck is Annie thinkin?

"But look," she saysta me, "if it's for the greater good, we can call that a necessary and justifiable expedience."

"A necessary an justifiable wha?"

"Expedience. Means it's shit but it makes sense. You can collect her tomorrow. They can't keep her without charging her, and I'll see to it they don't."

Sayin this, she finishes off her drink. We both stand.

"Right. C'mere, I really appreciate this."

"I know you do. And I appreciate *you*. Just be careful, OK?"

There's this weird moment'a, like, do we do a handshake, a hug, a kiss or what? In th'end she juss squeezes me arm an lets her hand drop so it slides down an ar fingers meet an the tingles oh the tingles down below by god they're there. Fuck me. Could I fuck a gard? Maybe it's different, her bein a detective an that. I'll haveta think bowt that.

I duck out the back. Best we don't get seen leavin together all the same. Not round here, anyway. Seatown in particular is full'a eyes.

The next day I go on upta get her in any way, Annie I mean. I've had enough'a the hams up there in the cop shop. Kelleher's an exception, but y'know what I mean. The mulpin on reception, a proper thick-lookin feen, he juss grunts at me. S'pose it's better bein a gard than doin security at car parks or whatever it is the poor bucks do that don't make it through gard school. Spas.

Eventually, Annie comes down, lookin dead annoyed. She's thinkin like *what took you so long?* She doesn say it obviously, but I can tell by her that she's thinkin it. We say nathin an juss head off. She flips off the poor feen on reception. I'd sorta startedta sympathise with him, poor cub, thinkin'a him guardin a car park, y'know, some empty car park in Ardee or somewhere pointless like that, an it rainin all the time. Poor lad, sure he's juss takin shelter.

Still. A pig's a pig.

Drivin back in Shamey's yoke, I pull down a dead end an stop the car. The prickly outrage, juss steamin off her. So I start talkin before she lays inta me.

"Look. I was only ableta get y'out on one condition."

That put her on the back foot.

"Oh. What's that?"

"I'veta take y'out'a the Town for a bit. Out'a the country."

"Oh," she says, half bewildered, but kinda, well, not unhappy bowt it.

"An I've juss the job for us."

"Where will we go?"

She sounds, well, almost meek. Like she's all earnest. It's strange.

"UK."

"Oh!" She sounds pure happy now. She sits back, kinda thoughtful an that. "That could be fun."

"Aye. We'll take the car. This car. Shamey Hughes's yoke."

"Nice! A road trip."

"Yeah. A road trip."

I start the car again an turn her round. The glint's back in her eye. The hungry glint.

"What's the job?"

"Awah, I'll tell ye when we're over there," I say, sorta pushin it aside. "Part'a the deal was that it stays quiet. For now at least. I mean I can't say nathin until we're on the road like."

She muttered somethin kinda as a mock bowt secrets an spies an that. But she knew she was in no positionta push it. An in any way, she loves th'idea, I can tell by her. The prickly edginess is gone from her.

"Anyway," I says, "we can go wherever we want. Juss hasta be out'a Ireland. The Narth is out too, obviously. So you'll suss that bit. We can go see yer pals an that."

"Really?"

"Aye, sure y'know England much better than me."

"You don't know England *at all*!"

"Yeah, that's what I said, *you* know England much better than me."

This got herta lighten up at least. Her eyes start dartin, I see it th'odd time as I look round drivin. Sorta seein things. Maybe rememberin. Her lips, movin. Not quiverin. Not scared movin. Countin maybe. Countin without even thinkin.

A TINKER'S FUNERAL

The first time I worked with the Rat King, that was long before Annie cameta Dundalk. Before we met like. Back then I mostly worked alone. I worked with Shamey Hughes a'course. Otherwise when I teamed up with folk for a job it was strictly business. Until I started teamin up with the Rat King.

Word got round t'me that there were some lads under pressure above in Newry an needed a dig out. See they had a hape'a fags needin moved. They'd set up a workshop, more like a wee factory really, makin fake fags. Well, counterfeit ones, ye could still smoke them an that. Grand so th'are too, ye'd never know the difference sure. They had a bunch'a Polish feens workin for them there, an y'know how them Poles are bowt work, mad for it so th'are, so they had a glut'a these fake fags. Victims'a their own success, cause the narthern cops were onta them, checkin warehouses all round Newry town. Closin in on them. The PSNI, y'know, they're real cops, they come in hard an without knockin. Make the gards below look like a bunch'a pussycats, y'know, so these feens needed their stuff moved so they did, quick.

It was two fellas runnin th'operation, a lad from Newry who was sound enough, an another fella from Belfast. Typical West Belfast hardman from the Falls a'course, droppin hints bowt his connections in *the Organisation* an that, tryin t'intimidate me so he was, an me after comin up alone, to see bowt givin them a dig out like. Fuckin prick.

So I asked him if he maybe knew me cousin Marty Match from the Falls. That fairly smartened him up. Everyone knows the Match. Second in command'a the Belfast Brigade so he is, a real live wire too. That's how it is with these Belfast hardmen, always yappin away til they hear some bigger dog bark.

Anyway, I said I'd help them move the stuff. Problem was that with the cops onta them it was no easy thing. But that was a good problem sure, I got a good deal on the haulin. Still, I knew I'd need some kinda distraction for the PSNI, cause we'd need a wee fleet'a vansta shift all them fags.

That's how I thought'a the Rat King. See, if there's one thing the peelers are afraid'a, Narth an South, that's the travellers. Cause if they touch them it's a scandal, whether they've done somethin or not. Discrimination an that. An then again they might juss get hit with a hammer in the back'a the head. Everyone discriminates agin the travellers so they do, so I figured we could use this t'ar advantage.

I knew the Rat King was a reasonable sortofa fella, from the meetins at Smokey's so I went to see him. Didn need t'ask which caravan was his, the stares juss got that much harder the closer I got to it. But they knew who I was, so no-one was gonna stop me. An bein a beor, feens always tendta think yer harmless. I could'a juss gone right in an cut his throat like. Pure sexist that.

I rapped on the door an someone moves inside. This lad

pulls it open, proper lanky fucker. Gives me this smile full'a teeth, all bucked an yellow, big porter stains all down the sides'a them. Sits me down an goes backta what he was doin, feedin his pet rat. Back then it was still totally wild but.

"Right, whaddya want?" he saysta me so I tell him the craic. As I talk, he's sittin there, starin at me, real deadpan like. But playin with his rat, teasin it with a lump'a bread. The rat keeps tryinta bite his hand but he always moves it juss in time. I catch meself lookin down so I do, but he never does, juss keeps his eyes set on me, as if he trusted me less than that dirty auld rat tryinta bite him.

In any way, he liked me plan. We put a rumour out there'd be a big traveller's funeral in Newry three days from then. Easy done, ye juss have a traveller call round a few pubs lookin for a venue for th'afters. Sure then the pubs do the rest'a the work for ye. Get all in a big panic an call each other up n'all. Half the pubs in Newry were closed when we came, a proper tinker's prohibition so it was. An a'course the cops had wind'a it too. Juss what we wanted. For the rest, the Rat King brought in his whole crew n'all their cousinsta make a big show sure. That way most'a the peelers in Newry town were all at th'one place—perfect distraction. Left most'a themta have the craic an took the vans roundta pick up the fags an that. Yon prick-ofa Belfast hardman didn even open his mouth. When we had everythin loaded we had a drink arselves, juss enough timeta let the lads in town calm down a bit. Later on we went to pick them up, th'ones that the peelers hadn already arrested. But sure that was part'a the plan, they'd be paid for their time sure. Hadta make it believable for the pigs, let them pat them-selves on the back for restorin law an order n'all. Ye should'a seen the look'a relief on the cute wee piggy faces'a the peelers when they realised we were takin them away sure. We were doin them a favour like, so they didn even askta take a peek in the vans, an y'know, the cops up Narth are dead nosey pricks. But I mean ye don't go lookin a tinker's horse in the mouth. Fucker'll bite ye.

BOAT TO LIVERPOOL

The itch. I hate it so I do. I do. But I can't help it. All scratchy an fidgety an frantic the way it is at times when me hands get goin. Thinkin. Pure thinkin. What bowt. An if. Fuck. The things that could go wrong over yonder. Even on the way over. Would there be dogs? Boundta be dogs. Sure isn that the thing they always do. Sniff-sniff. Scratch. Fuck. A spot.

I was startinta think maybe goin t'England was a bad idea. That's another fuckin country, an I'd never been there but what I'd heard didn sound good. An goin on a boat? I didn like that. Never been on a boat. I like the sea, to look at it like, but gettin right in the thick'a it? The sea's fuckin huge—people die in there. I didn wanna. No fuckin way. But see them waves haigh? The way they crash n'all? The fury.

I was thinkin all this drivinta the boat. Looked across at herself. Cool as a fuckin . . . I dunno, somethin cool. Easy for her, she knew England inside out. Asleep so she was, an in fairness it was early as fuck but that was her idea anyway. I hate mornins. A 9 a.m. sailin, what kindofan idea was that? A lost day, that's what that means. Ye never recover lost sleep.

Full'a this shiftin down in the belly'a me I was, this squelchin movin mad thing that seemed like it was tryinta get out, an I'd only had a drink or twota settle me nerves sure.

Gettin onta the boat was mad, goin up this big ramp. But actually bein on the boat? Feck. Y'know, all them truckers an that, they're usedta it, ye could see it by them. Away for feeds'a fries like a pile'a pot-bellied greyhounds as soon as they were on the thing like it was no botherta them. But the front bit'a the boat'd go up an then dip down an the whole thing'd move th'other way an it a huge boat n'all an fuck. Movin, the whole thing movin. There's even a bit'a the boat too where ye can stand out in th'air an watch the sea if ye can believe that. For fuck's sake, lads.

Annie was dead sound that time so she was. We sat in a kindofa couch bit an Annie let me put me head on her lap so I could sleep even though I couldn sleep. Who'd be ableta sleep at sea sure? Knowin all them sharks an fish an weird watery things are flowin an slidin round ye, an that ye might fall in with them at any minute. Still n'all it was dead nice'a her, lettin me lie down like that, real comfortin. Sat there hummin an runnin her hands through me hair an hum hummin real soft. I sorta snuggled in an let the smell'a her, clean clothes an that lovely skin cream she wears juss fill me. I didn fall asleep exactly but I did kinda drift off a bit. Felt less sick at least. Less thinkin.

Annie got me up when we were comin in towards Liverpool. It was a mucky auld day, grey clouds an grey sea an then we startedta see the land out in the distance. At first it was dead centre distance, then it stretched across, like a tear between sea an sky. Real slow, like a blotch'a ink spreadin across a sheet. Almost beautiful, but sorta menacin too, specially as we got closer. All these cranes an big buildins off in the distance. The size'a it.

Gettin off the boat there were dogs. Oh yes, there were dogs. Very obviously they pulled us over an I could see the dogs. Sat stewin there, waitin for the dogsta come for a good sniff all round. Three cars down from us. Then two. Some buck comes over an raps on me winda. Annie leans across an starts talkin in her plummiest Englishist accent. Fuck. Didn even know she had one'a them. Hands him her British pass-port too so she does. Didn know she had one'a them either. Then again it makes sense. I hand him mine. Irish. Oh well, it's the twenty-first century peace an love n'all that juss don't talk bowt the war an definitely don't talk bowt the border. What border? The dog's at the car in front'a us then, an yer man's leafin through me passport. Blank pages. Barely looks at hers. Juss two *girls* on a road trip. *Why?* For the craic sure. Fair enough. Overta the *mainland* for some culture maybe. Ha-ha-ha, *mainland*, where's that, Germany or somewhere? The dog starts barkin. At the car in front. Fuck. Unload every-thin. Search-search-search. Poor bastards. Probably juss a bit'a spliff. The peeler looks at us like we're auld pals now an raises his eyebrows. *Troublemakers. We'll teach them. Takin our country back innit, takin back control. You girls enjoy your stay now, have a good time. On you go.*

Prick probably thought he was charmin as fuck.

"Fuck me," I says when we get out'a the port an make for the city. "That was tight goin."

"Relax, honey. You did great."

"*You* did great."

An she still didn know what we were doin, or what was in the car.

"I think I need a drink," I says.

"Good shout. I know a place. Take the next left."

"OK, but juss one. We can't stay in Liverpool."

She put her hand on me leg.

"You think I'd forgotten? Just one."

THE ROAD

This thick feelin in me tummy, the queasy boat feelin, that stayed with me a good lock'a time on the trip, an it came back again an again, like somethin that'd swell up in me, like a wave, but in me belly, not in the sea, threatenin me, threatenin ta swallow me in me own words an wants an things. Now, it wasn juss a question'a me not havin much experience'a the road or that. I know the road. I've been on the road, I've been on the road plenty. Upta Belfast, downta Dublin, an everywhere in between. It's all the same. Dublin specially is juss a big bunch'a pricks packed in real tight. An anyway, down yonder they're all tryin too, pretendin they might go somewhere else like London or New York, or even worse, they act like they're already there. That does me head in, cause I think Dublin probably usedta be daecent. I'd never wanna live in one'a them places, say London. Where do them pricks pretend they'll go? Fuck knows.

I was eventa Galway once, too. Nice wee spot now in fairness, but a bit too clean for me, too pretty like. I felt like I was makin the place dirty juss bein there n'all. We went over on a bender, me an Shamey Hughes an Tommy. Feels like ages ago.

We went for no real reason. Juss took a notion an went for the spin in Shamey's yokc. Fuckin miracle we didn crash or get lifted like, fuckin balubas so we were. I s'pose if we hadn'a been so rat-arsed we'd not'a gone for the spin, I mean the notion wouldn'a took us sure. An without the pills we wouldn'a made it all the way. Who the fuck goesta Galway in any way? Tourists, that's who.

We didn have anywhereta stay, so we juss rolled around an ended up in some estate out in Salthill. Shamey had this class idea, to juss ring people's bells an blag it. Figured it'd haveta work eventually.

An sure it worked the first time. Some bleary-eyed feen in his thirties lands down at the door. Big gullible head on him. We tauld him ar mutual pal Johnny Murphy above in Dublin said it'd be alright for us onesta crash with him. Fucker didn even question it. Pure comatose sure. Good man Johnny.

He lets us in, the madman. A lovely gaff it was. Like proper nice. Real tasteful an that. Kinda intimidatin, cause none'a us ones were usedta anythin like that. An y'know, there was somethin bowt the way he treated us, proper generous like real guests an that, even sat down an had a can with us. Real disarmin so it was. Fuckin hell, I felt kinda bad so I did, an him a pure wee dote like.

"What's the craic with Galway then?" I saysta him, juss puttin it together that we were actually there.

"What do you mean?"

"What sortofa place is it t'all," says Shamey. "Are the people daecent or how are they?"

Yer lad cocks Shamey this look, dead quizzical like. His lip curved an he had a quick chuckle inta his can.

"I'm not tryinta be funny or nathin," says Shamey, an god love him I could feel he was serious. Worried bowt offendin the feen so he is. An not cause he's worried bowt us gettin turfed out or nathin, juss cause he doesn wanna like, hurt him or that.

"It's juss we've never been like. Juss curious sure," I said.

Tommy wasn really part'a this conversation t'all, the head on him. That third pill was one too far for the poor buck. Chewin the jaws off himself he was, an grippin the can in his hand like it was some kindofa handrail, on the bus or that.

Galway lad puts down his can an spreads his hands through th'air. Locks eyes with Shamey so he does.

"I think people are fundamentally the same the world over. I mean, at the bottom of themselves, there's the same amount of decency and muck in all of us. It's just the shit we're dealing with shapes it."

He took a gouge out'a his beer.

"In that sense, well, people in Galway are grand. They could be better; they're a lucky bunch. It's a good place to live, all things considered."

He swirls the dregs'a his beer round an downs it.

He goes away upta bed after that, but not before fetchin us ones blankets n'all. Like proper guests sure. Some craic.

Shamey tricks away with Tommy, tryinta get a bit'a craic out'a him, but I'm stuck solid in me own fuckin head. Them words, that *good place to live* bit, they stuck with me. I have this memory, me hand clenchin on the can, an them words goin round an round like some angry satellite stuck in me head, gettin sharper, gettin faster each time it went round, *good place, good place*.

I keep squeezin an squeezin til the sides'a the can crumpled an cut inta me hand. I can feel it threateninta cut through if I clench it tighter an so I do, an it feels good. Feels like release.

The next mornin, he comes down. We were thinkinta make a quick exit like, before he copped onta us. But sure he'd already copped it.

"You know, I don't actually know anyone called Johnny Murphy," he saysta us an him headin out the door. "And like, lads, it's probably the *least* imaginative name you could have come up with."

"Ah, yeah, we must'a got th'auld address mixed up, mate," says Shamey out from under his blanket, tryinta hide the big Shamey smile'a his.

"It's alright. I figured you just needed somewhere to crash. I've been in the same boat."

"Yer a sound man," says Tommy.

"I've got to go to work, anyway. But you guys can lie in. Just let yourselves out. There's food in the kitchen, help yourselves."

I sit up a bit, kinda thinkin I'm still dreamin maybe. "Ah, deadly. That's class. Yer a star so y'are."

"Any time," he says, an smiles. "I'm used to it. I host travellers all the time from Couchsurfing."

"What's that?" I ask the feen.

"It's an online hospitality network. Usually nice to get a little advance notice," he says with a wee wink, a real nice one. "You should check it out, it's very useful. When you're leaving, just close the door behind you, it'll lock itself."

Not a touch'a bitter in his voice or nathin. I'd be dead

annoyed if anyone woke me up in the middle'a the night an them half-cut I'll tell ye.

He gives us a hug an shakes the hands'a the lads. Pure legend. Pure gullible, innocent, naive, bullet-proof legend.

He fecks off an we juss exchange this look, fuckin eyes as big as they'll go. We go backta sleep for a bit. When I wake up again, Tommy's scramblin eggs. He gives us this, with smoked fuckin salmon, coffee an toast an juice n'all—the works.

"Did yon buck say there was a whole website for lettin randomers crash at yer gaff?" I says.

"He did, aye. Mad craic altogether," says Tommy.

"That'd never work in a hole like Dundalk but," came Shamey.

"Yeah well in fairness it wouldn be much use there anyway. It's hardly what you'd call a tourist destination."

I hated talkin bowt the Town like that but to be fair it's true.

The funny thing bowt all that was that after him bein so gullible an that, we couldn even touch nathin he hadn invited usta. I tried thinkin bowt it n'all, but it was like a magic spell, some kindofa shield. Mad craic altogether. Trust, it's a powerful thing. We even tidied up after arselves, an us never gonna see yon buck again.

Hellofa wayta start the day, I'll tell you. All'a us dead happy, an feelin clean, the feelin'a bein clean on th'inside. Rotten clean.

The whole day I could feel the cut'a the can from the night before. Crushin the can like that, the sharp bit stuck inta me, but in a funny kindofa way—it kinda scraped back the skin from the heel'a me hand. Was good though, good in a way, to have that to focus on. Groundin. Cause the lads, they were wild that time. On the drink as soon as the pubs opened.

Some lovely pubs in Galway, really lovely ones, all wooden insides an snugs. Felt dead proper, like proper old-school. Too nice for the Town, I remember thinkin, we couldn have them, someone'd fuck them up. An I hated them thoughts, too, the hand achin on me.

If it had only been beer the lads were swillin. Was gas— dead funny like—*me* bein th'one hauldin back, tryinta steady them. But that's the way it was with them pair. At one point the pair'a them pop offta the toilet together, like a pair'a beors, an I wonder what all this is bowt.

"Fizzybum," says Shamey, that big gern, the big Shamey smile on him an him on his fifth pint'a Guinness of the day, an it three in th'afternoon.

Pills up the bum, slow release. Fuckin hell. I could see I was in for a long night, so I did the same, but juss with the halfofa one so I could stay a bit sober. Fizzybum's a good high in fairness, even though I don't like fiddlin at me arse.

We hardly know where we are. It was one'a them days, one'a them nights when the time passes over ye like the tide, when each pint is like a punch, like some enemy onslaught in a battle, a siege like, but one yer happyta be fightin, at least for the night that's in it. We passed from pubta pub, until at one point I have this Galway lad, feen by the name'a Pól chewin th'ear off'a me, tryinta impress me cause he talks Irish dead good an folk who talk Irish dead good think they're dead class, like as though they're more Irish than everyone else—as if that's a good thing. It's mad, cause if ye think bowt it, not speakin Irish is every bit as Irish as speakin Irish at this stage.

Anyway, I don't much like it when lads tryta get their dick
sucked by showin how they're dead smart an that. Remember
thinkin that, rubbin the raw heel'a me hand, kinda pushin inta
the rawness'a it.

Th'other two were off upstairs on their third pill by then.
Was thinkin bowt howta ditch this lad an go upta them without a fresh round'a drinks or that.

Pól's still blatherin on bowt Connemara, somethin bowt
the stones an the rains an the miserable Irish experience, but
he's already lost me. Cause see there was this other fella. My
god, a gorgeous fella. Real slender, delicate. Looked like he
belonged in a magazine, advertisin fancy clothes, the way he
stood, how he moved n'all. It was like he was at one'a them
fashion shows or that.

But it wasn juss how he looked. There was somethin else,
somethin magic—like a magnet. An it wasn juss me. I could
see the whole room reactinta him. Not starin, but there was
somethin there. I watched him weave through the crowd, like
a fish or somethin, like in one'a them documentaries. Real
lively, n'all, hidin between rocks an weeds an things here an
there an then gulpin somethin down an dartin awayta the
next feedin ground. Pól, he hadn noticed that I wasn really
with him anymore, an I was vaguely aware'a him harpin on
bowt woolly jumpers or some shite. I thought this other fella
hadn noticed me watchin him. Thought I was bein discreet an
that. But I was already warm down beneath. Then he juss turns
around an locks gaze with me, smilin liketa say, *yeah, I see you.*

Beautiful fella he was. Rich reddish-brown hair, all slicked
back an that under this old-school kinda hat. Normally that
kinda craic'd put me off like, but it worked on him. The feen
had a fuckin moustache n'all. Scummy auld things mous-

taches, but see on this lad the package was good enough it all kinda worked. It was like his whole look had been designed by a team'a French flower experts overseen by Coco Chanel herself. But in a nice way, fuckin sexy, not some kinda weirdo perv way or nathin.

An then he's off again.

A bit later Pól goes offta the toilet. An yer man comes back, cocks his hat an sits down, casual as ye fuckin like.

"Hi," he says t'me, proper cocky like. I don't normally like cocky feens, an so many'a them're cocky. But on this lad it worked. Oh, it worked. I was already hooked—I hadta follow this, to see where it was goin.

"Andrew's the name."

Fucker shook me hand, even kissed it, an I'm juss there in a fuckin buzz like what the very fuck is this? An his hand, real soft hand, real smooth like. Don't remember a damn what we talked bowt, but by the time yer man Pól comes back I'm already hooked. Andrew juss takes me hand an leads me off. I follow him without hesitation.

Bit later I left the two lads after th'one drink an went home with him. Didn even text them, which I felt a bit shitty bowt the next day. But sure, it's not like they noticed, the state'a them. Andrew. Annie. Thinkin bowt it now, I could almost laugh bowt it. The things I should'a known.

Them two days juss slid by for me between the sheets, pure sexual decadence like. Gettinta know things I'd never thought'a before. At first the pair'a lads were grand on their buzz, but as time wore on their texts got edgier an edgier. They wantedta be gettin back home. Lookin back it's hardta blame them like, cause Galway's pretty dull if yer not mad inta someone. If I hadn'a met Annie, I'd'a left the next day. It's juss a couple'a streets that're too pretty in any way. It's all juss muck underneath, so why the fancy facade? Fake shite sure.

The third day I tauld them jussta g'wan backta fuck, but that I was stayin. Tauld them I'd take the bus. See at that point I juss kinda presumed I wouldn be seein Annie again, so I wantedta enjoy it proper. Didn think it'd last at the time. I mean Galway's fierce far away, an in any way, she had a fella on the go at the time. I mean a'course she had—at least one.

The night after the lads left meself an Annie went for a walk. She starts hauldin me hand, down by the water where it's lovely. I thought it was juss a sex thing up til then but this felt like a signal that naw, actually maybe there's more. I tried not to think too much bowt it like cause it made me hands dead itchy an that, which was awkward with her hauldin them. I could still kinda feel the pain, from the can, but it was well faded. Annie was sound bowt that, she didn even say nathin bowt the bandages so she didn, which was dead sound. But she asked loads bowt Dundalk an that, with this kinda shinin in her eye. At the time, I didn know what it meant like, but now I know. The vicious shine. She was thinkin. An where me thinkin makes me hands wanna tear each other apart, her thinkin sets th'eyes ashine an turns anyone who looks at them inta part'a her plan. Ye don't even realise it, that's the thing, but that's how it happens. Very fuckin few people I've knownta be ableta resist that sure.

I guess she knew rightly what I was bowt. I knew she was flirtin with the business too, but in a proper smalltime kindofa way an that. Sure the shine'a her eye, it was really juss her belly rumblin. She complained bowt Galway an that but wouldn say much bowt Belfast. At the time it really puzzled me, why would anyone leave a class town like Belfast for a dump like Galway?

That night she said she'd come see me in Dundalk. At first I thought she was juss coddin me, juss tryinta be nice but I didn know why. Wasn like I'd asked herta come. But a'course I didn say so, cause I was dead happy like, fuckin delighted, me belly on fire down below an the back'a me knees already startinta sweat.

THE HIGHLANDER

Lyin there kinda tangled together we were, the sorta way where ye lose track'a whose leg is whose. Annie puts her hand on me thigh as ifta remind me, slidin it up an up an I know what's comin next cause it's already the third time that mornin. That's the thing I love bowt girls like, bowt bein with beors, it's like they have extra hands, or maybe it's cause they know what to look for. Maybe it's juss patience. Yeah, it's probably patience. It's key. But then again, even when a fella takes the time, you'd swear he's sandin a plank.

With Annie though, it was pure magic. The crazy thing is she barely moved her fingers. She has this mad lazy way'a movin in bed, it's like the tips'a her are charged with some kinda electric or somethin. She juss lies there on her side, her eyes half open in a tired kindofa way that's dead sexy, an her tongue slidin around her lips like she can taste it an she likes what she tastes. The way ye might spend time eatin somethin real good.

She's sittin there touchin me an massagin her head at the same time, with the same rhythm n'all. Maybe that's where th'electric comes from, maybe it's a kindofa static charge an her whole body's one big coil creatin it. Hasta come from somewhere.

"I prefer girls, really," she saysta me, "more interesting. More of a challenge. Men are such basic creatures by comparison. I've always wanted to have a girlfriend."

Oooh, fuck me, that tingly spine magic, hairs standin still an shrill like flowersta the sun. Yes yes. Like me stomach inside out, but in a nice way. Excitin like, not like when yer feelin sick after a hape'a drink or that. A kindofa good sick, like ye'd feel before somethin big, a big payoff or that. It's sorta funny like, cause I never thought much'a bein with a beor, definitely not in any kindofa serious way sure, not til I met Annie.

Before her, I'd never really been involved in anythin too serious. I mean, I'd been with fellas an that, but that's mostly cause, well, ye juss figure that's the way things should be cause that's what people want ye to think things should be like an that, when yer young an ye don't know howta listenta yerself cause there isn really *yer* self yet, juss a bunch'a selves other people want ye to be sure. Not that that gets much better mind. An in fairness I do like th'odd fella.

There was this one feen I was even mad inta. Back home in Mullaghbawn. In a way, it was part'a the reason I left home when I did, cause I felt fuckin stupid, cause I'd let meself get caught up with his ideas'a things, the person he wanted me bein, he talked a lot bowt that before he pisst off like. Prick. I mean, I woulda left Mullaghbawn sooner or later anyway. Everyone leaves Mullaghbawn so they do, unless they're funny in the head.

He was fuckin beautiful. In me mind he'll always be around nineteen. Hugh, his name was. Big broad shoulders on him, an a big thick head'a long black hair. He was the most lovely-lookin lad I ever saw, Hugh. To think he picked me, an me juss a frumpy wee lump.

I loved him in the way every beor loves the first feen she fucks. I was two years younger, he hadta repeat a year in school cause he was a bit thick like. But at the time he seemed dead grown up. Experienced an that. He usedta scoot bowt on this shitty wee motorbike, moreofa moped really, but in Mullagh-bawn that seemed like a big deal. He never wore a helmet, an it looked dead romantic with his hair blowin behind him an that, like somethin out'a a film. I usedta get so mad at him for ridin round like that. Fuckin reckless. He was like that though. Juss didn give a shite. Seemedta think he'd live forever, that he was immortal or somethin. He was obsessed with this film, *Highlander*, see. Thought he was like the feen in the film, thought nathin could hurt him.

Fucker juss kinda disappeared. We had ar last night together an he gave me this big spiel bowt *findin himself*. Destiny an that. In any way, I saw on Facebewk he ended up drivin JCBs in the mines in Australia. Got fat an married. Sure some people have all the luck.

BIG ENOUGH

Sat in yon pub in Liverpool, an us only off the boat, that's when I decidedta tell Annie bowt the job an that. I mean, bowt why the fuck we were there t'all. I think I tauld her soasta reassure meself, really. To tell meself like, yeah, this was the right thing, definitely the right thingta be doin. This makes sense an I'm not mad an sure havin herta hear it did make it sound a bit better like, reassurin somehowta see how she thought this was a good idea, an that we could pull it off n'all. Cause on the boat it was all I could think bowt. An goin through customs, fuck me, that was somethin else. Thought I'd shit meself sure. So by the time we sat down in the pub an that it all came floodin right out.

One'a them proper hipster pubs, y'know, one'a them ones that look the same no matter where they are, Dublin, Belfast or Liverpool sure, with the same type'a auld wood an the same fancy fake auld lightbulbs that are actually juss LEDs an don't give out any daecent light. Y'know the type'a them sure. Thank god we've none'a them in the Town, though with all the new jobs an the money comin back an that there's still a risk, specially if more people start commutinta Dublin. Cause like, then, they'd wanna make it juss like Dublin. That'd be shite.

All the same the craft beers can be alright. Meself an herself, we snuggle on inta a sorta wee booth. I'm sorta lookin over me shoulder, cause'a that craic with the Liverpool gang back in the Town. But they didn look like hipsters, an besides, they're still below in Portlaoise—they'll be there a long time yet. The lads at the bar there, they looked like they were more interested in their moustaches than they'd ever be in us.

"Ye wanna hear why we're here? Aside from the whole get out'a town bit."

"Go on then," she says, sorta haughty like. See, she doesn like th'idea'a this bein her fault like, the same way the pup doesn like havin its nose shoved in its own shite sure.

I decided not to shove her inta it. Wasn really her fault in any way. That was juss me spun it like that. An in any way, there's plenty I got upta that she never knew nathin bowt, plenty. So there was no call for double standards—I'm not a man after all. Besides, things were good round then, I didn needta go ruinin that. I guess she understood that, appreciated it, that I'd thought bowt it, cause when I reached acrossta take her hand, she squeezed mine, dead tight so she did, like a wee baby might. Her way'a sayin thanks. Thanks for understandin. Things like that, they're hard for her.

"Well, here's the craic," I saysta her.

I lean in close, so close that the smell'a her gets all up inside me, down the middle'a me n'all.

"It's a coke job."

"Fuck. Really? You're not usually into coke, are you?"

"Indeed I'm not. But it's part'a the conditions'a yer parole, darlin."

She looks at me sideways a bit, her head tiltin up an her lips thinnin cold. She's not happy not knowin more, bowt not knowin the details.

"Is it big?"

"Big enough now. Big enough. Fuckin loads haigh."

She squeezes tight on me hand. Real tight again. *Trust me*, she's sayin.

"Ten fuckin kilos."

"Jeasus Christ. That's . . ."

"Yeah. Fuckin loads. An pure as fuck haigh. C'mere t'me."

She leans in an I give her a wee taste.

She sits back. Th'eyes on her, ye should'a seen it so ye should'a. Dancey magic, big, bold an beautiful. Her thinkin. Off her tits but still thinkin. Proper gourmet shit, this.

"An we've got ten—" she starts, full volume like.

"Would ye whist! There's no-one knows that an there's no-one that's gonna know that. Else we're fuckin dead when we get back home."

"Back home?"

"Backta the Town."

"Right, right," she says, kinda noddin, confused-lookin but. "Obviously. Sorry."

"You understand? Tell nobody nathin. Nobody back home an nobody we meet over here. Got it?"

"Yeah yeah, I get it."

That's the dead annoyin thing bowt talkinta folk who're off their fuckin tits an that, they take offence dead easy so they do. But sure, I neededta tell her.

"So where are we going? I mean, who are we meeting?"

"No-one."

"What do you mean no-one? Who's the buyer?"

"We haveta find them."

"Them?"

"Yeah. Them. This hasta be done quiet. A kilo at a time at most. Under the radar like."

"Shit. How, though? I mean that's a lot, a lot of stuff."

"We'll juss haveta play it by ear haigh. It was part'a the deal, the quiet bit, the dealta get *you* out'a lockup. But there's a cut for us too. A proper, daecent cut so there is."

"Like how much?" she asks, eyes on fire.

I hesitate. Me throat, me mouth an all, it's pure dry juss then.

"Like half. Straight down the middle."

"Fuck. That's a lot. That's gotta be worth . . ."

"Loads."

"Fuck! Great!"

"Yeah. It is."

Her eyes go wild again.

"Class!"

I burst me shite laughin. She almost looks offended.

"What?"

"It's juss funny, you sayin that."

"Would ye whist, ye mulpin, ye ham child!"

She chuckles sayin this, an she leans acrossta kiss me.

"That stuff *is* class, though," she says. "Can I have another taste?"

"Only if ye say *class* again."

"Class. Claaasss. Claaaaaasss. *It's pure munya haigh.*"

Now she's breakin her shite laughin.

"Alright, alright, don't go takin the piss would ye not," I saysta her, but I'm dead happy actually.

I give her another wee taste. Take a wee poke meself. Couple'a feens at the bar gawk at us. Fuck them sure.

We finish up ar drinks an bang on down the roadta Manchester. We're stayin the night with some'a Annie's pals. Now she knows the craic, she's in straight-up plannin mode. Juss like I knew she'd be. I felt so sure then, in that moment there, so sure that I could trust her. So sure'a the road, though I didn know a fuck what was round the next bend so I didn. Didn feel like I neededta, cause I had her with me.

I did feel a bit bad bowt not tellin her the full scéal, bowt this bein the Rat King's coke. I wasn lyin bowt it, not *exactly*, juss leavin out details, but I still didn like it. But sure it was one'a them things, what was it that Detective Kelleher called it? Ah yeah, a *necessary and justifiable expedience*.

Yeah. It was one'a them.

GOOD MAN GERRY

On the roadta Manchester a mucky big cloud was rollin in off the sea the way we went. The mood came over me, a bit mucky, like the clouds that seemed to be chasin us up the road to Manchester. Felt like it was a shame, y'know, a shame not to get to see Liverpool better. I've heard it's a daecent spot in fairness. I'd expectedta feel dead foreign, the way I do in Dublin, say. But I didn, not really.

Annie was drivin, an I was sittin watchin this wave'a cloud come over us. Felt pure wintery then, an it put me in a mind'a this one time, this time when Annie an me went for a spin. Early spring the year before, an she wasn long in the Town at that stage. I'll never forget that day, cause it'd been rainin the whole month before. Barrels'a rain, every day. We were startinta go stale stuck inside so we were.

Annie had movedta the Town bit by bit. I guess that's th'only way anyone movesta Dundalk really. She cameta visit a load'a times in autumn, but over winter, her movements kinda slowed, an she juss kinda stayed there—stayed with me

I mean. We'd been together a good bit by then, but still, we probably should'a talked bowt it. I'm sure she still had stuff back in Galway, things'a hers an a room an that to sort out. But she juss kinda abandoned it. An there was a fella was mad inta her, but that wasn workin anyway she tauld me.

Anyway, that day, she was itchinta take a wee trip somewhere. Where? It didn matter. Juss somewhere. *Somewhere round here.* But there's nowhere round here, I tauld her.

"What do you mean there's nowhere around here? We could go to Carlingford maybe?"

"Bunch'a spas out there. All stag parties an wee snide shites, cause they're from a place that looks nice."

"What about Clogherhead? I've heard it's nice."

"Waste'a time. Unless ye wanna go fishin or drown yerself, which probably *is* what ye'd wanna do if ye went there."

"What about Ardee?"

"They're all mad in the head up there. Can we not juss go to Toales for a pint sure? Be grand."

"For fuck's sake. No! I want to go somewhere. Somewhere nice. It's the first nice day all year, so while there's still some daylight I want to go see something. We're not doing anything today, anyway. You'd have said so. So come with me, or I'll go by myself."

"How would ye get there, an you without a yoke?"

"Sure you don't have a car either. I'll hitch."

"Hitch? Yer mad."

"Why not? I've done it loads of times before."

"Look, folk don't go hitchin round here."

"You can hitch wherever you want. That's the point."

"OK. Right, I'll go with you. But juss cause I don't like this whole hitchin thing. Lunatic. That's how people get murdered. I'll call Shamey Hughes for his yoke."

Decided I'd take her for a walk up in Anaverna, upta Clairmont Cairn. Y'know, up where the television mast is. Only place I could think'a at the time for some reason, a high place, felt far away but close somehow.

When ye get t'Anaverna, it's still a fair auld trek up the hill. Anaverna—quare namcofa place. We juss call it the fuckin mast! I wasn sure Annie'd really wanna go all the way up. Neither'a us had proper gear for bein out walkin the hills in March, even if it was a sunny day an that. We must'a been some quare sight to th'ones out trainin, what with Annie in that big fur coat she liked. Real fur n'all. Said it'd belongedta her granny once. Looked like she belonged on telly so she did, but then she often did. Spent fuckin ages every day agonisin over what she was gonna wear. She was always makin fun'a me cause I'd get ready in five minutes, so I'd have loads'a time before we'd go anywhere. Dead annoyin, that. The ground was like a big auld sponge someone'd left go mouldy, all black with water the way it'd ooze out when ye'd step on it. Mucky auld business walkin the hills.

The view at the top was mad. Up there at the mast, ye can see right round. On up inta the Narth, cross the Mournes, all down the wee towns an villages on the sea, an the Cooleys, stretchin on forever. They almost look like proper mountains from up there sure.

Annie was real quiet. Takin in the views an that I thought. An in fairness, things do look nice from up there. The Town doesn really. It's like this kinda big dirty spider, the kind ye usedta see in yer grandparents' toilet that'd frighten the fuck out'a ye. Annie was all quiet but I felt like talkin, I felt un-trapped then, all the scratchy feelins an tight feelin juss sorta floated away. Everywhere was like I could juss reach out an touch it if I wanted. Not like bein down walkin the streets with the clouds that feel like they're bowt three feet above ye sure, with some prickofa wannabe hardman givin ye the hard eye as he walks by.

The two'a us sat on a big rock not far from the mast, to look round I guess, an get ar breath. She's all heavy sighs an that, the way people do when they wanna talk bowt somethin. I rolled up a couple'a fags an passed her one. Even this got some big kindofa sigh out'a her. Then she starts talkinta me bowt relationships an confusion. I'm lost. So I tells her.

"Where're ye goin with all this haigh?"

"I just don't know what you want, that's all. And I don't know what I'm able to give you. You know, I'm still exploring myself. Still learning. I mean, I'm only twenty-five."

"Age has nathinta do with it, love. I'm twenty-eight an I don't know a fuck what I want, either. I wish *I* knew. All I know is that we have a good time together, an I enjoy bein with ye. I don't juss mean the sex."

"Right. Me too. It's just that, well, I'm not really into monogamy. And I've tried polyamory, and that didn't work out for me either."

She kinda stumped me with that, specially the second one, which I later learned basically means havin yer cake an eatin it.

She puts her hands on her waist, the one'a them kinda fidgetin, like it's lookin for somethin.

"The thing is, I just care about you too much to commit to

an exclusive relationship. I know myself too well. I know I'll fuck it up. I know I'll slip up."

I didn say nathin. She turnsta face me though, waitin for a response. So I light up the fag I rolled, an take a big puff.

"D'ye think I haven noticed?"

"Noticed what?"

"The way ye look at lads. The way ye talkta them. The way ye love how they talkta ye the way they do. The way ye play with yer hair. You bein on Tinder an that. Yeah, sorry, I wasn tryinta look or that, ye juss needta be more discreet."

"So you know?"

"Yeah."

"I'm sorry. Really I'm sorry. It's just that with you I thought it could be different."

"What're ye talkin bowt? It is different."

"How?"

"It is different," I saysta her. "I don't mind what ye get upta with fellas. It's grand sure. I might hook up with a few too. Or beors. As long as it's juss a sex thing, as long yer with me, I don't mind sure."

See, I'd already clocked that if I triedta hauld her back, I'd lose her in bowt two seconds flat. So I figured this was th'only way. I'd already accepted it like.

She looked at me then as though she were tryinta guess me weight. She had her lips all closed, buttoned like a purse.

"OK," she says, "we can try it like that."

An that's how it was. An mostly, it worked. I mean, mostly it was good, y'know?

We went on back down the mountain. It started gettin dark halfway back so it was bowt time, too.

The Town was buzzin though, as if somethin had changed.

We stopped in at Toales in th'end for a hot whiskey, warm us up like. Shamey came inta get his car keys, an ended up playin a bunch'a tunes, cause they know him real well in there. Left the car parked for the night in front'a th'office'a Gerry Adams TD.

Good man Gerry.

SOME FUCKIN SIEGE

MANCHESTER LAD
(FIRST DICK IN A WHILE)

Mad sortofa thing innit, bein at a big party when it's juss a load'a folk who don't know each other. The whole minglin thing. What's that all bowt, anyway? When I go to a party, it'sta buy somethin or sell somethin or spend time with people I already know. People ye don't know tendta be pricks—can't be too careful.

Times like them I've a kindofa feelin like yeah, no, yeah I dunno, I'll juss hide in me hat maybe, or under me drink. Nice an cosy down there. Or with a bunch'a folk already too far round the bend. That way they can't be too muchofa pain in the hole with all them questions they think are juss polite an that. Fuckin spas. Don't they know the violence in it, all that *what do you do* shite? I hate it so I do, I juss hate it.

We were at a party like that in Manchester so we were. Big mad party full'a randomers. But in fairness, that one time was a good time cause Annie was with me, an I mean really with me cause a lot'a the time she's on her own buzz, which is fair enough but this one time we were proper together an that was good cause I could sorta hide in her. An sure it was some siegeofa session, fuckin deadly music there was, loads'a drink an even grub an that, proper noble peck too. Me an Annie were havin great craic, juss watchin this crowd'a posers, off on ar own buzz the two'a us.

"What do you think that guy does for a living?" she saysta me.

"Yon buck with the hat?"

"Yeah. Him."

"Fuck. I'd say he works in property. Real estate agent. Speculator maybe. Rentin out crappy gaffs that usedta be council houses or somethin."

"That's very specific. But I wouldn't have put him down for something like that."

"Naw, see, course not. Cause if yer a crummy estate agent or a scumbag speculator ye hardly want folk knowin it straight off. That's why he has the gimpy hat an that idiot shirt. Wants folk thinkin he plays in a jazz band. Maybe even funk. Maybe funk the Saturday night, jazz the Sunday mornin, that kindofa thing, y'know?"

"Yeah yeah, I get it now alright. You're good at this! What about that woman over there?"

"Oh, her. She's an open an shut case as they say."

"Is she?"

"Surely. She usedta do webcam stuff, to get her through college. Kinky stuff. Now she's a teacher. Still a bit kinky but."

"Naaah, come on, be reasonable."

"That is fuckin reasonable! Look at them shoes. She wantsta stay grounded. But showin that kinda cleavage?"

"That's a bit presumptuous, isn't it?"

"Whaddya mean?"

"Like, surely a woman can dress how she likes. Doesn't necessarily mean anything, not like that. I mean if you were a man . . ."

"A'course, a'course she can dress how she wants. An I don't mean anythin by it. I'm juss pointin out the combo there, that's where I see it. See, I knew a beor in DKIT usedta do that. She made loads at it so she did. Like prostitution without th'inconvenience she said."

"Wow. You're so good at this. It's . . . surprising."

"Whaddya mean?"

"Um . . . I don't want to, you know . . ."

"Juss say it, fuck's sake."

"It's just, you never seem to pay much attention to, well, clothes and things. I always figured you just don't notice."

"Ye gotta be jokin. I notice *everythin*, love. Naw, it's not a question'a that."

"What is it then?"

"I dunno. I don't like bein noticed I guess. Not like that in any way."

She sorta bit her lip on th'inside, I s'pose she was tryinta hide it from me that kindofa way.

I looked th'other way, took a gouge out'a me drink. We went backta the game, but that look she gave me kinda hung there in th'air.

I was a bit annoyed, bein at this party full'a middle-class cunts who'd never buy more than they could sniff themselves, proper safe folk. An this after Annie's pals sold it t'us as a placeta make some good connects. There was class music but, th'one silver linin there was. At one point we end up upstairs an there's some feen gettin readyta play a few tunes. Now this wasn like the boom boom goin on down below. An two chill floors in between meant we could actually hear him n'all. So he takes this funny-lookin thing outofa case an starts tunin. The room itself is lovely too, all carpets an cushions. Feels like I'm somewhere fancy.

This fella starts playin an I swear it's like someone poured honey in me ears an me ears ableta eat it sure, taste it. Savour it like. An I'm thinkin, fuck me, Shamey Hughes should be here so he should. He'd love this. Some craic.

This lad's playin for ten minutes without stoppin or lookin up t'all. I lean overta some feen sat nearby.

"Sorry, d'y'know what this fella's playin? It's deadly."

"Arabian lute. Wicked, innit?"

"Pure class."

I reach for me phone.

Me: Shamey ye mucksavage, check out arabian lutes.
     Fuckin deadly.

We were sittin right at the back, agin the wall. This was somethin else. The bass from downstairs'd still come in an that, but it mixed in, had this mournful sortofa beat to it. Lovely. Like some soft remix stuff. But in a good way.

Anyway this Manchester lad leans in an starts chattin.

"Where you from, love? Not round here eh?"

Fuck's sake.

"Mullaghbawn."

"Mullawhat?"

"Mullaghbawn, y'eejit."

"Mullaboan. Sounds exotic. Where's that?"

"Armagh."

"Oh, that's in Arland innit? I have Ayrish family I do, on me dad's side."

"Congratulations."

"Is that in Northern Arland or Southern Arland?"

"The Narth. But I live in Dundalk."

"Is that in Southern Arland then?"

"Well, they're basically the same latitude, ye ham child, but someone came along an put a line between them."

"Who'd do a thing like that?" he says, with a wee smile as if it's a joke an that.

"Some prickofa Brit with nathin betterta do," I says.

He looked confused for a minute, poor cub, not sure howta respond. I knew I was bein a bitofa cunt, but I said it in a nice way so I did. It's always funny when ye call someone a spa in a nice voice. It's juss dead annoyin, cause in England no-one knows fuck all bowt Ireland an they expect ye to know all bowt England even if yer talkin some random shithole like Manchester. Which is even worse like, cause yeah, we do. Fuckin pure humiliatin in a way, surely if I haveta know bowt Manchester they should know bowt the Town. But they don't. I didn meet one prick over there who'd ever even hearda Dundalk. Shockin, really, when ye think bowt it.

Anyway, poor chap was juss tryinta be friendly an that. Wasn his fault that th'English never paid attentionta the places they trampled through history. An he wasn bad lookin either, had a lovely accent too so he did. But I kinda couldn help meself, for the pure divilment'a it.

"You like the music anyway?"

"Like it? That's a fuckin dumb thingta ask."

"Erm, sorry?"

"It's fuckin devastatin this stuff. Like the proper heady sound. Sufferin an joy an fuckin everythin in there so there is. Proper life like."

"Yeah. Powerful."

Spa. Cute, juss not that smart.

"What do you do then?" he saysta me, showin no sign'a givin up. Points for persistence.

"Avoid thick conversations, that's what I do."

"I'm sorry?"

"Awah now don't be sorry. It's not yer fault. Ye juss don't wanna know, buck."

"I wouldn't've asked otherwise," he says. "Look, it can't be worse than what I do."

"Try me."

"I'm a fuckin undertaker, innit."

"I dunno. Is it? You tell me."

"Sorry?"

"Don't be. Undertaker. That sounds shite."

Poor lad. Really did sound shite.

"Well, yeah. But the pay's good and the hours aren't too bad. It's only in winter it's awful cause loads of people die all at once. That's a pain. Otherwise it's bearable."

"Deadly."

"Hah!"

"Wha?"

"It's just funny, innit, cause you said 'deadly' and I work with the dead."

"Hilarious. Are ye religious or somethin then?"

"Fuck no."

"Mad."

"Why?"

"Juss, I'd'a figured ye'd haveta be off with the fairies an that to wanna work with corpses."

"Nah. I mean I grew up kinda religious. My family are Jewish. More just as a tradition though, we're not orthodox or nothin, we don't go to temple, just for special occasions. But when I went to work as an undertaker, well, all of the religion in me sorta evaporated. Must've been the formaldehyde fumes. Happened round the third time I had to shove a cotton wad up some grandad's arse. Nothin much holy bowt that I'll tell you."

"Innit," I say, takin the mick out'a him, the way he talks an that.

"Nah, love. That's not how you say it."

"Sorry."

"You're fine."

"I juss don't wanna go appropriatin yer culture an that. Will ye forgive me?"

"Is that meant to be irony?"

"Ha? Are ye jokin? Sure yous ones never appropriated shite. Yis should'a. Would'a done yis a power'a good. All yis knewta do was destroy."

"Didn't I tell you I was Jewish?"

"I thought ye said ye were Irish."

"Which means I have even less to do with the destruction of your culture, or appropriating it, or whatever. I'm a bit of both, innit."

"Is it?"

"Yeah. I'm Irish and Jewish."

"An English."

"Well, Mancunian. But yeah. My point is that I've got

plenty of culture. Plenty. So don't you worry, love, no need to go appropriatin nothin."

I was actually startinta like this fella. I notice Annie kinda observin an that an I see a wee smile on her face. Me phone buzzes.

Annie: You want to fuck him?
Me: I dunno. Maybe. He's cute.
Annie: Go for it!
Me: Yeah but I'm not sure tho.
Annie: Why not?
Me: Dunno. You OK with it?
Annie: Yeah! Of course. Go for it!

It's easierta hide yer phone than whisper in front'a someone in fairness. I looks at her an she's beamin at me so she is. An I know it is, that she won't hauld it agin me or nathin. She squeezes me thigh then takes off inta the party, away back downstairs.

"So what is it that you do then?"

I turns an looks at him, full on like.

"I sell booze. Illegally distilled vodka an gin. An I run counterfeit fags across the border. Sometimes I boost stuff from people's gaffs, but I'm tryinta get out'a that. Bad profit/risk ratio so there is. These days I only do it on a consultancy basis, y'know like, help smalltime thicks muddle through. But here in England I'm sellin coke. Don't tendta do much'a that so I don't but I'm doin it soasta help a friend."

"Fuck. Must be some friend."

"The best. The feen is fuckin weapons grade so he is."

"You're not pullin me leg are you?"

"Lad, if I pult yer leg it'd come right off."

"Hah! I believe you."

"Ye'd better. Were ye lyin bowt shovin cotton up yer granda's arse?"

"Whoa whoa, not *my* grandad."

"Yeah yeah. Sure it's all the same. Sounds awful in any way."

"It is. That's why I've been gettin inta a bit of dealin meself innit."

"Ha?"

Me phone buzzed. I take a sneaky wee peak.

Shamey Hughes: Aye. Fuckin sublime. How's tricks?
                          Miss u.

Manchester lad's babblin away bowt the scene there.

Annie: Well? How's it going?!

Me: Grand.

Annie: Tell me!

Me: What does sublime mean?

Annie: Really? Already?

Me: Tell me.

Annie: It's like, something really powerful. Something that breaks barriers. Transcends, but in a delicate way. At least that's what it means to me. But no man's that good.

Me: I know. NVM. Love u.

Annie: <3 love you too! Have fun:*

Weird seein Annie use so many emojis. Remembered that I'd forgot to reply to Shamey.

Me: I miss YOU. Ye've no idea.

Manchester lad pipes up.

"Sorry, did I bore you?"

"Ha?"

"Am I boring you?"

"Naw. Yer grand so ye'ar."

"Yeah yeah."

I look at the fella playin. It's like he's bowt to cry, an I can tell it's totally sincere. He's givin it his all like. Fuckin beautiful.

"Well, anyway, like I was sayin, I'm dealin too. I'm gonna save up enough so I can quit this shit. I don't wanna be in the undertaking game all my life. Kills you on th'inside bein round dead people all the time."

"Good idea, cub."

He cocks his head an looks at me.

"Yeah. So I'll take some gear off you."

"How much?"

"How much you cartin?"

I give him a look jussta say *walk on pal*, an look back at me phone.

"Ye don't ask questions like that."

"OK, OK, how about I take a kilo?"

I look back. He's got that same sad look as the musician. Dead sincere n'all.

"Yer no good for it."

"I am. Just give me a good price. No questions asked."

"I'll give ye *the* price, feen. It's good stuff. Pure as it comes."

We slip out after the lute lad finishes his set—no question'a missin a minute'a that. We head backta his on the pretext'a havin a sample. Samples bein all I have on me at that point. Rules'a the job—ye gotta have rules when yer on the job. No punters knowin where the gear was stowed. Even if someone looked into the car, they wouldn see it, an it in the doors'a the yoke. An no carryin round proper amounts—samples only.

Anyway, I'm not worried bowt this feen. I know rightly he's as interested in what's in me knickers as he is in what's in me handbag. Still, it was a bit weird, bein with him. An not juss on account'a him bein a fella an that, though in fairness it'd been a fair while since I'd had a bit'a dick, like more than a year. Cause all the time me an Annie were together in the Town, well, I didn do it. Not cause I couldn, I mean obviously I could. Juss didn feel like it so I didn. But somehow juss this thing bowt bein abroad an that was what changed it. We were right far away from the gaff we were stayin in, so I stayed over with him. An that was the weird bit, y'know, after a year'a mostly wakin up beside th'one person, or wakin up without her but her meant to be there, wakin up beside another. Some-one who wasn her, with her smells an that. Even if she was OK with it.

Fuckin some craic though. David was actually deadly in bed. Real curious sortofa fella so he was. I tauld him bowt Annie an me an he wasn a bit weird, not like I think the fellas'd be like back home. Or, I dunno, maybe they wouldn, but I always had this feelin like they might be an even if they weren, fuck, could be worse, they could be excited, they could think maybe they'd get to watch us playin with ar titties together, dressed in fancy underwear or whatever it is they think we get upta. Spas. But naw, David was dead cool bowt it. Probably cause he really knew his way round a beor's body, almost like, well, a woman. Though he kept tryinta put his fingers in me bum—I didn like that. That was th'one thing that he did that was a proper lad thing, cause beors know it's no fun havin fingers in yer bum for girls. That's a pure male fantasy, cause really *they* want somethin stuffed in their bums, most'a them juss won't admit it. An like, I wouldn mind, we could'a used a dildo for him or somethin, but naw, he kept stickin his fingers in mine an I kept pullin them out. Everythin else was great though, the way he'd slide his dick in an out from the side an then gently in again onlyta ram-ram-ram an then oh fuck oh yes that was class with him touchin me clit at the same time. The want on him was somethin fierce. But I still couldn come so I couldn cause it was dead distractin havin fingers in me bum. Still it was good though. Like good sex with a fella kinda good.

We were lyin up in bed after, juss lettin the day slide by. I guess he was dead happy cause he'd gotten a kilo'a coke at a daecent price too, but I think he did kinda like me. An in a good way, not in a kindofa *now I'm gonna own ye* way the way fellas get, but juss happyta be spendin the time together which was dead nice in fairness.

"Y'know, before we started chattin last night I was fit to punch the next prick t'ask me one'a them dumb English questions."

"English questions?"

"Aye, all that *where are you from* an *what do you do* shite."

"I dunno. Just makin conversation I reckon. Don't people ask that kinda thing back in Arland?"

"It's Ire-land."

"Huh?"

"Never mind. They do surely, but it's not the first thing out'a their mouths. Well, it probably is below in Dublin, cause all they care bowt is money too. Probably cause yous ones learned them it. But elsewhere, naw, it's not like that t'all. I'll give y'an example."

"Go on then."

"Well, take me pal Tommy. I've known Tommy ages an ages so I have. But I never knew what he did. Always juss figured it was somethin proper, I knew for sure he wasn in the business an that. Always dressed real proper an that ar Tommy. An ye'd only ever see him on the weekend really which is usually a good sign that someone has a job, y'know?"

"So you don't know what he does for work?"

"I do. But I juss found out by accident like. See once I was in the Credit Union an saw him in there workin."

"What's that?"

"Credit Union? It's like a bank, but not run by pricks."

"Hah!"

"Wha?"

"It's just funny innit, you havin a bank account."

"It's not a bank. Not really like. But ye get the point."

"Yeah, what was that again?"

"That Irish folk are juss sounder than English folk."

"What? No I didn't get that *at all*. Fakk. You really have a problem with the English, eh?"

"Doesn everyone?"

"Nah, love. I don't, for a start."

"Yeah, but that's cause you *are* English."

"Alright. But I'm Jewish too."

"Them's different things."

"Well, yeah. But let me explain. See, I know the politicians are scum. An now we're gonna live in a Tory hell for the rest of fuckin forever. But there's still lots of decent people."

"Where but?"

"Everywhere. There's lots of confusion. Lots of fear. But great decency too. See, when my family came here, in the thirties, Jews were bein chased out of Europe, hunted down like animals. And they found haven here. I'm not sayin everythin was peachy, right, there's anti-Semitism here too, yeah, same as everywhere. But still, they came here and they were treated the same. Same as everyone. My grandparents were sent off to the country to be safe from the bombers, like everyone. So like, that's part of me, bein an Englishman and a Jewish man. You gotta be decent, that's all. Treat people the way you wanna be treated. So like, I know there was the English of Bloody Sunday and the Black and Tans, yeah, I know all about that, but there was the England that took my family in, kept them safe. Life's complex, that's all I'm saying. There's more than one England, and you can't hate them all."

I kinda wantedta keep arguin with him so I did, juss for the divilment'a it. But it was hardta, an him after sayin that. An he was rubbin the back'a me head so he was an it was real nice an that. Not in a *shut up woman let's juss fuck* kindofa way, but like a nice way, like helpin me listenta him kindofa way, like he really wanted me t'understand n'all. That was dead nice so it was. Dead nice. Like I was th'only one person in the world juss then.

An I did understand. I did, even if I didn really understand like, I got it so I did, what he was sayin. I still don't like *my*

England, th'one I know an was always tauld bowt. But I like him an I like his.

A long mornin we spent that way, chattin an ridin, ridin an chattin. Was bowt two by the time that I got roundta callin up Annie. She was still half-cut—she'd stayed up most the night with her pals an they were back at ar flat havin fuckin Bloody Marys if ye don't mind. I ask herta get the gear ready without anyone seein. We meet out front, the three'a us, an she's got the stuff in a plastic shoppin bag.

I can't keep this stupid smile off me face but, an she's makin it worse with the noises she's makin, wolf-whistles an that, tryinta embarrass us. There's this strange tingly electric in th'air when the three'a us are standin together. We make the handover an Annie asks David if he'd liketa come in, an this electric, this tingly electric feelin goes mad, it's dancin in th'air, all round us. It's like, it's like a thing I can't keep hauld'a, a wild thing from the sky, searchin the ground. I can feel meself gaspin a little, cause I want it to go through me, I want it to go through me again. An her, I wanna share it with Annie.

David looks at her, looks at me, raises that eyebrow, real suggestive like, an I'm thinkin, fuck, I don't know what I'm thinkin, an Annie, she takes me by the hand. David kinda hangs his head with a little laugh.

"I'd love to. Really. Love to. But I better get goin. Got some stuff needs doin. Next time."

I am actually bitin me lip so I am, like a proper ham child.

"No worries. Any time, David."

Bitofa headfuck, the whole thing.

BREAKDOWN

On the road between Manchester an Birmingham it was. Hadta pull off the road cause th'engine on the yoke's makin this mad noise. Proper nerve-wrackin, the weird noises auld cars make, not knowin what's wrong with it, the thought'a havinta go to the garage with it n'all. Especially with nine kilos'a coke packed inta the sides'a it.

Pull off inta this dumpy wee town on the side'a the road. Wolverhampton. First things first. Call Shamey Hughes, see if he knows what the fuck this is all bowt.

"Well!" he says t'me down the phone. "It's yerself!"

"Who else would it be?"

"D'ye think yer th'only one that rings me? There's loads'a ones rings me."

"Aye, the Shamey Hughes's cock appreciation society, I know all bowt it," I saysta him an he breaks his shite laughin. "But I'm not callin bowt that. C'mere, yer yoke's makin an awful strange sound. Pure horror show like. Listen."

I give the nod to Annie, an she starts up th'engine. I feel

like a dope there hauldin a phone up to a car, but this car's almost like a person. I mean it's got personality, an a lot'a memory.

"Shite," he saysta me, "th'engine's idlin fierce rough haigh."

"An what the fuck's that mean?"

"I dunno. Could be loads'a things."

"Such as?"

"Were ye drivin off-road? Maybe there's a stick got caught up there somehow."

"We were fuck. It's all motorways over here, Shamey."

"Right, right. Fuck, y'know what, I don't know a fuck." He paused, a heavy kindofa worry. He loved that car more than anythin, more than his guitars even. "Ye'll haveta take her to a garagist."

"Right. Fuck. Grand," I says. I hate garages. But fuck it. "I'll let y'know how it goes."

"Sound. Talkta ye."

We pull up the nearest garagist on Maps an bang on down the road to him. One'a the worst drives ever that, the sound'a the car. Like treachery. Like a fuckin threat.

At the garage, I let Annie do the talkin. Works a treat. First they say they can't see us until next week, then it's maybe tomorrow. A couple'a minutes later we're next in line.

Meself an herself sit down in some wee cafe on the side'a the road beside the garage. Empty, an with the sense'a havin been that way a long time, like they stopped doin things up in th'eighties. All faded lino an tea-stained tables. But grand for a cuppa like.

"Why does Shamey drive that old car, anyway?" she saysta me.

"That yoke?" I says. "Well, it's a long story. But it breaks down regular as clockwork. I remember this one time, back in th'auld days. Must'a been ten years ago. Back when we were startin off with the gin an vodka job. We were comin back from meetin the lads beyond in Forkhill, an we broke down. So we juss sat there, almost right on the border. I remember askin him, would ye never think bowt gettin a daecent yoke."

I took a sup'a me tae an glanced at Annie. She was listenin, like proper listenin, not even on her phone or nathin.

"Anyway, he says somethin like *sure this yoke's class haigh*, an I'm laughin cause I juss mean a car that won't break down all the time. An he goes, *d'ye not remember? I got this car from yer brother.*"

Annie gasps, juss a little, juss a sharp breath in.

"I tauld him I did surely. It juss wasn somethin I thought bowt, y'know? For me it was his yoke an he should send it to the scrap sure. But Shamey? Shamey's a sentimentalist. *Naw. Naw*, he says, *I'll keep this car on the road. I'll change th'engine if I haveta. Fuck it.* An I thought that was that, or that it should be like. I don't really like talkin bowt me brother. Don't like thinkin bowt it, thinkin'a him wastin away. I was lookin out the winda tryinta hauld back the tears as we waited for the tow truckta come. Then he saysta me, *y'know I remember cyclin down this road with yer brother. Loads'a times. We had a great scam goin so we did.* He tauld me all bowt it. The two'a them, the wee pair'a bollixes, they figured out that they could photocopy raffle tickets for the local GAA club raffles. So they went round, houseta house like, floggin them any time they needed a few bob like, the pair'a chancers."

Annie chuckles an chimes in, "Not bad, you have to admit."

"Wait til ye hear. They'd report th'odd one, an one time one'a th'ones me brother, Liam, one'a th'ones he sold an actually reported, it won first prize. The fella who won even gave Liam fifty pound if ye don't mind."

Annie's nearly breakin her shite laughin, I can see the same sparkle in her eyes as when we're talkin bowt a job. She loves it, even this teenager craic.

I'm laughin too, but I can't help a stray tear from takin off down me cheek thinkin bowt it. Thinkin bowt that time, thinkin bowt the tear that started runnin down Shamey's cheek an him talkin bowt me brother. Bowt Liam.

"The pair'a them, they took that money upta Jonesborough. See, it was comin on Halloween, an Jonesborough's the place for the fireworks. They have big markets there every weekend. But round Halloween it's where everyone goes, Narth an South, for the fireworks. Anyway. Shamey tauld me bowt this image'a watchin me brother cyclin in front'a him, skullin a tin'a cider, two big bags'a rockets an bangers hangin down from each handlebar."

I'm in proper tears now, an Annie's hauldin me hands, strokin the tops'a them real soft. Lookin in me eyes, an bitin her lips. An I'm thinkin'a that time, I can't help but laugh, thinkin'a Shamey laughin an me laughin an both'a us cryin.

"I remember him sayinta me, *it'll be five years this winter*, an me sayin backta him, *aye an sure this yoke was already a banger back then too*. The two'a us broke ar shite so we did, an when we calmed down, him wipin the tears off me face. *He was some man, ar Liam*, he said t'me. That was the funny thing though, cause when I remember me brother, I remember him as a child, as a wee cub like, even though him bein me big brother n'all. I tauld Shamey bowt this one time see, when Liam swallowed a Lego block so he did."

Annie's also startinta cry now, juss a bit like, cause she never knew me brother or that, so I guess she's cryin for me. I rub her arm an wipe the tears from her eyes.

"Well, the wee cub decided he was gonna die. He went an lay down under the bed so he did, an it took agesta find him cause he wouldn answer cause he thought he was dead. Only found him cause he started coughin. The wee mulpin. Anyway, meself an me mam hadta drag him out'a there, cause he had asthma an that an it was dead dusty down there. Wee Liam. Even him bigger than me at the time, he'll always be wee Liam t'me. Shamey broke his shite again when I tauld him this story so he did. We couldn convince wee Liam that he wasn gonna die like, that he'd juss shite it out eventually. The wee lad spent the rest'a the day lyin up on the couch, his wee arms crossed over his chest. The wee eejit. The wee size'a him. Ah Liam! An him. An ten years later, y'know, there he was. In the coffin. The wee size'a him still, after the leukaemia had ate him up sure, an him juss twenty years auld. His wee arms crossed over his chest."

I was overtook by this, it was like a wave rushin over me. An us still drivin round in his yoke, in *his* car. I juss remember Shamey puttin his arm round me an sayinta me *oh love, oh love, c'mere t'me*. An Annie puttin her arm round me, sayinta me *oh love, oh love. Come here.*

All'a these things, stories. Images. They all collide in me head like. Annie an Shamey an Liam an me an Shamey in the yoke years back an the tow truck man comin rappin on the winda, seein us huggin an cryin an us not carin a fuck, an Liam lyin there on the couch an then in the coffin an th'arms

crossed on him the wee size'a him an then the garagist, the
mechanic lad comin inta that shitty wee cafeta tell us the car's
ready an me an Annie huggin an the tears all down us, an us
not carin a fuck.

Like a fuckin pile-up so it was.

THE CARRICK JOB

That fuckin car. A prison'a sentimentality so it is, hauldin onta it juss for the memory'a me brother. But it was class at the same time, I mean ye felt class drivin round the place in it. It was a presence, y'know? Had personality. I know fuck all bowt cars, but Shamey was a genius with them, an he had this yoke fine tuned. *When* it was workin mind. An that was a pain in the hole when ye were on the job.

One time that happened t'us beyond in Carrick. Carrick-ma-fuckin-cross. Th'engine started makin the same kindofa grindin noise, the nasty menacin groan, givin out like. As if it was pisst offta be tookta Carrick. Question'a personality. An in fairness like, who wantsta go to Carrick? Was worried we'd get stuck in some ditch on the way though.

We were there for a job, me an Annie an Shamey Hughes. Sure why else would ye go there t'all? Could call it consultin, or project management. An providin technical assistance. A flat fee for helpin some locals get inta some feen's house. I don't really like the whole burglin thing, so this was the last one I did. Juss too many thingsta go wrong, an sure it's usually only spas wanna go breakin inta people's gaffs. That was definitely the case here.

This was the craic. We were down in Doyle's havin a drink with this local crew'a hardmen wannabes. There was this hobo chap watchin the gaff, below on Cross Street. I didn like that for a start, relyin on a hobo for anythin. An fuckin Cross Street? In Carrickmacross? Are ye fuckin jokin like? Apparently though, that's where this fucker who owns Mulligan's lives. An the head barman there had a boneta pick with the feen, somethin bowt not payin him right an that. In any way, this hobo fella was meant to throw a brick through a winda at Doyle's an cause a big scene when th'owner'a Mulligan's went out to work. Get the attention'a the local gards like. Distract them.

It sounded good, on paper at least. But hobos are fuckin unpredictable as fuck so th'are. Ye can never be sure will they show up, or what'll they do. But these feens vouched for the hobo, fuckin insisted on it. It was a cousin'a one'a them see, so they wanted jussta throw him a few bob an that. Fair enough, but I saidta them sure, if yer payin me for advice ye should at least listenta it. Could'a juss given the hobo lad a bit'a cash an left him be like. Fuckin smalltime arseholes. Ye should never let yer feelins get in the way'a work. First rule'a the business.

Now, apparently this feen who owned the Mulligan's, Boyle he was called, he was one'a these lads hated puttin cash in the bank. Trust issues. But that's pure stupid if ye've got a proper business n'all. Jussta cheat the tax sure, an the pubs rakin it in. All the more stupidta keep yer money at home an then cheat people who know bowt it. This guy was juss askin for it.

Anyway, one'a these Carrick wise-guys, Donal his name was, he was fuckin hell bent on gettin wired. Said it helpt him think straight. Now, I can understand that, but I did tell him he was thick as shit—juss due diligence like. Annie was bored as fuck, so she was fake flirtin with this big wannabe hardman, Fred. Dumb name. Big dumb head on him, too. Big mad beard he had an a big head a hair the like I've never seen before. Too thickta realise she was only playin with him sure. Never been out'a Carrick I guess, by the shite he spouted. The bigger issue, though, was this Donal chap gettin Shamey drunk, as if Shamey needed any kinda encouragement.

That's the problem with crook publicans an hobos. Unreliable. It was well past midnight when I convinced one'a them Carrick amateursta pop overta Mulligan's an see if the prick was there, or see what the craic was up with the hobo chap sure. Proper pain in the hole when y'know far better than them what to do but these feckers juss hit ye with these condescendin smiles an say somethin like *don't get yer knickers in a twist, darlin*. Spas.

A'course, yon lad Boyle was already out in Mulligan's. We went roundta his gaff for the look. These thicks had given the hobo chap an advance, an a'course he juss spent it gettin drunk. Passed out after two bottles'a Buckfast. I said it didn look good, to do it another night. They didn listenta me, an y'know what? After a while ye get tired'a shoutin at spas. In any way we'd already been paid. But without the distraction, we'd be sittin ducks so we would. None'a these feens seemedta realise there's nathin—but fuckin nathin—that goes down in Carrick.

They wouldn listen. Got past the first alarm easy-peasy, but I tauld them, I fuckin roared sure, anyone I said, anyone paranoid enoughta keep that much cash at home would'a more than one alarm. They insisted on goin ahead with it though. Fuck it.

I kept Annie out front. Said we'd keep sketch. But I knew how this'd go down. I tauld Shameyta go round the back, then texted him.

Me: U readin me?
Shamey Hughes: Aye
Me: Get u the fuck back upta Doyles. Now!
Shamey Hughes: Right So.

Anyway, them lads went on in. I grabbed Annie round th'arm an tauld herta play along. The pair'a us staggered up the street arm in arm, singin some shite as if we were off ar tits. A'course, we made it to the top'a the street juss in timeta see the squad car flyin round onta Main Street. The feen had one'a them silent alarms, hooked straight upta the gards. Another dumb name for a street, *Main Street*. Fuckin inspired they were when they built Carrick sure.

We went back for a drink in Doyle's. Casual as ye like. The Carrick boys got done, the fuckin ham children. Men. Can't listen like, most'a them. Annie said it's cause they're juss a walkin sense'a entitlement with balls. Sounds bowt right. Fuckin amateurs.

The best bit was a wee while later yon hobo feen started feckin rocks. Smashed in *all* the windas'a Doyle's an him foamin at the mouth sure. Took it as a sign an piled back inta Shamey's yoke an banged on up the road backta the Town, th'engine grindin all the way.

MORAL HIGH GROUND (A DUMP)

It was in Birmingham that we really realised the size'a what it was we were doin. That there one chunk'a the work was worth more wedge than we'd ever seen before. *Ever.*

We'd been travellin for nearly a week already, an we were fairly worn out from the road an the drink an that. So Annie said we should stay in an take her handy for a night. She seemed a bit down too. Probably juss the tiredness. But if ye don't take the timeta come down proper ye get dragged down. Like gravity sure.

Th'early part'a the day she spent on her fuckin laptop watchin vlogs. Now, see, when she'd do that back in the Town I'd juss head out an do a bit'a work or somethin. Pure stir crazy so I was, stuck inside. I'm bowt to go lookin for a sheet or somethinta hang meself with when I decided I'd better get out'a the flat before I really do.

"Right," I says, "I'm headin out. Should I get somethin for the dinner?"

"You know, I was just thinking, let me take care of that."

"Ye sure?"

"Yeah. I have an idea. And I want to treat you."

That was dead nice'a her actually.

That was mad, juss out wanderin without properly knowin where I was goin. Like, I always walk bowt loads, but usually juss goin from one thing t'another, one job or a pint to talk bowt a job. I don't own a yoke sure, though when I need wheels I can always get them. Like for this job. I like walkin even, it's juss I'm not usedta wanderin without a purpose. Was nice in a way, but felt weird too. Scary somehow. Not that I was scared'a anythin particular, juss this kindofa *what am I even doin here* feelin that I didn much like, y'know?

I thought bowt maybe doin some tourist shite but the thought'a bein round tourists made me teeth itch. Besides I'd haveta figure out what tourists actually do, an that seemed like a proper pain in the hole. Tourists are dead annoyin, juss a bunch'a idiots bumpin inta things wonderin where they are, cause sure isn it the same shite everywhere? We're lucky in that way, back in the Town, cause we don't get many tourists on account'a the Town bein a bitofa hole but sure that's juss the way I like it. In a big city like Birmingham there's boundta be tourists an that, at least folk that go there by accident, wanderin round, selfie sticks at the ready. *Selfie sticks*, they're like Gangnam Style or Donald Trump—proof that humanity is doomed like, we juss can't hack it so we can't, else we'd have more sense sure.

I wander round til I realise I'm followin this lad. Kinda looks like David, see. Now, that's a funny one, eh? A woman followin a man round for a change. But I wasn doin it in a creepy, leery kindofa way the way that fellas do. Naw, I was juss curious. I juss wantedta explore the town an that, so I decided somehow I'd let *him* be me tour guide though he didn know he was doin it. Fuck it sure.

Birmingham David pops inta some pub, don't remember what it was called, the King's Mickey or somethin. So I go in after him in any way. Jussta see what it's like. I sit up at the bar, few stools away from him, an he keeps lookin at me like *are you followin me or somethin?* but I juss look down at me phone refreshin Facebewk or somethin even though nathin's happenin, nathin t'all, but I don't wanna get inta some conversation bowt the followin thing cause that'd be dead awkward. I was juss doin me tourism sure. Drank a pint'a warm bitter piss an flipped through a paper talkin bowt how deadly Brexit was.

Then I get a text off David, the real one.

David_Manch: How you doin love? Where are you?

Me fuckin belly took a hellofa jump when I seen this. Gotta be cool I saysta meself. Can't text back right away. That's the shit thing bowt them seen notifications but, they give y'away, when yer tryinta be cool n'all.

I down me pint an leave the pub. David, the fake David, he's lookin at me like he wantsta stop me an have a chat or that. Probably thinks I fancied him cause a fella always thinks that if ye look at him twice, but naw, sorry, wrong David. He wasn bad lookin or that but it'd be weird, y'know, ridin one David after another.

When I get out onta the street I realise I've actually been out for ages so I have. It's near dark. I hurryta get back t'Annie. Fuckin waste'a time, all that tourism bollix.

Annie's already cookin when I get back, but I notice this

weird sortofa smell in the flat when I land back in. Not juss the cookin.

"I've been dumpster diving!" she says, all proud'a herself.

"The fuck's that?"

"You know, finding food that people have thrown away. Shops and that mostly."

"Yer messin."

"No, honey."

"So we're eatin rubbish?"

"No, I'm feeding us without engaging with the capitalist system."

"Didn ye say ye were gointa the shops?"

"Yeah, I got this at Tesco's, from their dumpster!"

"Ye mean the bin?"

"Well, yeah. But they call it dumpster diving."

"An why's that better than shoppin?"

"We're going round in a circle here, hon."

"Yeah, cause I don't get it. Juss seems like a wayta be cheap an feel better than other people at the same time if y'ask me. Sure we've plenty'a money."

She gives me this look then like I'd juss shat on what she was cookin. S'pose I had in a way. Then she gives her eye-rollin look like her *I can't believe I have to explain this oh my god* kindofa eye-rollin look. She loves that look. It's her favourite.

"I was watching a vlog earlier about alternative living and ethics in the twenty-first century."

"The fuck's that?" I says, crackin open a tin. I was skatin on thin ice here an I don't even know howta skate so I cracks her one too.

"It's the vlog about how to resist capitalism in an everyday way."

"Awah right, that's th'one that the fella does, th'one who wears the dresses an make-up an that?"

I was tryinta be nice sure.

"She's a woman, *OK*? A trans woman."

"I thought it was juss like the way you dress up sometimes."

"It's completely fucking different—what is wrong with you? It's her life. That's just something I do."

"Hey, I'm juss tryin t'understand s'all. It's grand. She's a woman. What did she say?"

"Well," she says, kinda comin round, "dumpster diving is a more ethical form of consumption because the food is already out of capitalism—it has no monetary value anymore—so we're not engaging in the exploitation that's inherent in the system."

"Grand so."

"And it's even OK to eat meat that way."

"But sure, we eat meat anyway."

"Yeah, but I mean it's unethical the way we do it. But if you eat from a dumpster, then you're not supporting industrial agriculture."

"Class. Did ye get any meat? I'm starvin."

"Well, yeah," she says, relaxin a bit. "But take a whiff. I think it's rancid."

Fuck me, yeah. It was.

"We can be vegans tonight, love. No bother."

She even smiled at that. Finally.

"We're not gonna get sick though, right?"

"It's all pretty fresh otherwise," she says, hauldin up a mouldy auld carrot.

Mad craic. Shoppin in the bins an that, juss soasta make yerself feel better bowt livin in a shite world an that. An the

thing that really got me was that Annie saw nathin weird
bowt all that sure. Sure the night after, when we made the big
deal, she insisted we go to this fancy joint to drink champagne.
From France n'all, an that jussta feel better than other people. Fuck me, I'd'a been happy enough goin backta the King's
Mickey if only their beer wasn shite.

The grub was still dead nice, even if it came out'a a bin at
the back'a Tesco's. So was the champagne the next night an
neither'a us gave a rat's arse bowt bein in or out'a the capitalist
system juss then. Sure we didn know where we wereta fuck.

I tried not to replyta David n'all. Thought that'd be better, y'know, jussta let it go. But I didn wanna be rude either.
I couldn help it sure. It was harmless in any way, juss a bit'a
craic.

ANTS

Y'ever seen a colony'a ants? Isn that what it's called sure? A colony? Must be. Wee colonialist bastards. That's what th'are, with those thousands, tens'a thousands, probably hundreds'a thousands'a legs all marchin, walkin one after another. Offta colonise somethin, t'ate it, take it over completely. They move by smell I think it is, an they don't even have noses. Mad. Anyway, it's somethin like that, the chemicals n'all. I remember it, see I usedta watch these shows on telly. Bug shows me da usedta call them, laughin, tauntin like a hyena, *he-he-he*, thinkin he was dead funny. But they mostly weren bowt bugs, they were mostly bowt animals an that an I loved them. I loved watchin them. I could spend whole days on the couch with meself watchin them.

Watchin the shows bowt animals, that was how I triedta understand people. See people are juss like animals really, I mean we are animals. Pure instinct an that, juss hid behind other shite. So if I could understand animals I'd be ableta understand people, an maybe manageta fit meself in with them. Be a little less lonely. But it was a pretty superficial kindofa way not to be lonely, cause I didn really get them, even with David Attenborough explainin everythin all bowt them an that, an he's class at explainin. I mean it's his job like.

Me thoughts were like ants sometimes. Like a fuckin load'a them, marchin along like a big troop, out lookin for food or spoilin for a fight or whatever. Sure that's the same way thoughts work. At least it's how *my* thoughts work. Like a big column'a ants, marchin away, wee colonial cunts cominta take me over.

Bein with Annie, I got plenty'a these big circles in me brain. Deeper an deeper they went, every day. An mostly it was good like. Juss the repetition'a havin her round, y'know? The fact'a talkinta the same person every day. A'wakin up beside them. Gettin usedta their moods, their habits. Knowin howta smooth somethin over, an howta piss them off if ye needta. It was like a path gettin more familiar. In the beginnin it was a forest or some wild place, all overgrown in a big mess. But the more th'ants passed through it, the more the feet pressed down again an again an again, the more regular it got. The more used ye get to it. Yer own feet follow it. So even the jagged bits, the things that frightened y'at first, ye get usedta them. Part'a the path sure. Like Annie gettin in a strop or fightin with people—I was usedta that before too long sure. An sure the good parts made up for the bad. Even when I'd get upset meself, say if she went an spent a couple'a nights with some fella, that might make me trip up a bit, but I'd get right back up an keep walkin. An with paths like those, the deeper they go, the longer ye think they're gonna keep goin for. Why else would anyone go to the hassle'a makin it otherwise? Doesn make sense sure.

Y'know wha happens if someone drops a rock on a colony'a

ants? They all start rushin round, all crazed beyond confusion, rushin round, all angry, sprayin acid an attackin anythin they can find. Pure murderous like. It was the same with me when I lost Annie like, an juss like th'ants with the rock, ye can't kill somethin random that arrives out'a nowhere, somethin without reason or fleshta even bite down on. That was the worst'a it. An I was left with loads'a her words, words that feel pure foreignta me. I wanna give them back. Like *inexplicable*. That was one that she used loads, but I only really ever understood it when she left me.

There were lots'a little crashes along the way, but loads'a times I thought it would go on forever. Good times. Times when I was so sure'a the road like, so sure there would be no need for anythin but juss her an me after all the jobs had been done. Maybe we'd be like Smokey Quigley an open a wee pub somewhere, step back from the game, somethin like that. Juss make time for each other.

One'a them crashes came when Annie went backta Galway for a bit. Now she said it was for a friend, but I knew it was at least partlyta do with a fella. The fella she was seein when we met. That much I knew from her phone. I didn go lookin or nathin, I juss couldn help seein. It was like she wanted me knowin leavin them notifications on. Didn even haveta unlock it like.

So I says I'll take a spin home. Didn make a big deal bowt it, so I juss put a note on the bed, y'know, in case she'd come home before me or whatever. Which she didn, a'course.

Now, I'd invited Annie to Mullaghbawn before, but she always had some excuse not to come. This time at least I wouldn be botherin her with that. I was always usually comin up with excuses not to go home meself, so I think me ma was a bit worried when I juss called upta say I was comin home for a few days. Like worried somethin'd happenedta me or somethin. I was juss tryinta distract meself from the messy ants, give them a chanceta reorganise an for Annie to come back like.

I dunno what I was thinkin, goin home. I hate it like. Mullaghbawn is a grand wee spot I s'pose, but at the same time it's a village like, no action, nathinta do.

Mad, too, the thought things might be different. Sure why would they be? Home was the same as it ever is, juss a prison'a memory. Like when I opened me wardrobe an saw there was still me school uniforms. Why hadn they thrown them out? Should'a fuckin burnt them. Touchin them, the cheap scratchy polyester'a them, that was rememberin squeezin inta the sizes that juss weren meant to hauld me, sizes for *normal* kids, an me ma cursin me cause'a th'extra cost'a havinta get them altered, an that after a full fuckin hour'a humiliation tryin on bowt two dozen sets that don fit an nathin bein right cause either me boobs were too big or me belly wasn right or me hips, an her cursin me like, pure cursin me. Fuck that. An I can understand her like, th'expense an that. But still.

The worst was seein me ma an da, seein how they'd changed. Which was not t'all. Her still puttin up with him, still takin shit off this coward an him juss full'a bitterness cause he never lived upta his ideas'a himself, the self that he was back when he still had work which was a long fuckin time ago I'll tell ye. Shoutin at her comin back from the toilet, *make the tea would ye*, an then when she's on her way in with it, *I'd love a sandwich*. Finally, *is there any cake?* Fuck's sake.

A'course the worst part was her actually goin backta do it, without sayin a thing, expectin himta get it from the way she'd shove it at him, but sure he didn care. Naw, not as long as he was fed an warm an didn haveta move his arse he wouldn notice anythin t'all.

An the banter out'a them was bowt as good as out'a a poor wet pup pawin at the door.

"Well," I'd say, me eye caught by the telly, ads for accident claims an life insurance an that.

"Well, now," one'a them'd reply. Didn matter which.

"Any craic?"

"Awah now. Quiet enough. How's work?"

I tauld them I worked at a Tesco's in the Town. Kept them from worryin, maybe, though I don't know if they would'a.

"Grand. Yeah. Eh, y'know, Liam's birthday is comin up. Maybe we could do somethinta mark it."

The pair'a them shifted in their seats, the cheap leather crackin. Da clears his voice.

"Like what love, what're ye thinking?" says Ma.

"I dunno. Go out to the grave. Go to the pub. Y'know. Jussta remember he was there."

Da starts mutterin, cursin an fouterin at the remote. Ma says somethin that sounds like agreement but it's not. Says she'll talk t'me sister bowt it, but I know she won't. An see, that's what I hate. I fuckin hate it. They won't even talk bowt him. It's like he never even existed. But he existed. He fuckin did, an we was thick as thieves, an I juss wanna remember, I juss wanna have that part'a him still. The fuck is wrong with people like?

Me eyes'd wander round the room an onta the bookshelf mostly used for these dumb wee porcelain bunnies me ma likes. There're th'only two bewks me da ever bought, pride'a place. Biographies'a Gerry Adams an Sir Alex Ferguson,

CBE. Looked that up cause I didn know what it meant. *Commander of the Most Excellent Order of the British Empire.* Someone needsta send them lads across the water a wee message an let them know the sun's set on all that.

Mad craic altogether. Wonder what Gerry'd say bowt sharin a shelf with a *Commander of the Most Excellent Order of the British Empire.* Still n'all, it is Fergie, so he'd probably be OK with it.

Then I'd realise I'd been asked if there was any banter with me, an there I was juss in this weird trance state lookin up the different grades'a pretend knights n'all that ye get to be if the Queen'a England thinks yer class.

"Ha? Awah. Naw. Quiet sure."

Jaysis. This was desperate.

I called roundta me nan which was grand actually. Me nan, see, she was always dead sound. I practically grew up at her place, I was always tryinta get away from home. Bein at home was always bein in a cage, specially after Liam died. Thank god Nan was there like. Goodta see her at least. No questions, nathin, juss dead happyta have the cuppa.

That night I call up Shamey Hughes again. He's already on the drink sure, but it doesn matter, I tell him it's an emergency. An it fuckin was sure. I was fit to do harm.

I didn give them any warnin. Better that way. They were still watchin telly sure, comatose on the couch. I say somethin's come up an I gotta head backta the Town. I tell them that I'll be back soon, not to worry, that everythin's grand.

Shamey comes an gets me. Thank fuck. What was I thinkin?

A WEE TASTE

The day after ar lovely dumpster dinner, Annie brought me roundta meet a couple'a her Brummie pals, a pair'a lads by the names'a Larry an Simon, a couple as it happens. Pair'a headers, they were mad inta EDM, bein DJs n'all, but sold yokes on the side. Pill-heads, but Annie reckoned that they'd be good for a wee kilo on the sly maybe. Sounded like a daecent enough idea, an sure I had nathin betterta go on so I says yeah. Give anythin a go th'one time like.

Anyway, we head down by the basin, where the canals an that are. Nice spot that, kinda made me feel at home somehow. We pop inta this pub, another King's Mickey kindofa job, but at least it's not one'a them hipster spots. Stuffy sortofa spot but not a bad shout all the same—hidin in plain sight like.

The first half hour has Annie all chitter-chatter like she always is. An mostly that can be a fuckin pain in the hole with pals'a hers, cause they can be awful stuck-up, Annie's mates. Most'a them are artists, see, middle-class yahoos with no sense'a the world an fierce notions'a themselves. So mostly

I'd juss step back a bit from moments like that. Which could be a prickofa thing, gettin left on th'edge'a things like that.

But when it comesta business with folk ye don't know, it's not a bad thing bein a bit on the side'a things, until the moments ye needta intervene like, until ye haveta get stuck right in. There on the side, ye can get a proper look'a what's goin on—when yer in the thick'a things, that's when they wanna take hauld'a ye, to get ye buck blind. I mean, moments take on their own forces, an no I don't mean that in some dumbass yoga kindofa way, but juss that things gather momentum, y'know, specially when there's drugs an money an such at stake.

Sittin there on the side, I saw straight off Annie's mates hadn a hope'a dealin with any sizeofa chunk'a charlie that big. No chance like. They were only in drugsta support their DJ habit sure. Fair enough haigh.

Annie starts pressin them for the sell, but I can see them all evasive, so I sit back an watch how this is gonna break, with a crack or with a crumble. Have a sip on me gin tonic like it's Sunday lunch or somethin. An in a way, I have respect for them takin it this way, cause there's not many smalltimers know the size'a themselves.

"Look," says Simon, this big feen. Really big like, but juss in the proportions'a himself, his head, his hands an all, an him scratchin the back'a his head, tossin his floppy head'a hair round an round, nervous like. "We couldn't take the risk. I mean, we'd be getting ourselves in over our heads."

Th'other lad, Larry, pipes up in between puffs'a his vape yoke, which he's blowin inta his jumper so the pub landlord doesn notice.

"If we was talking a hundred G, say, that'd be fine—lovely jubbly. We could space it out a bit and mint ourselves a little romantic weekend away or something, innit? But more than that and we'd get the kind of attention we don't want, frankly."

"What, from the cops?" says Annie.

Yon Larry lad starts hackin away in laughter, an him blowin fake smoke down his jumper. He looks like a spa so he does, cause the vapour still gets out, juss slow, out'a his sleeves an places where the threadin's thin.

"Nah, love," says Simon. "From people further up the food chain."

I'm kinda warminta this pair, even with their nervous smalltime carry-on. I can see that the pair'a them are on the lookout for each other like, juss like Annie an me I'm thinkin. But still, it's dead annoyin wastin time on this smalltime shite, so I'm thinkinta juss sell them a hundred grammes an get on up the road out'a this kip. An that only petrol money like.

Then Larry stops scratchin his arse an looks up with a dead thoughtful look on his face, as if this is his eureka moment, he pipes up an says, "But maybe there's somethin we *can* do."

Simon shoots the feen this confused look, an Larry pats him on the knee, reassurin him, an I can see it's somethin he's done a thousand times. He has these lovely soft eyes ar Larry does, ye juss feel straight away he can't be a cunt for the sake'a it. So I say nathin, but juss let him babble on.

"We *could* just bounce you further up the food chain."

Simon shoots him a look again, almost hurt somehow.

"Are you joking? To Fitz?"

Larry nods. I smell somethin here.

"Who's Fitz?" I ask the lad, the first time I've said a word in ages, an I can feel me mouth all dry.

Simon looks at me, sorta startled like, as if he's surprisedta see me sittin there or somethin. I feel like laughin.

Larry pipes up.

"Fitz is our supplier. He's the big fish in Birmingham—has the place more or less sewn up. A proper old-school cut-throat kind of geezer. Shoot first and fuck the questions. Very connected."

"Yeah, exactly!" says Simon. "I don't like it. The guy's a cunt. I wouldn't trust them not to cut your lovely lily-white throats and take your gear. Two more bodies in the canal—no biggie."

Annie's drummin on the table.

"More or less," she says, an this pair'a mulpins gawkin at her, wide-eyed wonderin what she's meanin. But I see where she's takin this, an I let her sure.

"More or less. But not *completely*."

"Well, yeah, love, I mean it's a big city," says Simon.

"So who's the next biggest?" asks Annie. Clever. Fuckin clever.

"That'd be Big Dom," says Larry. "Why?"

"Well, why don't we go pay a visit to Big Dom? May be a safer option—someone looking for a leg-up is less likely to break yours."

I loved hearin her say that. I was dead proud'a her—she was thinkin like the Town at last.

Larry an Simon sit there, squirmin. Simon starts shakin his head.

"We couldn't make the connect, love. Wouldn't be worth the skin on our backs if that got back to Fitz. We get all our stuff off of Fitz."

Larry pipes up but.

"But," he says, an hauls up his handta stop Simon interruptin, "we could tell you how to get to him. He's easy to find. Just don't tell him who sent you."

He puts his hand down on Simon's knee again, an gives it a squeeze. That seemsta quieten the big gom, who juss nods real slow, his big fat lower lip hangin slack like a loose fitted sheet. Larry puffs a bit'a vapour down his jumper an then the pair'a them share this look, big sad eyes on the pair'a them full'a forlorn impotence.

Turns out this Dom fella's got a club. Like a nest so it is, his safe place, with a bunch'a lookalike heavies hangin out, lookin nonchalant like they're not his muscle. I'd not be surprised if he never left the couple'a streets there—ye had the feelin walkin in that ye were enterin some kindofa resistance den or somethin. An I was aware'a the risk, walkin inta a spot like that, but I was one with Annie's instinct here. Him bein the down dog tryinta gain th'upper hand, he might be in lessofa habit'a stampin people out jussta keep them small.

In we go. It's a class wee joint, Dom's, proper retro like, disco style. They do all these kinda retro nights, seventies, eighties, nineties—all that kinda thing. It's early still, broad daylight like, so the place is empty cept for Dom's crew.

I thought better thanta bring the piece, cause I figure, we want this in good faith done, an the minute ye bring a gun inta the room somethin changes, it juss does. So when we get frisked goin inta Dom's office there's no nervousness.

Anyway, they don't find me blade, not where I keep it hid. A lad never thinks'a lookin there.

Dom is a fuckin legend, I can see that straight off. Caribbean British, an he has this dead nice way'a talkin, all lilty like, it almost puts me in mindofa Kerryman. Dom's dead fat, but has a smileta charm the socks off ye. He's a slick operator, an I can see he'd do ye like, but not for no reason. So I let this go ahead.

Before he even asks what we're in for he sends for drinks, asks us if we want any peck or that. He's proper gentlemanly, old-school but not in a prick kindofa way, not the way men play the gentlemen bit when they're tryinta make ye feel small.

Annie tells him why we're there, an gives him a wee taste'a the product. I'm still watchin, a bit held back, see.

The fuckin eyes on him b'y.

He leans in—t'me—talkin straight at me now. I can feel Annie gettin prickly, but she knows not to say nathin.

"How much you say you're cartin, love?"

"I fuckin didn," I says, an the smile near cuts his head in half.

"Anyway," I says, "it's moreofa question'a how much can y'afford."

He starts laughin, hauldin the sides'a himselfta keep from burstin, as if this is dead funny, an me not jokin one bit haigh.

In th'end we settle on three kilos, an I make it seem like that's all we have on us. Figure it's not safeta sell any more than that. Already at that there must'a been a voice in his head if it wouldn'a been better jussta dump us in the canal after we hand the stuff across. But I could see by him that if that voice was there, it was quiet enough. Not the way this lad does business.

He gets us the wedge in any way, no messin, no fuckin bother haigh. We stow it away nice an safe, an Annie an me go on the razz, juss the two'a us like. We might'a sampled a bit too much'a ar own gear but that's grand too once in a while.

Halfway through the night, Annie gets this mad glint in her eyes an makes a call, arranges for a case'a champagne—bubbly stuff—to be sent overta where we're stayin. A bit much, I'm thinkin, an us ones already half-cut, but see it's only half for drinkin. This gaff we're rentin see, it's got a lovely big jacuzzi bath in it, big enough for the two'a us, an Annie takes me hand an leads me in. She has the six bottles'a bubbles there beside us an the bubbles pourin all over us an other bubbles comin up from beneath an Annie's electric fingers on me clit an her eyes in me mind, in me head an I remember thinkin this, this is it. This is us. Juss a wee taste'a thingsta come.

WHY DON'T WE STAY?

The mornin after the big deal, the Birmingham deal, that was tough. One'a them hangovers ye remember for years after, where ye'd almost feel like goin off the drink. Almost. I lay there in bed, full'a fear, before finally movin. Real slow like, an I felt dead stiff, like I was ten years older, an me head like a jackhammer.

Annie was in great form that mornin. She went an got us coffee, brought it backta the flat, another manky Airbnb. Annie had coffee an eggs n'all on the go, an that was juss the ticket I needed out'a this hangover.

Lyin there in bed I could hear her cookin away in the kitchen. The coffee all warm in me hand, not too hot but a proper good warm. The smell'a the rashers, but no sausages cause she knows I don't like sausages. Thinkin bowt all'a that *we* business, her talkin bowt the things *we* could do with the money, juss the two'a us. Places we could go an that. I'd always wantedta visit Kerry actually. Heard it's dead nice down there, even if it'd be a bit weird cause ye can't understand half the chat out'a them. Cometa think bowt it, there's loads'a places

I'd never even beenta in Ireland, lovely places, an that made me feel dead sad bowt bein where I was. Out drivin round this dumpofa country, when I'd never done half as many miles at home.

Annie bursts in with two trays'a peck, a lovely wee fry with mushrooms an *no* sausages an eggs an even some tomato. I'm already popped up in bed thinkin, with me coffee that's doin wonders for me hangover. We're there, eatin an juss touchin, juss a wee bit, juss enough like. An I remember feelin great. Fuckin deadly like all warm everywhere. I remember thinkin that we were dead close an that this could juss go on forever sure, an so it should. Fuck everythin else, fuck the world, fuck what they think. I even felt better bowt the whole sharin carin open thing, specially since Manchester. In fairness that helpt a lot. But this was still better. Much better. Juss the two'a us, juss her an me. An me full'a pride, the pure pride'a her'a havin organised the big deal. Three kilos in one go, fuckin some job haigh.

Then she hits me.

"I've been thinking. You know, we don't even have to go back."

"Ha?"

"To Dundalk."

"Sorry, wha?"

"I mean, with the cash we'll have. We don't have to go back. We can stay here. I know there's stuff waiting for us at home. The gin job, a few other things. But with this, you know, we could really set ourselves up. Here. Where there's some real action."

I didn know what to say so I said nathin.

"I mean, in Ireland, it's all such small-scale stuff. Even in

Dublin. Here, well, here we could really make a mark. We could move up in the world, properly. We could be happy here, you know?"

The peck in me mouth lost all taste. Like munchin wet cardboard. I asked her what the fuck it was she was talkin bowt, tryin not to sound too rough, cause I did actually wanna know an not juss start a fight. She juss repeated herself with this look on her face like it was dead obvious. Like I was maybe a bit thick for even askin. Me heart went off like a fuckin Lambeg on the twelfth.

"You do realise that we're not th'only ones involved in this? I mean I got the charlie off someone, it didn juss pop out'a thin air," I says, tryinta stay calm.

"Oh, come on. Don't give me that. You're smarter than that."

That's a prickofa thingta sayta someone. *You're smarter than that.* As in, *yer stupid cause you don't agree with me.* She kept talkin.

"Whoever got their hands on that—and I won't bring up the fact that you refuse to tell me—well, they robbed it from someone else. Must have. That's the only thing that explains the price."

"So?"

"So? We don't need to be bound by slavish morality. Look, it's just work. It's just a transaction. We're far beyond the pale here already. We don't need to ever go back to that shitty town. No-one can touch us here. And there's nothing we have back there that we can't get here a hundred times from all the money we'll make. It's our chance to start over. To build a new life. *Together.* To change if we want to. Go straight. Whatever. Fuck it. It's *our* chance. Things can be different."

"Go straight? Are ye mad in the head? An here, what happened t'all yer socialist thoughts? Right an wrong n'all that?"

I'm juss blown away. I feel each bit'a me throbbin.

"Look, whoever it was gave you this stabbed someone else in the back to get it. This is just business, this is logic. Don't be naïve."

"Are you fuckin jokin me? This is business, yeah. Exactly. I'm ten years in the Town buildin me position. That didn come out'a nathin. That's trust. That's fuckin work. That's life. That's *my* life. An ye want me to throw that away now? For wha? To move *here*? Are ye fuckin jokin? I hope y'are."

She haulds her head in her hands, massagin her temples an that, sighin. Real condescendin. I fuckin hate that. Like I'm talkin some stupid shite but I know I'm in the right here.

"I'm sorry," she says, "forget about it."

"How the fuck can I forget bowt it? That's some bad fuckin shite yer after comin out with."

"Do you have to curse?"

"Do you haveta be a cunt?"

She looks at me like I'd juss slapped her crossways up the face. Like I was dead in her eyes, there an then, in that moment. Proper anger. Real burnin an that. I triedta be calm. I triedta sayta meself, she doesn understand. How could she sure, she'd only been in the Town a wet week at th'end'a the day. An she didn know. She didn know it came from the Rat King. An him a brotherta me. For fuck's sake.

She does the temple thing again. All sighs an a shaking head. I hate it.

An juss like that, she changed. Sent the shakes right up me that. She juss changed. Everythin. The look'a her. Th'eyes'a her. The talk'a her. The stiff in her bones sure. Left me fuckin flummoxed so she did, again.

"You're right, hon. I'm sorry. It was just a silly idea. I just got carried away with it." An her rubbin me shoulders, leanin inta me, now with both hands. "Can we just forget about it?"

Well, sure the rest tells itself. That was a slow mornin, but fuck me, I couldn forget that. Naw. Naw, that stuck in me, right in me, all the wayta the back. Like a splinter that goes right the way through ye. How're ye meant to forget, an you bleedin all the time?

FIRST JOB WITH SHAMEY

Screechin up one hand an down th'other. There's really no other wayta describe that so there's not, the way it feels when the shit gets inta me fists. It's like, well, like somethin tight, pulled across above ye. Pushin down on ye, an out at the same time. But juss in the hands. Not the way it gets in me chest. That's a different way. A tight way that. This isn tight, it's hard an down an th'only wayta get it out is scratchin. Feels good, but juss while yer at it sure. After, bloody, an then there's some relief until it starts again, but a different problem then. Fuck it sure. It's not as bad as the chest one at least. Them times it's like I can't breathe, juss these small short shallow things, real ragged an fast, me lungs pure hostileta th'air then.

Lucky that time it was juss in me hands. Real itchy, but hot too. Makes me wanna tear them open sure, jussta let it out, whatever is in there. So sometimes I do. I scratch all the way downta the red. Whenever I'm thinkin hard it's like that. Proper prickofa thing, that. The bigger the thought, the worse the scratchin goes. I fuckin hate it so I do, specially cause I don't even notice it anymore, when they start bleedin an that. But other folk are always real shocked so th'are which is stupid like, cause it's juss a bit'a blood at th'end'a the day. Ye'd swear I was playin with me period in front'a themta see the disgust on their faces. Cause it's like that. People want ye to keep yer problems inside. Like yer period. No-one wantsta know, lads specially not. It's not an excuse for nathin, even if yer bein ripped in two an can't stand. But a lad with a headache— watch out. It's the same with the scratchin. Makes people uncomfortable, cause they can see that shit. It's weird for them. They'd prefer cancer, deep on th'inside. Then all they'd haveta do is somethin they've all done before, dressin in black, sayin some shite bowt it bein real bad even if they hated ye. An maybe gettin locked at th'afters. But if they see ye bleedin? Fuck. They might haveta actually help—fuck that.

Me hands are always kinda half bandaged cause'a that. One half or th'other. I wear long sleeves mostly, but it's an awful pain in the hole cause I'm always thinkin. Always worryin them away, me hands. Dead annoyin.

Drink usually helpt more than anythin. It's great so it is, drinkin. But this time, well, it was kinda where the bother got started. Naw, not drinkin it, juss thinkin bowt drink. This is goin back now, real far back, when I was still makin a name for meself so I was. Way back before I knew Annie. Before I knew the Rat King even.

See, some lads above at home had got themselves in an enterprisin state'a mind. Gone an repurposed a bunch'a auld poitín stills they got off farmers round South Armagh. No-one really drinks much poitín anymore, juss hipsters an auld lads. But these stills worked, they were ableta make stuff, well,

I don't know if it was really gin or really vodka, but they got it tastin like it. An sure with the cheap stuff, fuck, does it really matter? People are juss lookinta get pisht.

Six auld stills they had goin. It's up t'eleven now. Fuckin serious work. Spotted all round farms in Mullaghbawn, Drumintee an Jonesborough. Them feens, auld schoolmates'a mine, they run round between the different farms an soon they had the stuff pumpin out at a steady flow. Sounds risky, but people in that neck'a the woods, sure they juss get a kick out'a buckin the law, or any type'a authority figure. Even more than the rest'a the country sure. There's a proper rebel spirit in them that never went away. All they were in want'a was a market for the stuff they were pumpin. Sure the Town was juss too obviousta resist.

This was when I was still back in the smalltime all the same an that's what was stressin me out. Back then I was only really sellin hash, to teenagers mostly. Fuckin shite-all money there was in that. This was a chance for me. This was *my* chance. No-one was doin that so it wasn like I'd be steppin on no-one's toes an sure if things got tight I could always call on the lads above at home for a bitofa dig out. They'd wanna protect their investment so they would. But it never quite cameta that. They knew me from school an that an sure me granda had been pals with theirs, an cousins'a ars had been in the RA together back in the day an that. So there was a natural trust there so there was. Didn needta be discussed. The plan was simple. Stupid-proof. Get used bottles, refill them, sell them at half price. Cash in the claw sure. The pubs are swimmin in money, they always are, an th'only thing that people with money want is more. So that was a no-brainer, the sellin bit. Still, I reckoned

I needed someone based localta help me out. A bit'a muscle. Someone I could trust, too.

Down I went to Smokey Quigley's. We were havin a lock-in, auld Smokey puffin away behind the bar, havin the craic with two sergeants from above at the barracks. I wasn too well known round there yet but still enoughta get in. Shamey Hughes was playin that night see. Usedta be a great wee lock-in session in there of a Thursday. The great thing bowt there bein so many gards drinkin there was that we'd never get raided. Sure even the poor wee piggies need some- whereta go after so many hours'a sittin on their arses above in the barracks.

Shamey now, he's from Forkhill so he is, an Forkhill's only over the road from Mullaghbawn really. Me an him'd always had a dead good understandin. A lot'a people think Shamey's maybe a bit thick or somethin, but it's not like that t'all. See Shamey's a genius. He's juss on a different wavelength so he is. He's an artist, so his interest in the business, well it's only ever partial. Which is good like, worked perfect for the two'a us. It's like a part-time job, so he has the timeta write songs an that. An I respect him for that. Them thicks who say he's a bit dim, I'd loveta see them write a song sure. Usedta play the fiddle too, an write lovely poetry. Though mind you, I don't know anythin bowt poetry, but Annie said it was dead nice an she knows bowt stuff like that so she does. So yeah. It's dead nice, his poetry.

Anyway, all I know is that Shamey's a great feen. Trusts me like. I always kept him in work so he could be a poet an a musician an that.

He was juss finishin up the set when I landed in. Middle'a

winter it was, fuckin freezin n'all. But the feelin in there was enoughta put warmth back in me bones once Shamey smiled at me, this big Shamey smile that only he can. When he gives ye one'a those ye can't help but smile too. It's one'a his superpowers, no matter what an utter prick ye might be t'everyone else, Shamey's smile brings out the best in ye. An him a bitofa hardman, I mean naturally like. Fuckin giantofa fella so he is. Rarely even hasta hit anyone or anythin. Though once I saw him hauldin some feen down so tight he broke his wrist by accident, juss keepin him down. The fuckin ham child—sure it was his own fault. But Shamey still said sorry an paid him a taxi upta the hospital. See, that's the kinda fella ar Shamey is. Must'a been some headfuck for yer man but.

I was actually dead nervous an that, cause this was the first big proper job I'd sussed. But Shamey smilin as I talked bowt it made me feel better. Calm. Safe. *Not a bother*, he says. *A'course. We can do that.*

It was all I needed, cause after that it *was* simple really. The two'a us, we were a deadly team so we are. I called the shots an he backed me up. Never any messin between the two'a us. Juss pure trust.

We set up a shed near the ramparts. Sorted out gettin empties from the pubs all round, an fillin them. Well, Joško does that. This fella from *Croatia* I think it is. Great feen, no questions asked. He looks after the bottles, washin them an fillin them. Goes back ta Croatia every year for a few weeks but always stocks up so he does. Treats it like a proper job, a normal job like, an I really appreciate that bowt him. Juss the kindofa fella ye need for that sorta thing. Th'idea wasta keep her flowin real steady, keep the shit movin, so even if we got raided it wouldn be th'end'a the world, there'd never be much in stock. An sure Joško, he'd juss repeat *know nathink, know nathink*, an that's fair enough cause he was kept in the dark'a the details'a it all. That was his idea. Didn wanna get involved. Juss wanted a daecent job where he could make a bit'a cash for his family back home an see them at holidays. Ye gotta respect that like.

That was the first big thing that I got together really, it made me in a way, gave me my place in the Town. I had Smokey's backin, an it helpt that I wasn steppin on anyone's feet, either. Was class like, cause then I was a proper part'a the scene, brought to the meetin an that.

Not many people know bowt it, which is the best thing. Keep her country, that's what I always say. Still, most'a the Smirnoff ye drink narth'a the Boyne is brewed in Mullaghbawn, Drumintee an Forkhill. Fuckin first-class stuff too. Gets ye where yer goin sure.

PATIENT ZERO

Cardiff. It's not actually England, is it, Cardiff? An I thought we were skippin Wales. Was actually quite happyta get out'a England at the time but it was like we didn. Poor Cardiff like. Too closeta Englandta be good I s'pose.

Now, I don't hate th'English. Really like. Loads'a English I met over there were actually grand like. Sound so they were. But there *is* somethin bowt the place. It's not in the ground. It's not in the people per se. Naw. It's an idea. But it's different from most ideas what juss drift in an out'a the brain an that. Naw, England's a different kindofan idea. A brutal, vicious, infectionofan idea. Grips things, doesn let them go. An as far as I can see it's spread everywhere they went an sure they've went everywhere with their fuckin empire. Empire. See, that's part'a th'infection. This idea'a bein better than other people, cause it is there, isn't it? Otherwise why would they be draggin everyone back inta the Middle Ages in their Brexit fuckin time machine?

At least we've got the sea mind. Still n'all though the thing that's in Cardiff is in Dublin. Worse in Dublin too. Dublin is where Ireland goesta forget itself—pure paralysis like. Not that they go in for th'imperial bit. I mean th'idea'a Irish pretendinta be better than anyone else, that'd be some joke sure. But this want in themta sell-sell-sell, it's right deep down inside Dublin town too. Sell what but? I'm always askin meself, where does it all come from th'economy'a clickbait that runs Dublin, turnin the place to a wasteland'a tech companies and chain coffee shops. Sure Irish economic policy is nathin more than us bein the cheapest hooker on the street as far as I can see. Which is grand, I juss don't get the politicians an that all pattin themselves on the backs an them thinkin they're dead clever for bein a bunch'a scumbags.

I'm not judgin or nathin. Well, OK, I am a bit, but mainly I juss can't wrap me head round it sure. Like sellin gin an vodka an swipin stuff, *that* makes sense, even the coke. Grand sure. That *is* somethin. But juss sellin with debt haped on debt for more sellin? I don't get it. Maybe I juss listenedta ar Annie too much with all her anti-money socialism craic. Who knows, but that's how I feel bowt it. Th'only things th'Irish are really fit t'export are misery an the craic, an that's some quare combination b'y.

Royal families. Debt merchants. Brexit. Crappy cafes, the same on every street. Airport shoppin. All that. The Queen puttin her label on brown sauce an shite like that. Snide hipster pricks groomin their beards in the corner drinkin shite coffee an callin it class. I tell ye, the world is juss fuckin mad.

Aside from bein real closeta England, Cardiff's not bad. Good craic like. An we made a wee sale so we did. Juss 100 g though. Hardly worth th'effort but fuck it sure. On out we went for a wee gargle in any way. See the sights'a Cardiff town n'all that. Ended up in a Wetherspoons. See what I mean bowt th'Englishness? Cheap swill though, so it was grand all the same.

This feen saunters upta us. Big dirty black beard on him, loads'a tats. A hipster's wet dream, but this fella doesn waste his time with flat whites, I'm quite sure. Cocky-lookin feen. Annie loves cocky men. They do me head in though I'll tell ye. Mad accent on him, I couldn hardly understand shite all.

"Awri, dolls, howreye doon?"

Scottish. Words all roll inta each other sure. Hamish is his name. That name is a fuckin nail through me heart I'll tell ye.

Now, Annie's kin are from Narth Antrim, so she's no problem with the Scottish accent. She's a fuckin linguist so she is, she can even understand people from Cork an that. An she speaks Spanish. Dead sexy that. Ulster Scots? Less so. An that's nathin agin the Proads an their heritage an that, juss that *ola chica* sounds a right bit better than *daftie wee'uns*. Though ye gotta admit callin Orange marches cultural heritage is sorta takin the piss. That might juss be part'a the culture though, who knows—some sorta wry sense'a humour.

Surprise surprise, he's mad inta her. An she has her hand runnin through her hair the whole time so it's clearly reciprocated. I can nearly smell her like, I wonder if he can.

He's at the bar gettin us a drink an Annie whispers in me ear.

"We could do it together if you like."

"It?"

"Yeah, it—*him*."

The glint in her eye b'y. I was almost tempted. But naw.

"I'm not really inta pricks, honey. But g'wan ahead sure," I saysta her.

Didn wanna be a spoilsport after all. An I still felt a bit bad after the Manchester thing so I figured this'd cure that. Funny thing, guilt like that, what with that bein me first time with someone else, yet I'll never know how many beds she's been in back in the Town. Don't wanna know. Better not to.

She juss laughs.

"He seems nice! Are you sure?"

"Bowt the threesome? Yeah."

"I mean are you sure it's OK if I go with him? I don't have to."

I smiled. I didn mind her gettin a bit'a dick sure. She liked it more than me anyway. Besides, no matter what she'd say, her body always spoke the truth. I knew how much she wanted it. Deny her that an I'd be left with weeks an weeks'a resentment. Last thing I needed, after that last day in Birmingham.

"Yeah. It's grand. I'm not really feelin the drink the night so I'll juss drain this next one an leave yis at it."

"You're a sweetie," she says, an kisses me. "I love you, you know that, right?"

Her voice was all thick, practically purrin so she was. *Sultry* I think they call it.

"Yeah yeah. G'wan. Have yer fun."

Biggest fuckin mistake I ever made, I'll tell ye that for nathin.

THE CRAIC

This one time, a car job came along. Came by Shamey Hughes. Car jobs always came by Shamey. See car jobs are fairly run'a the mill for him, he has his own connections in that world. Shamey's dead good at hot-wirin cars an alarm systems n'all that. The job was real simple. Some prick from Dublin see, came up drivin a Ferrari, if ye can imagine that. In Dundalk. Doesn work, does it? Th'image like. But still n'all, up he comes. Big football fan see. It was Shamrock Rovers play the Town out in Oriel Park. Anyway, there'd been an order out on this car since it was still in the warehouse like. Car boosters, they're fuckin nuts like that, they watch these fancy cars everywhere they go, waitin for the right minuteta pounce. Anyway, word got round, an everythin was arranged. It wasta be picked up above in Newry. Smart like. If there ever is a united Ireland like, it'll be a great lossta everyone in the trade on both sides'a the border. Which is sorta ironic, ye gotta admit, given how many'a them are in the RA. They'll do themselves out'a a job if they're not careful. But sure, we could always make a new one. These days, anythin goes.

Anyway, Annie got this Dublin lad's attention the way she gets men's attention. Fed him full'a drink an I kept sketch so I did. She kept yer man busy an we got the feen's car goin. Like bein in the movies or somethin it was. Felt like we were floatin. Took spin upta Newry, doin bowt 150 mile an hour on the motorway. We were there in five minutes sure. There were no peelers out, an even if there were they'd not'a caught us. Dropped it off in the shed, got out, cash, yes, thank ye very much, an took a lift back home. Weren gone an hour even. Annie gave the feen a blowjob in the toilet'a the pub so he wouldn be suspicious or nathin, which I thought was a nice touch, though she didn needta go tellin me.

We went backta Shamey's gaff for a few drinks. Shamey lives in a pokey wee place in Seatown. One'a them wee terraced bungalows. He had it done up real nice, like a museum'a guitars. He doesn even play half'a th'ones he has hangin up there. We went out back cause it wasn rainin an he has a nice wee garden back there too.

"Some craic haigh," says Shamey. "Y'know, that's the main reason I'm in this game. The craic. Sure it's th'only reasonta keep drawin breath really, when ye think bowt it. Y'know what I mean?"

Annie shoots him this dead hot sortofa look.

"No, Shamey," she says, "what *do* you mean?"

"I mean craic's the fuckin meanin'a life. Routine, fuckin structure n'all that? That'd kill me. I need the spontaneity'a this kinda life. Bein in the fuckin mill gettin ground down an down an down til there's nathin left'a ye but dust, I couldn stick that. Don't know how folk manage. That's why I'm in this craic with yous ones. It's like the music. Every gig's a little bit different, an ye haveta be sensitive bowt how ye do things. Juss like the craic. Ye need sensitivityta keep it goin. An when ye think bowt it, craic's a great word. Craic, like crack. That's where we live. In the cracks between things. Cause there are like, there's cracks in life, in the system, the routine—whatever ye wanna call it. That's where ye can escape from the drudgery, that's where ye find real life. Havin the craic."

Must'a been some hellofa joint he rolled himself, cause it's rareta hear Shamey talk like that bowt somethin. But I couldn fault his thinkin like.

Annie could though. All scowlin she was. See she's a pure craic addict so she is but kinda hates herself for it. In a way she wantsta be poor, wantsta have this thing, this kinda weird justice or sense'a bein right she thinks comes with bein poor. See, she thinks bein poor makes ye right, like it gives ye some kindofa licence. But bein poor gives ye fuck all. Real poor people, like properly poor people, they're juss too busy tryin not to be poorta waste time with all that self-righteous chat. A fuckin luxury in itself. I know it's not her fault like, I juss think she shoulda been more easy on Shamey, an herself. An me. It's not ar fault the world's in a fuckin mess.

"I don't think that's what craic means, Shamey. It just means fun, that's all. Which is OK. But there are more important things in the world," she saysta him.

Now, Shamey usually haulds back, he's fairly reserved like. But not this time.

"Like wha?" he says.

Her eyes get all narrow an she uses her schoolteacher voice. Annie'd be a great schoolteacher so she would, but meself I hate that voice.

"It's so fucking indulgent. We're so privileged. Most of the world live in misery. Your *fun*, the craic, that's just some shit we're sold by corporations, alcohol companies, the fucking state . . . Just to maintain the status quo."

"I don't agree with that t'all haigh," he says, "we're pretty fuckin far from the status quo. That's the point like. An the craic? The craic's fuckin anti-corporate! If ye want yer resistance, have the craic sure! That's the best form there is, cause that, the feelin'a really bein with other people, they can't bottle that up an sell it so they can't. Ye don't need the drink for it like, that's juss a wee bonus. Craic's a natural thing."

"Come off it, Shamey," she saysta him, "we might like to think we're different, but the only difference is that we don't work. We're like fucking parasites, man. And the only good thing about that is that at least we're a little further from the machinery of commercial capitalism. But we don't live outside it, don't kid yourself, and neither does craic."

"I never said we live outside it! An anyway, I'm not the one on a crusade agin capitalism, it's *you* that's always bitchin bowt it. I'm juss tryinta have the craic like, to live in the little cracks here an there."

"Yeah, Shamey, I don't think craic comes from crack. I'm pretty sure it's from Ulster Scots. It just means fun."

Sayin this, Annie folded her arms like. End'a fuckin conversation like, I'm right an that's that. She did that all the time like, an people usually juss changed the topic cause they didn wanna argue with her like, cause arguin with her can be a real fuckin pain. Annoyin as hell like, with her schoolteacher voice, all sure she's right most'a the time. But this time I was pretty sure she was wrong. So I went on me phone.

"Ahem," I says, doin me best schoolteacher voice, "now this is from *Wikipedia*."

Craic or *crack* is a term for news, gossip, entertainment and enjoyable conversation, particularly prominent in Ireland. The word has an unusual history; the English *crack* was borrowed into Irish as *craic* in the mid-20th century, and the Irish spelling was then re-borrowed into English.

Shamey breaks his shite laughin.

"That's you tauld! Hah!"

We toast to that. I mean I can't help it. Not juss cause Shamey's smile is so infectious like, but cause he's fuckin right. Life *is* bowt the cracks. It's somethin that happens best in the cracks an the corners, out'a sight. All the rest is juss pure farce.

I do feel a bit bad though. I know Annie's starin daggers inta the side'a me head. But fuck it sure. She was often like that, an there was nathin ye could do bowt it. A wee knot'a frustration an judgement she was. Couldn feel good bowt nathin less she could talk herself inta thinkin it served some big purpose. For *emancipation*, whatever the fuck that is.

Mad, ha? Cause at th'end'a the day she'd always forget bowt th'emancipation bit when the want'a somethin'd fill her up. Then when she got it she'd juss go backta the start again, all frustration, judgement, an grief.

But like I says, Annie's a pure craic addict. An sure after a few tins she even let herself relax. Started quotin Wikipedia at *me*. But that was grand, we were juss havin the craic so we were.

PURE MENTAL

The next day there in Cardiff, I spent the whole day waitin for Annie to get back from her night. Y'know, with yer man. Yon Scottish buck. *Hamish*. Cunt.

The whole fuckin day I spent in that flat, alone, th'only response I got out'a her bein them fuckin seen notifications. They'd drive a personta harm, them yokes. Feckin freezin it was, like a damp chill in the walls, an it still summer sure. Couldn get warm. Mould in the bathroom n'all. I'd'a complained so I would'a, cept that would'a meant talkinta the prick that rented us it, an arguin over money. I hate arguin over money. Makes me feel fuckin worthless. Miserable, like some dog fightin over a bone. An besides, I'm not oneta complain. I'm juss sayin like.

It was bowt seven when she lands in. With him. Hauldin. His. Hand. Jaysis fuckin Christ like, what planet was she even on? I don't even get a peck on the cheek or nathin, they juss plonk down on the couch an I'm there thinkin, *am I meant to make them a cup'a tea is it?* I actually thought that like, fuckin mental.

"How're you, missus?" she saysta me, as if this is all normal, cept not really normal, more like we're juss a pair'a pals. An yon prick all over her for fuck's sake. "Did you get out to see Cardiff in daytime?"

"Yeah," I says. "It's shite."

Hamish chimes in, as if I wantedta talk to him. "Och aye, it is fookin shite. The warst town in the haul country."

"The fuck're *you* doin here?" I asks him.

Cunt thought I was talkin bowt Cardiff.

"Ah y'know, A'm just here oan a wee job, doll. Bit like yerselves."

"Yeah," says Annie, "he's a very well-connected man. I was thinking that you might like to talk to him."

"Bowt what?"

"About the rest of the trip," she says, casual like. Looked roundta him, the cunt kissed her. Right there, a big sloppy— uugh. I can't. I just. Fuck.

Anyway, she says somethin then like, "It's not like we have a plan or anything. And I don't really know that many people in the South. Definitely nobody who'd be into that."

"So?" I saysta her. "We'll fuckin play it by ear. Be grand sure. People love coke, everyone does, we'll get it shifted no bother."

"Well there, lassie, it's just that A could save yew a lot'a bother," he says. "The South'a England's fairly sewn up like. There's load's folk ye wanna steer clear'a, y'know? Dangerous folk, proper dangerous."

"Was I fuckin talkinta *you*?"

"Well, just wait . . ."

"Naw. Naw, I fuckin wasn, so juss butt out."

"Just listen to him, would you?"

"Fuck off."

"Come on, be reasonable."

That did it.

"Be reasonable? Be reasonable? Would y'ever fuck off, would ye. An you comin in here. Not sayin a word all day. Juss actin like this is normal."

"What's she on about?" he saysta her. Men love sittin there, actin all calm, sorta collected an that, sayin things like that as if yer mental an they're the sane ones when all they really are is emotionally retarded sure. Would *drive* ye mental so it would.

"Did *you* not even *tell* him?"

"Jesus Christ. We've been over this. Like, literally . . ."

"Cop on, would ye? This is totally different."

"Look, I was only trying to help. To figure this out," she says.

"Ya, A only wan'a help, but A can see . . ." he says.

"Shut the fuck up. What world is this even? You didn go tellin him details, did ye?"

"How could I, you haven't told *me* any," she says.

Pure Annie move that, make it seem like it's all me fault n'all.

"I've tauld y'enough."

"You're paranoid," she saysta me, her voice full'a cold violence. "I sorted us out in Birmingham, I'm just trying to help out here. And he's just trying to help. But why bother?"

She stands up, with a wee stroppy sigh, like she's some kindofa victim. Th'eye thing n'all. She grabs his hand.

"Look, darlin," he saysta me, "just yew have a wee think bout it. A'm only tryinta help is all."

"Ye wanna help? Juss you fuck off an keep on fuckin off, *darlin*."

They leave.
An I'm backta mouldy solitary confinement.
That night I text her.

Me: I'm bangin on down the road tomorrow. Noon. You
    comin?

Took her near an hourta reply.

Annie: I'll be there.
Annie: He is just trying to help. I am just trying to help.

I don't know what the fuckta say, so I don't reply t'all. Bowt
an hour later, I get this.

Annie: You really hurt me tonight.

For fuck's sake like.

THE GULL

We *did* have loads'a lovely times, normal times, homey times, juss the two'a us times. Times when we were together, juss tight like, a proper couple—a real couple, y'know? Like this one time, of a Tuesday it was, she was full'a chat bowt goin on a spin. She's mad funny, like, when there's loads goin on, an plenty'a craic an people actin mad, she can be the source'a order, keep ye calm an focused—on her if nathin else. The still pointofa ship that sails best in a storm. But other times, calm times, when folk're tryinta take a break, she juss won't let up. Makes her nervous, I think, like she needs a bit'a chaosta keep calm.

I tauld herta take it easy, for the fiftieth time that week. Kept goin on bowt tippin downta Dublin. Why? For the craic sure. Fuck that, I says. We can juss pop downta McCormack's if we wanna have the craic.

Anyway, we don't go to Dublin, orta McCormack's. We juss lie up on the couch rollin joints, drinkin wine an watchin some bollix on Netflix. Can't even remember the name'a it. Some dumb American shite that even the Yanks probably can't be bothered with. But it was dead nice still, juss this moment'a bein normal, like a normal couple, cuddlin on the couch. Three joints in an I finally managedta get herta calm down. She wantedta talk bowt politics, bowt how Netflix is a form'a cultural imperialism n'all, but I asked her for the fiftieth timeta juss give me head peace an she did so she did. I really appreciated that.

All the same, it couldn last. Though she did it in a sideways kindofa way. See, on this shite we're watchin, some cunt punches a woman. She sat up an turnsta me.

"What do you think about that?" she says, pausin the show.

"Ha?"

"A man hitting a woman on TV."

"I dunno. Don't really care."

"Oh, come on, how can you not care?"

"It's juss telly, love. It's not like somethin that really happened."

"I'm talking about the representation of violence towards women. It's not a neutral thing."

"Ha?"

"Look, I mean that having women getting hit on TV, it's not *just telly*. Don't you think? It normalises it. Young guys will watch this and think that's OK. It's the same problem as them getting all their sex education from porn."

"I dunno. I've hit women before."

"Yeah, but you *are* a woman."

"I'm not proud of it, but they deserved it. Headers sure."

"Yeah, but I mean, you're *not* a man."

"Haven y'ever hit a beor?"

"That's not the point, love."

"I dunno. Isn it? Did ye or didn ye?"

"Well, yeah. Once."

I wrapped me arm around her moreta show her I wasn judgin or nathin.

"C'mon. Tell me bowt it."

"Uugh. I don't even like thinking about it. It was just once. At school. This teacher, right, we called her the Gull. She *literally* had a voice that sounded like a seagull on a rainy day at the beach. Whiney and shrill and just bad."

"Aww, that sounds awful. No wonder ye hit her."

"Yeah, but it wasn't that. I mean it wasn't just that. See she was really mean. And not just to me. It was like she was taking something out on us, some frustration or something."

"Fuck!"

"Yeah, like all the time. Awful."

"Bitch."

"Yeah. This one time, she had me in a corner, and she was poking me back further into the corner with these stubby little fingers of hers. Stubbing away at me, you know? Giving out about something. But there was nowhere to go, she had me right up against the wall."

"So ye hit her. That's normal sure it is."

"No, no, it wasn't because of that. It was her breath."

"Ha?"

"Yeah."

"Her breath?"

"Yeah."

"She had bad breath?"

"Awful. Just awful."

"What was it like?"

"Bloody fish! And not just any fish. Her breath smelt of tunafish. That's why I hit her."

"Jaysis."

"Yeah, like I didn't want to hit her. But I hate tunafish. Can't stand it. I don't mind salmon, or mackerel say, and I'd even eat a shark."

"A shark?"

"Yeah. They eat us, so it'd serve them right."

"Fair enough."

We *were* smoked out'a it to be fair. She kept goin.

"Yeah, anyway, I'd eat any of them, but the smell of tuna-fish, I can't stand it. Makes me sick."

"Nasty."

"Yeah. So there she is breathing her tuna-breath at me, squawking in her gull voice, and stabbing me with her stubby little fingers."

"No wonder ye hit her sure."

"And, and, there was a coat-hanger sticking in my back. I forgot about that bit."

"That's bad craic, that."

"Yeah. So, well, I hit her. A big slap across the face."

"What happened after?"

"Oh, she tried to get me expelled. I was in tears, you know, in the principal's office. But I told him my side of the story."

"Right."

"Yeah, and other students testified too. That she bullied us. She had *problems*."

"Right. Fuck."

"Anyway, she got moved to another school. I'd still see her around sometimes. She tried to pretend that I didn't exist."

"I think ye were right to hit her haigh. I'd'a hit her too so I would'a."

"Yeah, but that's not the point!"

"Ha?"

"I mean, violence against women on TV. It's not OK."

"Aye, but this was different."

"Well, yeah, it was different."

She shifted on the couch an leaned in closer t'me. Poured another glass'a wine in any way an juss kept watchin the shite movie so we did. Smoked another joint. Dead nice so it was, that one time on the couch with the wine an that.

MEDIEVAL REENACTMENT

Was a weird auld drive down the roadta Bristol after that, after the run-in with Hamish. The weirdest thing was how sound Annie was bein, dead nice, but not talkin bowt it. Figured I was gonna haveta pay for this in a month'a long silences an dirty looks. She didn though, she juss came over the next day as if it was normal. Made a point not to talk bowt it, just got her stuff, looked at me, dead straight-face like.

"Right," she says, "I'm ready."

This sorta firmness in her voice, like she was leavin somethin behind.

Was night time when we arrived in Bristol. Went for a wander round, went for a bit'a grub. Annie was still bein sound. Bit cold, but sound—not givin much away. No mood for banter, so we juss checked inta some gaff we'd booked on the fly, an I went to bed. Annie stayed up on her phone.

I woke with Hiroshima between me legs, an a cuntin ache inside me—two weeks early. Some wake-up call, that. Combined with th'usual confusion'a wakin up in a strange place, it was all the more bewilderin. I rolled round, reachin out for

Annie an the bed empty beside me, me mouth parched, the sheets bloodied.

I wandered out to the livin room, expectinta see her plugged inta one'a her vlogs or that. But naw. I saw she'd made it look like she'd slept on the couch, but it was hardta tell if she really had or if it was a prop. I staggered on inta the shower an stood under it for a good ten minutes. The hot'a it made me feel better a bit. Thoughts start creepin in like maggoty little ticks wormin their way under the skin'a me mind. I start with the scratchin. Fuckin pain in the hole.

The water startsta run cold so I dry off an wandered on out an saw she left me this shitty wee note.

Heya hon, you were asleep so I let you lie in. I got a lead from a friend, so I took a little sample. Won't be too long.
                                                                Annie x

The fuck? Who buys drugs in the mornin? Fuckin no-one. I smelt some shite in there so I did, but the pain in the middle'a me pure took over sure. Fuckin prickofa thing, an somehow it felt like an insult, happenin early n'all. When ye see it comin somehow it doesn seem so bad, but this way was like gettin harassed by some git on the street who think's he's dead charmin an then gets violent when ye call him a manky wee shite who should'a been aborted. The truth hurts people like that.

It was two a'clock by the time Annie got back. I was in a coil on the couch, with a cushion pressedta me belly all stab-stab-stab. I forgot eventa be pisst off at Annie it was so bad. An anyway, she disarmed me, bein dead nice an that.

"Oh, hon, you're in a bad way, eh?" she says, strokin me hair an that.

"Fuck off."

"I love you too. You're early though, aren't you?"

"Aye. Where were ye?"

"Just now, out walking. Bristol is actually really lovely. Much nicer than I remember it being. Maybe it was the weather but I was walking down by the docks just now and the light was perfect. Golden. Are you OK, hon?"

She was sittin on th'arm'a the couch. Lovely lookin. She always looks lovely, real fresh, after she's had the ride. I could fuckin smell the sex off her. I say nathin though. She gets mad antsy an that when I point that kindofa thing out sure. It's open. We're cool. We're free. Fuck's sake.

She was runnin her hand through me hair. I didn want a row anyway.

She went out to grab me some grub. When she came back she jumped straight in the shower. Not like herta slip up like that, mind you. Not if she really didn want me to know somethin. Sloppy like, so I knew there was one'a two things goin on, either she wanted me to know but she was afraidta tell me cause it was big, so she couldn talk straight bowt it, or she was too stuck thinkin bowt the feen t'even notice. Both options scared the shit out'a me. Me hands.

"So I went to see this guy. Michael. Friend of Hamish. From Cardiff."

There it was. Everythin I neededta know wrapped round that one word. The name. The face. The cunt. The little quiver in her voice an the coughta clear her throat. Fuck.

Me blood startedta quick a bit, an I sat up an listenta her with a serious face like this was juss business. An it was, now. Juss business. So even me hands went still. We're good at business. We fuckin know business. We can handle any prick out there, me an me hands.

"Yeah, g'wan then."

"Well, he says he'll take half a kilo. Real good stuff, he says. Not bad for a morning's work if I say so myself."

"Ye didn tell the prick how much we're cartin did ye?"

"No. He suggested the half kilo."

"Fuck's sake. It's a fierce lot for a first deal."

"We sold three kilos in Birmingham!"

"Aye but that was through folk ye knew. Ye juss met this punter, this Michael chap."

"Relax. It's OK. He's a friend of Hamish's. He put me in touch with him."

I sat right up then.

"An that cunt. Ye didn tell him neither, did ye?"

"For fuck's sake, do you have to call everyone a cunt? Hamish is fine. He only wants to help. You just reacted emotionally. He wants to make some money too, of course, but I think he could be really helpful. We're in over our heads otherwise. Like he said, this is unknown territory, but there's a lot of money around here, and a lot of people after it, people we'd best avoid."

"Would ye juss fuckin cop on? Juss cause he's ridin th'arse'a you doesn make him *ar* friend. Naw. No way. He's an opportunist, a pure opportunist. Juss like everyone else. I tauld ye not to tell him nathin."

"And I didn't, OK? *Jesus.*"

She stomped off, as if I'd been th'one off ridin behind me back, all secret like. Real dramatic an offended an that. That was juss the confirmation I needed that she was upta some-

thin with him. Still. That he was followin us. We got out'a
Bristol the next day. She wantedta stay a'course, but I insisted.
Hadta figure this shit out, an I still had the keys'a the yoke.
Wasn lettin them out'a me sight now b'y.

Annie got a review from the feen with the flat on Airbnb
in any way.

Annie and her friend seem like really lovely people, but
I am afraid that I cannot recommend them. They left my
place in a lamentable state. Sheets and a mattress ruined.

Lamentable state. Easy for yon mulpinta say. He's never
had a reenactment of a medieval battle happen inside him.

Annie an me'd always been more or less in sync, I mean we
had been the whole past year. But her own period was real late
that time. Must'a been.

LUXURY PROBLEMS

Cursed it is at times, good luck, cause it puts y'in a place where ye'veta think bowt bigger kinds'a problems. The kinda problems y'expect other folkta have. At least for me it was like that. Like, imagine, ye played the lotto or somethin dumb like that. Shh. Maybe ye did. Maybe ye were drunk. Juss go along with it. So ye won a car on the lotto or some kinda raffle or somethin. But then ye can't afford th'insurance or yer after gettin banned from drivin for bein drunk behind the wheel or somethin. The kinda thing that could happen t'anyone. Then the yoke's a problem as much as anythin else.

To be honest, I never thought I'd have the kinda problems bein with Annie gave me. The kinda problem'a bein with someone, bein with someone ye really like, not juss bein with someone cause ye wanna not be alone. When ye really love someone, fuck me, that's some craic. All the thinkin. The not knowin. The wantinta know an tryinta learn an thinkin an that an then bein stressed cause ye still don't know. Fuck me that's a prickofa thing. A real luxurious kindofa pain in the hole.

One'a these luxury problems was gettinta know bowt her past. An by that I mean anythin. Cause ye do get curious, don't ye? Sure it's only naturalta wanna know a bit bowt the person yer wakin up beside every mornin. Well. Most mornins. She never said nathin bowt her childhood or her family or that. An it's not like I particularly mind. I mean I know she was brought up Protestant an that. I don't give a fuck. Her granda could'a been Ian fuckin Paisley for all I care. Doesn mean nathin t'me all that shite. It's juss niceta know, all the same. Isn it? To know somethin like. I didn even know if she had brothers an sisters an that, or if she got along with them or any'a that kinda shite. Everyone tells ye like, that that's dead important an that, that sorta stuff, like they'll declare it with some kinda boom like it means somethin. *I'm an only child.* As if that makes it alright to be a prick or somethin. An in any way, it's juss a load'a bollix so it is, cause Tommy's an only child an he's dead sound. But y'know what I mean. It's still goodta know that kindofa thing.

This one time, we were above in Belfast for a bitofa job. Now, Annie's got tonnes'a friends, all over the gaff. But here's the thing. It seemed like I knew more folk up there than she did. An she's *from* Belfast.

We were in the Cauliflower, to meet some feens bowt a shipment. Funny pub, the Cauliflower, sorta half scraggy half fancy n'all that. An the punters in there, not yer usual Belfast hardman crew, but these sorta slick hipster types drinkin funny beers an that. They have a pizza oven out the back, the headers, with gluten-free dough an vegan cheese n'all—an they even serve it with a straight face so they do.

Now, I was only jokin like, but when we were waitin for this feenta show up an that I was slaggin her a bit bowt the fact that she said she didn know anyone in Belfast. Well, she juss broke down sure. Fuck me, I wasn expectin that. I'd'a understood her gettin thick at me or somethin, but startin cryin? Fuck me. An babblin. An her always so strong an strict an that.

"What is it? What's wrong with ye?"

"Leave me alone OK. It's not. I don't. Fuck!"

"Naw, c'mon. Tell me."

"Fuck! I hate that. This place. And all the. The things. Now."

"Sshh. Calm down."

"Calm? Fuck. I can't calm. This not. Not now. And calm? Here?"

I can't remember rightly all the words she was sayin t'me. All ragged breaths an random, like almost random but actually not random t'all. It was like talkinta someone else. At first she was real quiet an then nearly shoutin an pushin me away. All them poncey wee shites in there lookin at us. Sure I juss looks round with a dagger in me eyes. Like fuck yous. C'mon. Say somethin if ye want. Pricks.

I led her on out inta the courtyard, her pullin this way an that. Tauld herta smoke a fag. Smokin. Smokin always calmed her. It helpt, but then she starts whimper-limperin, her head in me shoulder juss a stream'a things an tears soakin inta me shoulder. I held her t'me then an tight an sure I couldn keep back from knowin that whatever I didn know bowt her, this was still the closest I'd ever beenta someone, there in that moment right there.

"Just this. And all and you and this town it screeches in me and oh and oh I fucking hate it. Them! No you *don't* know, don't say you know you *can't* know. And I don't, I won't let you know because I. No. Just no. I can't, I won't and none will make me, and now I know what I don't and what I don't *want*. At last. So fuck! Fuck! Fuck!"

She pushed me back an took these breaths, a barrage'a them, all short, sharp an shallow, each one seeminta need more. She seemed dizzy, but we were only on ar second drink like. She steadied herself by me an went on.

"I'll. Stay and away. I'm only here with *you*, because of *you*. I wouldn't set foot back into that and why and my life what it was. Before. Myself and past a long a long no never never NEVER no I wouldn't go. But here I am, and you *made* me that. And why soul, why am I here, I *even* hate it here. And no I want to go, can we go? And now and now. Please. Can we? *Please*."

It was th'only time I'd ever heard her use the word please, I think. It wasn part'a her vocabulary. An I don't mean that in a bad way. It's juss that she was different than other people. Imperial. When she'd say do somethin ye'd juss fuckin do it.

A'course there was moreta everythin she said an that. But fuck it. That was enough. I ordered us a taxita the train station. Waitin for the next train home, I called yon Belfast buck an tauld himta come meet me there. Fuck it sure, I was th'one doin him the favour. Though I s'pose he wanted t'impress me with how sophisticated Belfast was got, with their vegan fuckin pizzas, invitin me to the Cauliflower. As if I could give a fuck.

An as if vegan pizza is actually pizza.

Snide wee pricks b'y, tellin ye, ye'd best wanna keep an eye out for them.

THE WAKE

What is the future, y'know, what even is that? When ye think bowt it, it's nathin, all shite that hasn't happened. Mightn even. An I don't mean that in some kindofa hippie way, I'm juss sayin, all ye've ever got is now. An ye can only build that on the past. But ye want that nowta last. I wanted *my* now with Annie, I wanted it to last. So a'course when things are rough, ye think'a the times things were good, when they were workin well. Ye draw on that. Like the time when me nan died. I was in bits so I was. Me nan was deadly. Pure class act like. She had more craic in the tips'a her toes than most folk have in their entire existences.

Growin up, she was th'only one made me feel good. I think Annie understood this kinda instinctively like, cause she was dead sound bowt it all. She even cameta Mullaghbawn so she did, finally she did. Though she wouldn let me introduce her as me girlfriend, an that got me. To be honest it probably would'a made me ma dead uncomfortable an that, but fuck it sure. What do I care? Me mam does the rosaries an prays for me to find a *good man* whatever the fuck that is. She'll be a long time prayin I tell ye. None'a her business who I shag for fuck's sake, the whole thing's a pain in the hole, cause me sister's livin the dream above in Belfast, married, bored, with two brats. Fuck that.

Me nan would'a loved Annie. She wouldn even'a gave two fucks bowt her bein a Proad never mind a beor. She was someone could see the big picture, me nan. That was another thing Annie didn want folk knowin. I tauld her we don't eat Proads or nathin. I could understand that though, in fairness, Mullaghbawn being right down in South Armagh an that. They probably think we're fuckin savages above in East Belfast an places like that. Annie an me, we dealt with it mainly by not dealin with it. Juss didn ever feel important—we'd enough goin on.

Me nan though, she saw through shite like that. She's th'one taught me howta think for meself. How muchofa fuckin disappointment it must'a beenta see how me ma gave upta be with a prick like me da. Maybe that's why she put so much time inta me, me nan. Half raised me so she did.

It's mad. When someone has that kindofa place in yer life ye juss don't never think they can ever go. When they do, it proper shakes ye. Like I knew she was dead auld an that but y'know what I mean so ye do. There one day gone the next. Heart gave out. At least she didn suffer.

When I was a wee'un I practically lived with her so I did. Me granda died before I was born so she liked the company. We took care'a each other. She cooked I cleaned kindofa thing. She tauld me all kinds'a things so she did. An even if I can't remember any'a it, I remember the feel'a it if y'know that kindofa way. I juss liked bein with her for the beinofit, y'always had the feelin she really understood ye. An I think she even did, too.

Annie'd never been at a wake before. Not somethin they did much she saysta me. Fair enough cause when ye think bowt it ye can see why folk wouldn wanna keep corpses in their gaff an that. But that's tradition.

It was the second day when we landed up. The lot'a them already well oiled with misery an whiskey. Quare atmosphere for Annie to walk inta but fair playta her she handled it well so she did. She was always good at that. Freaked me out a bit, cause no matter if she's in a ratty kindofa mood, which she was, she can alway juss switch inta th'Annie everyone loves. It was all *ach, I'm so sorry*, an *sure, it was a grand auld age all the same*, an pourin tea an cuttin sandwiches like she'd done it a thousand times. Everyone loved her, as usual, which was actually kinda annoyin cause if they'd known the truth they'd be confronted by their own closed minds an that's dead annoyin.

I'd say it was bowt three in the mornin when the murmur starts goin round. Fierce quare talk, but I heard from five different folk that Nan came back from the dead. Yeah, I know. Wait til I tell ye.

People were sayin that they saw her breathin. Now, ye can't trust drunk people who're also grievin but I hadta see this. Sat there for ages so I did. Annie, she was pacin round the room, real restless like. Was bowt to leave when I sees it. Her chest! Heavin up an down it was an the whole room silent an makin the sign'a the cross n'all. Fuckin crazy haigh. This kept goin on right through the night. Startin an stoppin. Me auntie Mary Mini was ragged with the tears so she was, kept throwin herself on the body searchin for a sign'a life. Us ones hadta hauld her back sure.

Next mornin the priest was there, as if that was gonna help somehow. Big stern prick head on him sure, red angry cheeks an that, tryinta channel the spirit'a the 1950s or somethin, authority an that, as if he wasn juss a member of a glorified paedophile ring. They don't even pay taxes them bucks. But under the circumstances there was a sorta deferenceta the feen. After all, we didn know anymore whether it was a funeral or an exorcism we'd be needin.

Anyway, he saw it himself n'all that red juss pure drained out'a his face. Strugglinta speak straight he was, as if there might be somethin t'all this afterlife craic after all. An him probably juss lookin for a quiet life an a cheap sense'a moral superiority. Poor fella. Should'a gone South an joined the gards.

Put the funeral off for two days so he did. I called up the gin an vodka lads an got themta make a special delivery. Two more day's a wakin me nan after all.

Me poor aunt was convinced it must be some kindofa deep coma but me ma wantedta put her in the ground an be done with it. The lines were drawn between the lifers an the deathers. As if this country hadn seen enough civil strife.

The doctor came down later that day. Dead annoyed so he was. What was this superstitious nonsense, sure hadn he already pronounced the poor woman dead? A'course, it'd be mad embarrassin for him if he hadta reverse the diagnosis now. Rookie mistake for a doctor sure. Pulled me ma an auntie beside an tauld them in a voice somewhere in between outrage an embarrassment—for them—that she was dead.

Still her chest kept heavin, though I don't think the doctor stayed long enoughta see it. The hard-lifers wouldn accept his diagnosis. When someone threatenedta summon th'Archbishop'a the diocese'a Armagh, we managedta find a compromise, to get a second opinion on the corpse from a good Protestant doctor above in Armagh city. See people always put more trust in a Protestant doctor. Pure logical that. Everyone knows Protestants are better at doctorin, gardenin, an accountin. Common sense like.

Yep, she was still dead. An she'd soon be a public health menace he said, if we didn stick her in the ground. Poor fella, Grant McKenzie was his name, big fuckin doe eyes on him so he had. Looked afraid'a his lifeta break the bad newsta us for a third time an him without a police escort. Real meek an polite an that he shook his head an drank three cups'a tea before he felt sure that he wasn bowt to be sacrificed in some kinda voodoo papist ritual. *No, no, I'm afraid she's quite dead.*

The funeral went ahead, nearly a full week late. The church was packed. I called up Shamey Hughes an the Rat King to come down, y'know, juss in case anythin funny'd happen. Meself I was juss gladta be released from this bloody wake that seemed like it might go on forever otherwise. But Annie stayed with me the whole time, I really appreciated that so I did.

The hard-lifers triedta bar the funeral procession from gettin inta the church so they did. Fierce tense for a minute there, so thank god I had the lads with me. Between the stern look'a them an Annie bein dead sweet an that we got through easy enough. Fuck knows what might'a happened if they hadn'a been there. Me auntie hasn spokenta me ma since. She haulds her personally responsible somehow. Hardly seems fair, but they never got alongta begin with, bit like me an me own sister. Selfish bitch couldn even get off her arseta come to the funeral like. I juss wish me brother'd been, y'know, that he'd been ableta be there. He loved me nan too.

It was only much later that I found out what actually happened. Out on the spraoí we were, Annie an me, an she was three pills in when she says she hasta tell me somethin. That she hasta confess. She neededta tell me but she could only tell me if I promised neverta tell Shamey or the Rat King. Well, what else was I meant to do?

It was her. She'd been keepin me nan breathin. Cept she wasn really breathin, she juss looked like she was breathin. See, on them cheap coffins, if ye press down on the wee handle thing at the top the wood under the chest pulls up. Cheap plywood like, all glued together. So it looks like the body's breathin. She discovered by accident. An it really does work, too, I did it meself once since so I did. Try it sure.

It was pure divilment made her do it, but in fairness I could understand th'appeal. Good craic watchin all the drama. Too good a chanceta pass up sure. Like a potted history'a Narthern Ireland, with all the grief an stupidity an drink an everythin. We juss would'a needed an Orange march come an collide with the funeral procession an it would'a been perfect so it would'a.

PENIS ENVY

Wedgin itself down between two thoughts, like a tick on a dog's arse, a big ugly black yoke, wrigglin a way what ye can't ignore. No hope. Th'idea. Or Feelin. Fuck knows. Jealousy maybe. To be pure jealous'a some prick. That's what Annie said, but th'idea didn sit right with me. Bein jealous, of a man? Naw. She said it was juss a bit'a fun, like the fellas before, an I'd never been jealous'a any'a them pricks so I hadn so why would I be jealous'a this buck now? Didn make sense.

But she kept at it. Meself, I figured it was somethin else, in me gut like. Me guts'd always kept me safe til then, that sorta squirmy feelin I get when I knowta stay well shot'a some cunt. By god I had it now. Annie called it *penis envy*, an said she'd learned bowt it in psychology but that makes no sense cause she studied art. I think? Didn she? She said she did, so why did she talk bowt psychology now? An anyway, I remember her sayin a different time, another time, *psychology is just spontaneous ideology written down and presented as science*. Makes no sense. Didn sound like she likes psychology, an now she's a psychologist? An penis envy? The fuck is that all bowt? What the fuck would I want a dick for? Some limp drippy little stick? Pathetic. Besides I'd look weird with a dick. Psychologists must be mad, comin up with craic like that. I'd say it was a *man* came up with *that* notion. Well, he can fuck off with his cock an keep it. I juss didn like her hangin round with yon Hamish cunt cause I knew down in me bones not to trust him. I know a cunt when I see one. I juss do.

But she liked it, I think, gettin used. So usedta usin people, to usin feens, usin me too, an knowin I'd not use her, at least not in the same way. She must'a liked gettin used by him. Wasn her fault, not really. People love gettin used, y'know, even though they won't admit it in their heads, deep down in their guts they love it. They need it. To feel needed. A need, a fierce needta be needed, an sure if yer used, like proper used—used deep—ye must be needed. Can't juss be casual. Can it? I'm no spa, y'know, I know well she was usin me, since day one. I know it. A'course I know it. But I liked it. Made me feel strong, y'know, that someone like her would wanna use me. Y'know people say looks can be deceivin an shite like that—shite, cause mostly it's not true. Mostly when someone seems like a spa it's cause th'are. But I was different. Cause like if she was with me, then I must be different. I must be good. More than juss me looks. There must be somethin good there, somethin strong. So I liked bein used by her. Made me feel powerful. Fuck it.

This Hamish craic was somethin else but. Changed everythin. I don't even understand it, still like, I don't get what happenedta her. I don't get what happened t'me, either, the fear an the, I dunno, the *venom*. Not jealousy, no, I wasn jealous. Not scared either. I juss hated him. Not her, though. But I was disgusted mind. How she could act like this, all over a feen like? Didn make sense. That's why I did what I did, but lookin back it still doesn make sense. See, he must'a been manipulatin her, but I knew her better. It wasn her fault, not really.

Me: Where r u?

Annie: I'm out.

Me: Yeh, but where?

Annie: Out.

Me: Who u wit?

Me: Hey?

Me: WHO U WIT!?

Me: Annie?

Annie: Jesus. Chill. I'm just out. I'm trying to find a buyer.

Me: U wit that Scottish buck?

Annie: Calm down.

Me: U fuckin are, arent u?

Annie: Look, I'm just trying to get this stuff moved. I'll be back soon. x

Yeah. Now that seems OK, but it got worse an worse. Eventually she didn even mind tellin me the truth. The worst was bein left alone in these places I didn know. These ones here're from Brighton. I remember it well, I was sittin in some pub by meself. Fuckin lost. Some fuckin navy pub it was, an they were sendin round a collection for veterans. The fuck? British military veterans like. Pure bewildered so I was, I even gave them a few pennies jussta not be noticed. Gave me a wee sticker with the Union Jack on it. The fuckin butcher's apron like. Wonder what they'd make'a that back home.

Me: Annie where r u?

Annie: I'm with Hamish hon.

Me: Yeh I no but where?

Annie: We're with a friend of his. Talking business.

Me: Whcrc.

Annie: I don't know. His friend's place. What's the problem?

Me: Cunt

Annie: Look, we'll talk about it later. He just wants to help.

Me: Wants to ride u more like.

Annie: Jealousy doesn't suit you dear.

Me: Fuck off.

Annie: We'll talk about it later. Xx.

See what I mean? Him usin her usin me. The fuck did we need him for? I'm very picky bowt who I let use me so I am. No way I was gonna let yon buck get away with it. Hadta put a stopta this. Hadta. Cause the way I figured, he was only followin her like that for meansofa wayta get to the stash, ar stash.

Them ones was off talkin bowt the Rat King's coke, an it in Shamey Hughes's car. Cept I was th'one with the key. I wasn bowt to let Hamish get his hands on it. That was the Rat King's coke like, an ar money. Fuck that. Th'awful thing was juss I knew I couldn count on Annie then.

So I did th'one thing I knew she'd never expect. I went to London. Alone.

SAY NATHIN

TRUSTIN THE RAT

Words an trust an words like trust an then actually trustin. How d'ye do it sure? If all ye hadta go on was words, I don't think trust'd even be possible, even the very notion'a trust. Naw. An sure words are juss the messengers, ye can't go puttin all the blame on them. But at the same time ye need somethin more, the feel'a it right down in the back'a yer eyes, in the thick'a yer bones. An trustin the wrong fucker, that's like a cancer that gets right in there an eats it all up, turns it to muck. A slow death, a lingerin one, a death that stays with ye the rest'a yer life.

There are people I always trusted though. Always knew I could. Like Shamey Hughes. That's juss a real natural kindofa trust. No one big thing built that or nathin, juss loads'a little things like watchin him in different kinda situations sure. Like when he'd get annoyed, an wantedta hauld himself back, he'd scratch himself on the belly. Twice. Always twice. Seemedta work, cause fuck me b'y, that feen has some bank'a patience in him. He could put up with even the most sour'a pricks so he could. Sure he put up with me. Was always like that, even

when he was pallin round with me brother, back in the day. Ye
could even count on the feenta be pisht three nights out'a five.
Rhythm. Must be the music.

The Rat King's another lad I'd trust with me life. But see
there's moreofa story there, cause I don't know him as long.
An he's a traveller so he is, an they're a breed apart. Proper
aloof an that. But I understand why, from knowin him. At
the same time he's a rare one, he could be anywhere an do
anythin I'd say which makes him all the more interestin for
stayin in the haltin site. He could work in a bank sure, an lots'a
people think that's a good thingta do so they do but naw, not
him. The Rat King knows better. An a bank'd probably loveta
have him so they would, they could say *look at us, we give jobs
to women an travellers an handicaps an one day we might even
give a job to a black fella or a gay sure aren't we deadly?* Pricks.

An the clan, they're dead welcomin once they get to know
ye sure. See it usedta be dead common, goin off an joinin a
tinker's clan. The road, it's dead romantic as an idea. That's the
craic with the Rat King, cause see his ma, she wasn a traveller.
Yeah. She married in. One time, the Rat King said I should
marry inta the clan an become a traveller meself. I don't hate
th'idea, but I juss don't think marryin's really for me. An he
suggested marryin Sammy Squeaks. Can y'imagine bein in
bed with Squeaks? I couldn keep a straight face sure.

But that's juss the start'a it. I trust the Rat King an he
trusts me. See we've seen th'insides'a each other. We've seen
what's down there, at the very bottom like.

It wasn long after we started the fag job, the counterfeit
cigarettes an that. The Rat King's crew was handlin distribution, but them lads above in Newry still wantedta work
through me. Like a pair'a gloves, so they didn haveta touch

the travellers. Fuckin cunts. But it was alright, the Rat King liked havin me along an I liked bein there. Always enjoy time with that man, whether we're on the job or not.

Anyway the Rat King an me went upta do a run, loadin the big van up. Juss me an him an Squeaks. I went offta chat to the pair'a thicks, tweedle-dee an tweedle-dum what run that show an reassure them a bit sure. Whilst I was off with that pair, we got raided.

Wasn the peelers though. Naw. Much worse. Worse even than the thickest narthern cop ye'd never wanna meet. It was this crew, from beyond in Mullingar, a real nasty pack'a bastards. They were in a feud with the Rat King an his people, a feud goin years back.

See they'd never have come after him near Dundalk. Too strong there, his folk love him an sure half the Town owes him favours. Even the gards'd be on his side so they would, cause he keeps smacht on things. But in Newry? Grand sure. S'pose we had let ar guard down cause'a the border bein there, but sure the border means fuck all at th'end'a the day, specially to the likes'a them.

I was comin back from the drink with these two gobshites an we saw another van, Meath plates on it. Tweedle-dee an tweedle-dum twig it too, an sure they juss flap round like a pair'a grannies. But the silly kind, not like me nan. Would'a been deadly havin her there. She'd'a sorted them bucks out no bother.

Anyway, I know I've no choice. I've only me blade on me, didn take Stripes Maguire's gun. Kinda regretted that. Regretted not bringin Shamey, too. But fuck it. No choice the way I saw it. I could see two feens, big hapes'a fellas, unloadin the truck from ar vans inta theirs.

I go round back. Me chest is poundin, but not in that mad nervous kindofa way. Naw. Mad steady. A war-drum then. Me hands, no traitors them, they're dead still, like I'm bowt to go cut cheese, not cheeks.

In I go through a wee side door, the way I'm well hid by crates'a cigarettes. I go round the side an I see the Rat King's tied up. Squeaks too. Pretty bad hidin they got, but they're alive at least. Fuck. Squeak's jaw is bleedin somethin awful. There's one lad watchin them with a crowbar so there is, an two more loadin up the van. The feen with the bar's the boss. See he wouldn stoopta shiftin crates. Took them by surprise they did. Well, they weren expectin me neither.

The two doin the luggin are real slow cause they're arguin like a pair'a hams over who does what. This other lad juss bellows at them from timeta time, but he's mainly on his phone. Cocky bastards haigh. I know I gotta move quick though.

I see me chance. That cunt's back's turned. I come. On out I come. Everythin's movin real nice, juss like it needsta, that one time an that. The knife in his leg, moves through it real easy too. Take the crowbar before the bangin. Lotsa screamin though, like a wee piggy cut bad. Sure he is so he is, that's exactly what he is.

Quick now. Cut them ropes. Then th'others. Fuck. What. Fuck, that's someone. Has me by the hair an I'm bein pulled backward across the floor. Lost the bar. Doesn really feel that bad at the time, but the *knowin* that it *will*? That's bad. Fuck it. The Rat King. Then this noise, but inside me head like, not actually a noise. A kinda metal thing, but crunchy too like munchin on chicken bones but real quick. An then I can. Can't see. Fuck. Movin hands juss cold an blood. An cold. Fuck. I'm bleedin. Bad. Bad. Lots'a bad an blood an I can't feel where it's comin from but I'm gaspin cause there's lots an lots an lots.

Sight. Red. Not *my* blood. Good. Fuck. The pain. It's. There it is. It'll be OK. *Can ye stand?* I can. Can I? *Take my hand.* OK. We stand. A big bright fuckin bloody mess we are, but there's a quick smile there. Cause we're standin now, the three'a us. He hugs me so he does, the Rat King, an Squeaks too. Proper tight. Cunts. *They had it comin.* I know sure. Besides—they'll live. *It'd be bad luck killin them juss like that.* Juss won't walk right again. *That'll learn them.* Then I fall. Sleep.

When I wake again, I wasn there. Wasn home neither. Was in the Rat King's trailer. He wasn there. I was alone but it was grand. Warm, an he'd taken the stinkin fuckin rat with him so that was good. Clean sheets in his bed.

Stayed there for a couple'a days so I did. Got to know them right good then so I did.

Never talked bowt it much. What need sure? That's what trust is, it's not somethin ye needta talk bowt. If someone *asks* ye to trust them? Take me word. Don't.

THE CATERPILLAR

Gettin me head round London was some quare bit'a business, I'll tell ye. The size of it like. I called up Shamey Hughes for a bitofa steer on that, him havin been over several times giggin. There was no question'a takin the yoke inta town with me—drivin in London? Fuck that. Still, I needed somewhereta leave it, safe, but not fancy, somewhere where it wouldn attract attention, y'know. Somewhere it'd be safe. I left it out near Heathrow, end'a the tube line, in some estate that looked OK. Stuffed the remainin gear inta me backpack an took the tube, Stripes's piece weighin heavy in me pocket. But I was glad then, glad I took it, on me own in unfamiliar ground, an the ground openin upta swallow me. I'd never took an underground train like, an nathin prepared me for that. Not juss for the wee size'a it, the claustrophobia an nasty-smellin air deep down there, but for the looks on folks' faces. Deep down despair, distilled inta oil an rubbed on daily for the commute, the hopeless, grim plod of it.

On the way in I found somewhereta stay. Picked up a couple'a bottles, juss for some help switchin off, hopin for an early night's sleep. Some chance, with the way the thoughts were goin round me head like, light-speed relentless, an rattly. I'm no strangerta nights like them though. I'm often th'one left squeezin away at the last dregs'a the night, wrcckcd past tiredness, the sorta way where ye feel ye could keep at it if only it'd stay dark. The dark, the drink, an the banter, that's all ye need, it's the best'a life. Sure after that there's juss the fuckin tomb. Remorseless, the night. Messy, brutal, an happy. I could juss live there, not like I really miss the sunshine when the time turns round an I'm up all hours an sleepin durin the day. Even when it is day sure it's cloudy as fuck most'a the time anyway. An sure light lacks anythin in the way'a subtlety. Real kitsch in that way, flattenin things. Removes all that dark detail'a imagination, the good feelin ye get seein somethin in the dark through the struggle'a it. I reckon that's why the world's in the state that it is. People aren comfortable with the dark, most folk anyway, they're always tryinta banish it. There should be more shadows, all I'm sayin.

London's an awful place for the shadows. Awful place juss in general like, yet half'a them ones seem in constant celebration'a it. I don't get it, I really don't see why people think it's so deadly. Fuckin epicentre'a all that's fake far as I could see. Maybe that's juss me, maybe I'm ruined, a *cynic* like Annie'd say, but to be honest I feel sorry for all the folk tricked by this place. Probably good, honest folk, daecent folk, good hearts, juss scared maybe. Buyin this dream that isn even theirs, an payin through the nose for it. An I thought Dublin was bad enough. Fuck me b'y. At least Dublin still has its shadows, some'a them at least.

Neededta think. Walkin helps me think. Neededta walk. Walked half the city so I did, more maybe. Felt like I was th'only one out walkin, what with everyone stuck in the tube an the cabs an that. An them fuckin growlin at each other. Jaysis. Not for me, all that craic. The weary disgust, it was growin in me belly like a kindofa slime, percolatin right the way upta the stem'a me brain. Like a fuckin cancer it was, a hungry cancer.

I walked from Covent Garden, cause that's dead centre, right, an it's real famous an that. Load'a bollix. Juss a load'a people traipsin over each other. I wantedta go to Hackney cause I heard it was a daecent spot. So I did. Walked for fuckin hours so I did.

Central London was everythin I imagined, an less. Juss all these fancy buildins built'a the money the Brits plundered'a the rest'a the world, full'a shops that are probably all owned by th'one manky geriatric in America somewhere. Who actually has the time for all that shoppin anyway, that Oxford Street an that? Can't be the Londoners by the way they run bowt. D'ye know, I heard people take holidays jussta come an do their shoppin here. The fuck like, what's that bowt? Like payin the lad who robs yer house sure.

At least this way me legs could do some thinkin too, an it wasn all juss down t'me hands tearin themselves apart sure. Thinkin bowt me next move. I was worried bowt her. Naw, I knew what this was. Holiday fling. Happens all the time. But this feen, he was like a tick, right in under the skin. Insinuatin himself. He'd been directin Annie's movements. Leadin her round by the nose. I'm no coward but. I'd fuckin stare a rabid dog right down sure. There was no timeta be angry. Hadta walk. Hadta think. Hadta thinkofa wayta get him away from her, an her textin me ten times a day bowt meetin *us*. Pure prickofa thing.

I even called Caroline—Detective Kelleher. Thought she might be ableta help, get him lifted maybe, do a bit'a that cross-border magic. She was willin, but I'd need somethin on him, some proper dirt. An what did I have? Me gut. Fuck it sure. That was enough for me. Felt very far from home. Very alone. See this craic? This'd be no bother back in the Town. This wouldn even happen back in the Town for fuck's sake.

I remember thinkin, there must be some vicious cunts in London. Lucky enough I slipped right in under the radar. I remember thinkin that round Liverpool Street. Feelin glad no-one knew me here, that no-one could spot me. Made me more calm a bit, realisin that, considerin all the gear I had on me an the cash I didn want lifted. Tryinta get out'a this wilderness'a chain coffee shops an big buildins that look right like dildos. Fuckin oppressive. Do the lads—cause I assume it's feens design buildinsta look like dicks—do they never stopta think bowt what kindofa message they're sendin, all them nasty auld dicks up in the sky? Fuckin skydicks, as if there weren enough dicks on the streets.

London city's full'a sharks. Must be. Sharks that juss swam up the Thames an took a look at it, all the grey faces, the grey hearts. Bankers, politicians, property speculators. Lawyers. They must'a thought *here, here it is, this is a deadly feedin ground here so it is*. I figured the ones in the business must be proper rotten like, juss pure teeth like. They must make ar lads back home look like kittens. Heart wallopin, as if I was bowt to get fuckin swallowed by all them teeth. Walkin real fast I was then, away from all them skydicks. Poundin it was, me chest, all itchy me hands, an damp. Hadta get out'a here so I did. Get somewhere green so I could think bowt what to do with the stuff. Howta get the rest'a it off me hands without them sharks noticin? Without Annie noticin? Without Hamish noticin? Without gettin swallowed up.

This was goin round an round like. Fuckin really pissin me off, an then out'a nowhere I found meself at the farm. A fuckin farm in London. Yeah, that's a thing. A real good thing it was too. Fake, a'course, but sure what would ye expect in that town. At least there was a bit'a green though. A park. An the name'a the park was Haggerston Park, which reminded me a bit'a Haggardstown, near Blackrock in Dundalk. But not posh like Blackrock, like, daecent enough. Haggerston, Haggardstown, sure it's basically the same, an that's juss a wee wander out'a the Town. I know people there. Was like I'd left London behind for a bit, with all the rats in the cages an dicks in the sky, an sharks lost too far up the river t'ever go back, juss turnedta tooth an bone, but like, vicious bone.

I sat there, I dunno, a good long while. I don't know how long, but it felt good. Must'a been ages. Out'a nowhere I noticed these shadows creepin in, cause we were in the park an that, so it wasn so spoiled by the city an the light. An me hands were dry an still, an I could breathe normal again. That's when I met the Caterpillar.

This fucker. Juss sits down beside me. Nonchalant as fuck sure, right beside me, an there plenty'a other benches free an that. A'course, I'm not worried or nathin, I've always a blade up me sleeve so I do. Juss I wasn in the mood for any messin, a'any prick tryinta show me his willy or anythin like that. Seriously, specially not in this town where all ye needta do is look at the sky if ye want a dick-pic. An I'm only jokin, cause no-one ever wants a dick-pic, ever.

This fucker starts talkinta me. Bowt the weather an that. For fuck's sake sure. The fuck do I care bowt the weather?

It's sunny. Yeah. Deadly. Bit'a wind. Lovely. No-one ever talks bowt the weather when they wanna talk bowt the weather though, they're juss tryinta find a wayta get inta what they actually wanna talk bowt an them without the ballsta juss say it sure. Real fuckin stupid wayta start a conversation.

"The fuck you talkin bowt the weather for?" I saysta him, real sharp sure. "An what's with the fuckin clown costume?"

Dressed real weird, yon buck, I forgot to mention that.

Fucker actually looked shocked n'all. An him the spa out talkinta randomers bowt the weather.

"Alright, alright, calm down, calm down!" he saysta me.

"Do you always say everythin twice or is that like some kindofa speech impediment that I'm meant to be real sensitive bowt n'all? Cause I should tell ye right now, I'm not. So juss walk on, buck."

He starts rubbin his knees, but I see he's still smilin. Or maybe even smilin more I think. In any way, he's smilin, an I'm wonderin what's he still doin here but I don't mind him that much cause he's got a real nice voice actually, a proper London cockney voice. Much better than yer average English toilet voice. All the same, he could juss be puttin it on for me, him hearin I'm not from there an that. As long as he doesn try talkin bowt the weather again he's alright I guess. But still, I think he's not gonna show me his dick so that's good. No interest like. None.

So he starts tellin me why he's dressed that way, in this funny blue suit. Kinda looks like an old-school pimp from an American movie, but he says he's the Caterpillar, an acts like I'm meant to know the fuck what that means.

He leans in an says t'me, "Whooo . . . are . . . you?"

I still don't have a fuckin clue like. I say as much an sure he starts babblin like. But I still don't know a fuck what he's on bowt.

"The fokin Caterpillar innit! From *Alice in Wonderland*. Wot, didn you have a childhood, lav?"

"Don't you fuckin *love* me, an don't go there, ye fuckin weirdo. An you a grown fuckin man, callin himself a worm from a cartoon. A children's cartoon. Ye some kinda pervert is it? Or juss soft in the head?"

Poor lad seems kinda shocked again, so I tell him I'm juss havin a bit'a banter sure, an not to worry like. I tell him me name, that I'm from a place he's never heard'a, cause in fairness who in London would'a heard'a the Town? Would'a been weird if he had. I was usedta Brits bein shite at geography by then, god love them.

We get talkin anyway, an he's really not so bad like. Talks a lot, in this leadin kindofa way, an I'm wonderin what it is he's gettin at. I know when someone's scopin me out. Sure that's half the game.

Pretty soon I realise he's a dealer. That's why he came an sat beside me. Proper smalltime like. Probably has half his stock on him sure. He wants me to buy a bit'a spliff. I can tell by the look in his eye, this sorta shiftin look, that he's new enough in the business. Why else would he be sellin in a park? But I figure it might be goodta know a feen like that, all things considered.

I hated that. I hated how alone I felt. I hated the way things were then. When Annie talked bowt it bein open, the relationship, it was meant to be all bowt trust an love an open shite an not juss her off ridin someone else for days on end an pretendin it didn matter a fuck when we both knew it did. A'course it did.

She said it'd be different, when we got home. An that was all I had, cause I didn have her like, not then. She said things'd be easier, with the money an that, but they'd never been really hard. She said we'd go on a wee trip together, juss the two'a us, juss for the craic sure, but sure we could'a done that at any time. But I held onta that idea so I did, the thought that things'd be different. That they'd be good.

Anyway, this Caterpillar feen, whose real name was John, we talked an I let him know that I was in the business too. Bought a bit'a spliff off himta make him relax, an we talked bowt the scene there a bit. I let him think I was juss smalltime like him too sure. So he invites me roundta his mate's gaff, an I said *yeah, grand, let's go*.

I could already feel the teeth growin on me so I could. Becomin a shark like. On th'inside. Figured it must be a London thing.

ANOTHER NED KELLY

Like a bunch'a fuckin kittens with their tongues caught in mousetraps we were that time when Smokey Quigley got done. Nobody saw that one comin, her bein so well connected an careful n'all. Sure even the peelers looked confused, an they the ones doin it.

Of a Thursday afternoon it was, I remember well. I get a text off Paddy. Now, I don't really talkta Paddy much or nathin outside'a business so gettin a text off him I knew somethin quare was goin on.

Paddy: Shit goin down at Smokeys. U R gonna wanna see this.

I was with Shamey Hughes, doin a gin run so I was. Don't know where Annie was, didn see her til the day after. We juss piled back in his yoke halfway through the delivery. Tauld them we'd come back. Fired it round the Town an in a few minutes we were parked up on Francis Street. Half the fuckin gards in the Town must'a been there. Special Branch n'all. We get out an walk up, as far as we can. Big crowd'a people round sure, hapes'a them. Smokey was well-got see, not juss by folk in the business, but by regular folk, other publicans n'all. An sure the gards loved her, which juss made the scene all the weirder. Shamey spots Paddy in the crowd wearin a farmer's flat-cap.

"Paddy!" he says, relief in his voice, as if Paddy was gonna explain everythin.

"Right b'y," says Paddy with a nod.

"Well, Paddy," I says, "what the fuck is goin on?"

"Y'know wha? I don't know a fuck, an that's no wordofa lie haigh. I can only tell ye Smokey's gettin done."

"Smokey?"

"Aye."

"Fuck. To look at it, ye'd swear it was Ned Kelly they had in there," says Shamey, pointin at the Special Branch.

"Aye. An see the cunt yonder," said Paddy, gesturin with his chin at a man in an overcoat, "he's pure PSNI."

"He's not. Is he?" says Shamey.

"He is surely. I've ran inta the buck before above in the Narth. Former UDA man, now a detective in the PSNI. Fuckin horror showta see Free State peelers doin their dirty work."

Paddy hocks a gob'a phlegm over the barrier in the direction'a the PSNI man, real casual like.

"The fuck's that all bowt?" I ask no-one in particular.

"*Cross-border cooperation* they call it," says Paddy.

"Fuck," says Shamey.

An indeed, what else are ye meant to say bowt a thing like that? I mean, what's the pointofa border if ye can't even hide behind it? Fuckin no point, lad.

A bit later, we see Smokey gettin carted off. People start to wander off, an the three'a us are left standin there shakin ar heads, repeatin *fuck* in a hundred different forms.

We went acrossta the Bar Tender for a pint. What else're ye gonna do sure? Didn even feel weird hangin out with Paddy like, felt like th'experience put us in the same place, though we'd never socialised before or indeed after.

"Fuck me b'y," says Shamey, "what'll happen now?"

"I don't know a fuck," says Paddy, "but one thing I'll tell yis right now is that there's some bad badness behind this. Someone's done Smokey in."

"Aye, she'd never be stupid enoughta let herself get done," says I, scratchin me head.

"An half the gards in the Town in her pocket sure," says Shamey.

"I tell yis, it's somethinta do with yon PSNI prick," says Paddy.

"C'mon now," says Shamey, "ye can't go pinnin everythin on the Proads."

"Ye can not, surely," says Paddy. "I've plenty'a good Proad friends. Even in the UDA an that. There's a respect there. But yon buck, he even got turfed out'a the UDA. Sure the PSNI were th'only ones'd take him after that."

"Fuck," says I, "is that right?"

"Aye, surely."

"Anyway," says Shamey, "she'll hardly be in too long. Not Smokey sure. She'll find a way. The Town wouldn be the same without Smokey like."

"It would not," says Paddy, takin a mad big gulp'a his Guinness. All the beers they have in that place an Paddy picks

Guinness. The feen clears his throat an then looks at me an Shamey like he's juss after noticin somethin.

"Wheres yon beor, *Iron* Annie?" he says. "Thought the three'a yis were inseparable."

Shamey clears his throat.

"Dunno where she is," I says. "She's always goin off on these wee turns, she'll show up when she shows up."

Paddy gives me this look, y'know the look lads are always doin when they raise th'one eyebrow an say nathin. Has another go at his Guinness, as if it's especially thick an hardta drink that time.

It was the middle'a the day, but the Bar Tender was full'a folk from Smokey's, bewildered as fuck. We were in the wee room inta the right. Must'a been a lovely wee snug at one point, but they took the doors off, so now it's juss a room. With no doors, we could hear this steady hum'a slow panic an conspiracy from the bar, this back an forth whodunnit chat. An none any the wiser. I s'pose it was comfortinta be confirmed by this common ignorance. I asked Detective Kelleher bowt it later, an even *she* couldn tell me much bowt it. I don't think she was lyinta me either.

It wasn the same after that, the Town. Smokey, she stuckta her code. Never breathed a word bowt nathinta no-one. I went downta see her once meself, below in Portlaoise. We talked bowt all kinds'a stuff, the tripta England n'all. She didn breathe a wordta me, but I could tell by the look in her eye that she knew rightly what went down.

An it wasn juss cause'a Smokey herself, though that was definitely part'a it. Her quiet way, the way she didn ask questions, the way she'd stand out in the street with the smokes in her hand, givin everyone that same nod, sayin *well* t'everyone, givin them the same respect. Smokey's was a fuckin refuge. Like yon church in the *Hunchback'a Notre Dame*, a neutral ground, cause'a her code. No-one'd touch ye in there sure. The Town needed a place like that, an it's bad missed. A place where the peelers an the wheeler-dealers could meet an exchange a civil word. Good craic too.

Things were a lot more tense in the Town after that. Suspicion left, right an juss everywhere, an nowhereta talk it out proper. Even ar meetins, with Paddy an The Maguire an the Rat King, they felt different. No space felt neutral enough for comfort anymore.

Loads'a theories went round bowt what might'a happened. For the most part I triedta ignore them. I hate gossip. Nathin looser than the lips'a some buck proppin up a bar an him knowin nathin bowt nathin sure.

Paddy finishes his pint an stands up.

"Right. I'll be seein yis," he says, stickin on his cap.

"Mind who ye keep round ye, Aoife," he saysta me, an I feel a hundred mile spring up between us.

THE ETHICS OF THEFT

Rubbin all up an down an round the sides an that, always movin, no settle, nathin still juss tryinta get an give at the same time. Couldn ever be still ar Annie. Mostly I didn mind, I understood it sure. But see sometimes it did get in the way'a stuff. She'd sometimes fuck a job up on purpose, or piss someone off so they wouldn wanna do a deal or that kindofa thing. Like that time in Bristol, when a lad I met was gonna buy a pile off'a us but she killed it callin him skinhead scum. Well, that was juss the price in a way, her notion'a ethics. An sure I was well readyta pay it so I was. No bother sure.

I juss had a hard time wrappin me head round it. I mean, a'course, I *understood*. That was juss the way she was an that. But I didn *get it* get it. I couldn relate it to somethin in me but I didn needta really. Them was juss her ways. Me, I had a hunger in me. Always had. Sure who doesn? Thought it's normal bein hungry an that. An see I accumulate. Put on weight an keep it on. Not juss the fat on me belly sure, but other things. Other weight. People. Ideas even, even dreams can weigh ye down. An money. Yeah, I liked havin money, juss the feel'a not havinta be worried bowt a few bob. But Annie? Naw. She didn like that. Specially not money. The source'a evil? What'a load'a bollix. Humans'd be evil over plastic spoons, used ones, if that was all left for themta fight over.

I usedta think it was maybe juss that she grew up rich. Like a rejection thing. It makes sense, ha? Since she never wantsta see them, sure she must hate them, her family I mean. She hates them. But I don't think that's all. Sometimes she'd come out with these things like that she liked what we were doin cause it was free'a the badness'a capitalism n'all that. But fuck, when ye'veta break some feen's legs, that's abuse too surely? I dunno. I mean it *is* more honest in a way, more honest than child slavery maybe. But still. It wasn juss that.

Annie's real skinny. Like a little too skinny. She gets sick, y'know. On purpose like. She didn want me to know. Didn want anyoneta know. But a'course I knew. I'm no thick sure. I juss didn say nathin cause I understand these kinds'a things an I know it's a pain in the holeta haveta talk bowt it.

But that's the funny thing. She loves eatin. Loves it. Has a pickier, fancier taste in peck than anyone I ever knew. For most people food's juss fodder sure, fuelta keep ye goin. But for ar Annie, naw. Naw, she'd only ate noble peck. An then later she'd throw up when she thought I wouldn notice. The same way as how she'd give loads a moneyta some junkie allofa sudden, or sabotage a job like. Jussta get ridofit sure. Hated havin, hadta keep takin but. Loved the taste, the buzz, the rush, the craic. Anythin she could get juss so she could throw it away. To be free, maybe. But freedom, sure that's juss a load'a bollix. She must'a known that.

A big nervous knot'a frustration tied real tight an twistin round her guts. I think it's her motor, that, it's what keeps her goin. Propels her on forward. Always ahead, in any direction. Sometimes we'd be out for a drink an she'd say she doesn want a drink an then rob yers so she would, or some randomer's drink an drink a bit an throw the rest out. Shit like that. Seemsta be juss fuckin bizarre on the face'a it, but there's somethin there. A wayta understand her. Once I found out she gave half'a the cash we earned from a deal t'Oxfam an spent the rest on fancy wine. Not like ye could be annoyed with her an her pourin it for ye, which was the really annoyin bit. Pure disarmin haigh.

She loved th'idea'a bein poor. Th'idea'a havin nathin. Somehow it was pure for her. A kindofa spiritual pure, like Jaysis pure or somethin. Mad craic. Like as if not havin nathin made ye better than other folk, an oh she loved bein better than other folk. She wanted that bullet-proof poverty, th'excuse for anythin, things that'd shame the divil. Sure all that was grand juss if ye had the right justification.

Maybe it's what she liked bowt me in a way too, cause I come from nathin, pure nathin like. But the thing that *right* people an *straight* people an holy Joes don't understand is actually juss that poverty is a pure prickofa thing. An bein poor isn really bein bullet-proof. It's bein vulnerable, dead vulnerable, t'each an every temptation, money an luxury an everythin that ye don't have. Sure a telly's juss a temptation machine. I should know, there was always one on at home, mornin, noon an night. Annie, she reads bewks. Wasn allowed much TV growin up. She likes *cinema*, not movies. She doesn know too much bowt the proper temptation that's in poverty. People like that never do. I know she's juss runnin away from that. But that's grand. I love her so I do. So I can let her run. Cause I know she'll come backta me. She hasta sure. I'm th'only one that really understands her.

LININ UP THE DUCKS

Fuckin no craic, feelin sorry for yerself an that. But in fairness, it was hard not to, them days in London when I was without her, without Annie, knowin she was out there, out there somewhere, somewhere with *him*, him gettin further under her skin.

Seven missed calls that day. Then she sends me a voice message.

Look, it's really messed up. I mean everything. I know it is. This isn't how I wanted this to go, not at all, but let's face it, the writing was on the wall. It couldn't last. But there's no reason to react like this, no reason to destroy everything. This time . . . It's been so important for me. I've learned so much. So much about myself. And I'll always be grateful for that. I want you in my life, you know, always. But I just need to move on I guess. And so do you.

This long big sighin moment then, yeah yeah, all emotion an that. But I know she's puttin it on. I know she's juss pure confused like. He's manipulatin her like, pullin all the strings.

We can still finish what we came here to do. And Hamish can help us. I mean, we need him really. He knows the way things are here. And he's a good guy, trust me. We need him.

What did we need yon cunt for? What was goin on in her head t'all? What had her so taken with this Scotch prick? Sure she said herself, sex with a fella is never *that* good. But the change in her, like night an day. Proper fuckin frightenin so it was.

Nathin helpt. Masturbation certainly not, that was the worst see, cause then I'd juss be thinkin'a her, an fuck me that felt bad. It was a bollixofa thing. An with raw-rubbed hands? The worst.

So I was actually dead happy when the Caterpillar invited me over for a smoke. Not for a ride like, naw, not me type t'all. A lad who calls himself after a cartoon bug, can y'imagine? It was juss goodta get out. Still, he talked loads. Kinda did me head in, that, even if he had a nice accent.

"Used to do a great trade in ket round here, we did."

"Ha?"

"You know. Ketamine."

"Fuck me. Yis take tranquilliser? For the craic?"

I was only humourin him sure, playin the wee bumpkin from the country like. Lads love any kinda sense'a superiority they can get over a woman sure. An it made total sense. If I lived in London I'd wanna be put to sleep too.

"Yeah, course, lav. But the cop's've been comin down real hard on it recently."

"Right. So that's why yer dealin grass out'a a schoolbag?"

"Excuse me! Briefcase."

"Oh, sorry."

"Anyway yeah. Less heat innit. An it's a good reliable product, weed. You can't deny it, this is good stuff."

"I can not, surely."

"Yeah. See I know a guy in Suffolk who grows it. My personal supplier. So I get a good margin."

"Great."

"Yeah."

I juss let the quiet'a that do the rest, y'know, I let it cement in the smallness'a what he was upta. When I could see it in his eyes, that wee sorta sad, defeated look, defeated juss by life, the way life defeats everyone, I starts again.

"Y'ever think bowt tryin anythin else but? Somethin different?"

"What, like gettin a job?"

I broke me shite laughin at that one.

"Ye header," I says, "a'course not. Naw, like sellin somethin with a bit more added value."

"For example?"

"For example cocaine."

"Well, I mean I'd love to. But this is London, lav."

I fuckin hate it when London people point out that they're in London when they're actually there. Th'only thing that's worse is them pointin out that they live there when they're somewhere else. Like they're reassurin themselves'a somethin or somethin.

"Yeah. An?"

"Look, the supply of charlie is a strictly regulated business here. See if someone like me wanted to get in on that, the cost of gettin my hands on it means the margins end up the same as for weed. Or worse. An the risk is much bigger, see. Just not worth it, is it?"

"An what if ye could get a chunk, like a good auld chunk now, at a daecent price. Good enough that ye'd double yer money, at least."

"An what if I could get a blowjob?"

"Watch it."

"I'm juss sayin, darlin, I don't concern myself with hypotheticals. Not worth my while."

"What if I tauld ye I'm travellin with five kilos'a coke that's burnin a hole in me pocket. An I'd be happyta give it to ye for a daecent price like, enoughta make it proper worth yer while."

"What if . . . what? Are you serious?"

Ye should'a seen the head on him. Not sure I really trusted him, but I trusted that look in his wee beady eye, that proper hungry nervous look. Felt me teeth growin sharper an sharper so I did, proper shark sharp. This'd be the way. This'd be the best way t'avoid yon Hamish cunt. An the toothy London sharks. Stick closeta the ground. Proper smalltime. Timeta go backta basics.

THE CATERPILLAR CONSORTIUM

The Caterpillar got his mates togetherta meet me, an fairly fast in fairness to him. Bunch'a wee skittery shites in jumpers too big for them, 1980s tracksuits an that. Hand-me-downs passed off as vintage so these pricks can make-believe they're all unique an that. Pure clones'a each other so they were, the Caterpillar's London pals. He'd drafted them in, see, to help buy the coke off me. I had five kilos left t'offload, an sure he could never afford it all on his own. But it was good in a way. Predictable. Smalltime.

Now I liked the Caterpillar. Grand enough chap, juss he had notions'a himself he probably shouldn'a been havin, bowt his connections, his turf n'all that. He was a weirdo, a proper one, with a bit more weirdness than these ones juss pretendinta be weird, pure hipsters like. At least the Caterpillar had a bit'a imagination with his *Alice in Wonderland* thing. Showed character. See, folk say that ye shouldn judge a bewk by its cover. But that's pure shite. All the depth's on the surface of a person. An with a fella like the Caterpillar, I could tell he wouldn juss fuck me over juss for the divilment'a it. Like, he'd need his reasons so he would. Greed a'course, but he'd also need th'opportunity—he'd not force it. Someone like that's great to do business with. Predictable. His pals though? The problem was they were all smalltime, even smaller than the Caterpillar. I could smell the bit'a money off them, but comin from somewhere else. Didn much like that. They didn seem desperate like the Manchester lad either. Naw, I could tell that for them it was already tellin the story years later in their heads they were, bowt the mad craic they usedta get upta when they lived in London. I didn much like that, doin business with fuckers that don't really needta be doin it, but I was in a rush. An in any way I figured I could count on the Caterpillar, on his greed at least, to keep them in line. Had a dire want in him that lad, the Caterpillar, desperate it was. He'd been dealin hash out'a his bag for years so he had an he wasn gettin any younger. Felt sorry for him so I did, stuck in London like that. He was rarinta go, to spread his scummy little wings an fall. At th'end'a the day, there's not a whole lot'a difference if yer caught with one kilo or five, the risk's more or less the same. I think that's somethin the powers that be don't really appreciate. They're practically givin an incentive t'all the smalltimersta go big. Sure that's the cause'a half'a the violence between the wheeler-dealers out there, pure greed. It's a shame other places aren as civilised as the Town like.

We met in this fancy breakfast joint. Yeah. I know. In *London* they have places that only serve breakfasts. If ye come in in th'evenin, fuck ye sure, have yer breakfast. One'a them spots, all pretend shitty, looks run down, but really it's fancy, all bricks an wood n'all, so ye haveta pay twenty British pounds for yer breakfast. Typical hipster crap. I mean Londoners are juss mad in the head so th'are. Sure I know a place in Derry, above in the Bogside, where ye get a fry for a pound of a Saturday mornin. No messin. An it's a deadly wee fry, none'a this eggs Benedict messin. Who the fuck was this Benedict prick anyway? Ruinin good eggs like that—must'a been some kind-ofa pervert.

Four in th'afternoon an these mulpins are all eatin breakfast. Meself I have juss a cup'a tea. I'm wishin Annie was with me, but I know she can't be like, I know I can't let her know. Juss three calls from her that day. Givin up maybe. Fuck it sure. Get on with it. Business. Then I'll get her. But really, what kinda world is it anyway where adults go for their breakfast at four in th'afternoon an pay twenty quid for it?

Waitress saunters overta us. Real wholesome look in her eye, this lovely smile n'all. Says her name's Elise. What're you even doin here, Elise?

She spoke with a lovely voice, proper cockney an that. "Oh, I'm sorry, was you not ready? I'll come back."

Swim away from here, Elise, I'm thinkin, these waters are pure shark-infested so th'are. I went to the toilet, jussta clear me head like. Had a hape'a messages from Annie.

Annie: Look, OK, just answer me. I know you're reading the messages, I can see you've seen them you know. Just answer.

Annie: You don't have to work with us. You don't have to be our friend. Just give me what I'm due from the Birmingham job. I put that together, I deserve a cut.

Annie: Come on. You're a decent person. I know you are. Just give me what I'm owed, and that will be that.

Bollix. Those words, *us* an *our*, they were like bullets in me brain. How quickly that can swing from one way to th'other.

So, so, I neededta wrap this up, quick, an goin through smalltimers I figured I'd steer clear'a the big sharks out there, swim in under their noses an get out quick like, the real big sharks with all the teeth an that.

"Allow me to introduce you to the newly, er, incorporated, Caterpillar Consortium!" says yon buck, big stupid grin on his face sure. "This here's Billy the wizard."

"You can call me Billy," says th'other feen, lookin dead embarrassed, an him with all these dumbass cartoon tattoos all over his arms.

"This is Smithy," says the Caterpillar, gesturin t'an Indian-lookin fella with a turban. Lovely-lookin fella so he was, had this beard, real soft lookin, pure gentle eyes, the kind ye'd wanna go for a swim in. I bet he worked a nine-to-five.

"Olroight."

"An this, this here's Sue. Big Sue!"

Now, Sue, Sue I didn much like. Proper snotty look on her face, an these round glasses with lenses so thick ye couldn hardly see her eyes an that. Didn like that.

"Well," I says, "what's the craic?"

The lot'a them juss sat there pure starin at me so they did. Spas.

We decided on the deal in any way. Prices, whereta meet n'all that. Ye could feel the pinch when I tauld them the cost. But it cost what it cost. Still I felt a bit bad for them, cause it's probably dead awkward askin yer parents for that much money. But I didn feel that bad. Fuck em sure. I was still leavin them a proper margin so I was, an they knew it. I even gave them a wee taste, to go with their eggs. So they knew it was good.

Sue asks me, "So which borough d'you live in then?"

"Ha?"

"She's not from London, Sue," says the Caterpillar.

"Oh. Then where you livin?"

"I live in Dundalk."

Her face went blank. I might as well'a said I live in Timbuktu. Then again, if I'd said I lived in Timbuktu, at least she'd'a known where I was talkin bowt. So she took this proper condescendin voice, like, oh, the poor dear lives somewhere that's *not* London. Like she was talkin to a pure failure, someone who'd wasted their life an that.

"Wicked. You're movin to London then?"

"Ha? Naw. Naw, no way ye'd get me over here. Are ye mad? Fuckin kip. Naw, I'm juss passin through, that's all. I'll be gone once we get this done."

That was a laugh. I thought bowt it for a long time after so I did. I'd a lot'a timeta think so I did. It's funny like, them ones, or at least Sue, assumin I must wanna moveta London. Finally make somethin'a meself or somethin. An then the look on her face, on all their wee faces. Pure horror show like. Someone from *elsewhere* that doesn live in London an isn even remotely interested in livin in London. It was like I had AIDS, the plague, or listenedta shite music or somethin the way they reacted. It was like they were afraid it'd infect them, this idea that it was possibleta not wanna live in London, to be happy elsewhere. Cause really, big cities like London, they're pure predatory so th'are. They feed on yer flesh, yer life, yer time, an trick ye inta thinkin ye've made it, cause here's where it is.

Ha? Here? In some scummy little room ye'll never never call yer own bowt an hour in a tube packed full'a other troglodytes from anywhere ye wanna go. Yeah. Well done. Ye've made it.

Good one.

Still n'all, it was reassurin in a way, thcm bein a bunch'a smalltime spas. The weight pure lifts off me, an I'm buzzin proper. This is the business.

TALLAGHT THICKS

It *will* happen, though, havinta deal with smalltimers, for one reason or another. Fuckin amateurs like, they're always tryinta edge inta the game. An sometimes it will fallta you to be th'oneta hauld their hands. Like this one time when I was roped inta babysittin a hape'a Tallaght thicks up ar way for a job. Not in the Town, but near, beyond the border, an them ones needin a base.

Three lads. The three triplets—more like the Three Stooges so they were. Turbo, Razzer an Harry. An yeah, they really called themselves that. From Tallaght they were, which explains Turbo an Razzer. But Harry? See, Harry's ma was obsessed with yon Princess Diana, the dead English one y'know, the candle in the wind n'all that. Yeah. So she called her lad Harry. Must'a been proper soft in the head, juss like her son. Th'other pair, Turbo an Razzer, sure they wouldn let the poor bastard forget that. Kept slaggin him, callin him a Brit, singin Elton John n'all. They'd probably been goin on like that for years.

Anyway, these ones had a bank job planned. An inside job, through someone they knew up Narth. Bit auld fashioned

I thought, an besides that was someone else's game. I tauld themta be careful like, but they were fierce loose-lipped. Tauld themta leave it. It's not like I love the RA or nathin, least'a all these dissident cunts, but banks is their turf. Wankers with a hero complex for the most part. Thievin is juss thievin sure, I could never wrap me head round this Robin Hood shite. It was bad enough the preachin Annie'd come out with, all this social justice crap. Most'a them pricks are only juss linin their own pockets under the banner'a freedom or some such shite. Still n'all, ye should know better thanta step onta their turf. They take their murderin very seriously. Take pride in it so they do.

See the thing is these thicks from Tallaght, they had some contact above in Newry, the cashier in the bank who was in on it. A real network thing, an that's how we got involved too. See I owed a favourta them through a cousin'a Harry's. But I tauld them I didn wanna know bowt it. We'd help them, but we weren gettin ar hands dirty. Couldn sure. I haveta do business with Paddy th'odd time, couldn be havin bad blood between us, not too much at least.

Anyway, it was with one'a the Rat King's lads that I got them the lift to an from Newry. Got himta leave them out in Faughart. Shamey took them from there backta the Town. I didn like doin it, but at least this way I'd clear that debt.

It was too late for any bus backta Dublin, an in any way, I figured it was best jussta be casual bowt the whole thing. I juss triedta make them understandta haul their fuckin whisht sure. Triedta tell them this wasn Tallaght, but naw, they were deep in the post-game buzz. Fuckin thought they were kings'a the world sure. Kept sayin stuff t'me like *calm down, petal*. I fuckin hate it when men talkta me like that so I do. Pricks.

Real fuckin condescendin. Sure look, I kinda gave up on them. Could see this comin a mile off, th'amount'a chat they'd been spreadin round, fuckin screamin an yelpin in the streets n'all. They'd done a load'a lines in the van see, the fuckin spas.

I didn want this goin down at home so I didn. Neededta be somewhere safe enough, but it couldn be Smokey's. Wanted these ladsta learn their lesson all the same. So I call up Kevin an organise a special lock-in, below in McCormack's. Gave him a chunk'a wedge for his trouble, tauld him not to worry, it'd go smooth enough. Shamey Hughes an a couple'a his trad-head mates came downta play some tunes sure. This was grand. We'd be safe here. Havin Annie an Shamey with me made it more tolerable, bein with them spas.

No knock on the door, Kev juss got a call. I gave him the nod. It's alright. The Tallaght feens were still wired sure, off on their own buzz. This was juss damage control ye see. Before Kevin opened the door I leaned in an saidta them *I hope this'll fuckin learn yista keep yiser gobs shut. Spas.*

Ye should'a seen the heads on them.

In walked Paddy anyway, an his fuckin army, well part'a it, five'a them, real thick looks on their faces.

I stood up.

"A full hand'a fingers with ye, Paddy, that's a little much for a couple'a wee kittens surely?"

"Ah, Aoife, sure it's yerself is lookin after these kittens, is it?"

I shrugged, I think.

"Sure someone's gotta try an see they don't choke on their fuckin milk."

"Aye," he saysta me. "How bowt you an me juss step out a wee minute for a chat."

An not another sound in the pub like. These Tallaght thicks shut up n'all. See Paddy made sure they could see his piece. Fuckin-IR-fuckin-A types an their fuckin guns. Wankers sure, juss like anyone else once ye put a gun in their hands, they think they're almighty.

Anyway the two'a us went out inta the smokin area.

"Now what the fuck's with this?" he saysta me. "Thought we had an understandin."

"We do, Paddy, we do. But sure look, me hands were tied. See there's a debt an that. Favours. Y'know yerself. I wasn involved in the job t'all. Juss a bit'a babysittin."

He took a long drag on his fag, starin at me. One'a ar fags, th'ones we run with the Rat King. See I always send him over a couple'a cartons. Never know when ye might need a heavy hand all the same.

"Ye couldn'a juss said no, ha?"

"That would'a been hard done. Sure look, it's not like they robbed *you* or nathin."

"It's the principle'a the matter."

"Ach I know, I know."

"Usually I'd haveta do them y'know. Or knee-cap them at least."

"Aye. But it's daecent'a ye not to."

Paddy looked at me like he was tryinta guess the colour'a me knickers or somethin.

"Look," I says, "there's a job comin. The travellers are handlin somethin from below in Cork. MDMA. The Rat King wants me to take care'a the distribution'a it, but I can bounce that job onta ye. No bother."

"MDMA?" he says, noddin. "It's a good drug, Molly. Nice

clean fun. But what bowt these bucks? I can't juss let them go.
Be bad for discipline. Can't be seenta be soft."

"Sure I know. Look it. They have their takins with them
so they do. Yous ones juss take them for the drive around an
batter them round a bit. Don't break anythin that won't heal.
Ye can throw them out on the motorwayta Dublin sure. Leave
them a wee bit'a cash, but juss enoughta make them realise
it's not worth ever comin back. Tell them it's the Republican
customs for money robbed in foreign banks."

"Right. Dead on," he saysta me an stands upta go. Then he
looked back a bit an saysta me, "Juss don't go pullin this kinda
shite again, would ye not?"

When we came out Paddy gave a whistle an his lads grab
the three Tallaght thicks. I tauld them not to worry or that, to
keep their mouths shut in future but sure it was lost on them.
Kept flappin bowt, blamin me like, as if it was some kindofa
setup. Some people really have no gratitude. Always lookin for
someoneta blame. Still, I got a text later from Harry's cousin,
thankin me. He knew the score.

"Right b'y," I saysta Paddy.

"I'll be seein yis," he says.

SENSORY DEPRIVATION

Y'know what's class? Art galleries. Museums are alright too, but meself I prefer a good art gallery. Not for th'art mind you, though I've seen some nice pictures an that. Annie knows loads bowt art, so I'd juss let her lead me cause the way I saw it ye'd be ages figurin out all that craic if ye were doin it by yerself so ye would. She could even tell the difference between art that was good an art that was shite which I always felt was a bitofa minefield. But one thing that I learned traipsin in an out'a galleries an that was how funny the places were. Like little bastions'a middle-class politeness wherever ye find them, which, once ye get past the scummy fakeness'a it is basically a form'a naivety. Dead useful that.

For example, they're class spots for deals. There in London I was, for the big deal, the last big deal, with the Caterpillar an his weirdo pals. I'd checked out a bunch'a different spots. What I was lookin for was simple enough. Neutral ground, since I was on unfamiliar turf an that. No cops, but safe like. Loads'a saps floatin round who don't know howta see nathin, juss bodiesta take up the space sure. Now, that sounds easy enough, but in London it's actually dead hard. They might think yer a suicide bomber carryin round a big bag, n'all yer doin's a simple, harmless, drug deal. Now, I can understand people wantinta blow up the Brits, after all they've done an that, an them goin round pretendin it's grand, juss history sure. But the suicide bit, that's the bit I don't get. Sure what would I be wantin with seventy-two virgins in any way? Not really me thing. Too much hassle. What ye want is someone who knows what they're doin.

At first I wantedta do it at the V&A, big fancy gaff, with loads'a wee side-rooms an that. I went in for a recce. In case ye haven been, the V&A is a place where the Brits liketa show off all the kit they plundered back in the good auld days when they usedta have an empire an that, god love them. Must give them a lovely feelin in their wee Maggie Thatcher hearts that aren hearts t'all, juss some system'a pumps that slide the slime around. Deadly, we robbed that from there, an that from there an now we have it all in these wee rooms, one for each country we trampled. Ye gotta hand it to them though, it's quare'n brazen puttin all'a that kit on display. But I s'pose they probably think it's not theft if ye show it off sure. Some gumption. I'd never have the brass neck for that. Still, too much security at the V&A. Ye haveta open yer bag goin in so ye do.

But wait til ye hear what I did find. This real wanky gallery in Shoreditch. They were doin an exhibition'a anti-sensory art. Yeah. I know. Blank canvasses an loads'a stuff with basically, well, nathin. The highlight was a sensory-deprivation chamber. A fuckin quiet room, blacked out that didn let light or sound in or out or nathin. Apparently it'd drive ye mad, the quiet'a it, if ye stayed in long enough. Fits upta eight people at a time. It was practically as if the fella they flew in from Tokyo with it had built it juss so we could do ar deal in it. Now, a'course, this kinda craic ye'd haveta organise well in advance. But people who work in art are paid fuck all so it was dead easyta ply a bit'a wedge an get a slot that'd conveniently come free. Wasn even expensive, cause the feen runnin it thought I juss desperately wantedta be deprived'a me senses. Probably happens all the time.

Spa.

Art.

An sure yon box wasn even for sale. The fuck's the point'a that?

Now, I'm no thick. I knew at least one'a them was gonna try somethin funny sure. Juss didn know how it was gonna play out. Hence me pickin a nice neutral spot sure. An callin in some backup. A'course sure. A'course I did.

Now, I didn see the Caterpillar tryin somethin himself. But the whole thing was messy, I knew that, what with these fuckin randomers n'all. Still, I needed rid'a it, quick, before that Hamish cunt might track me down. Sure wasn Annie practically pleadin with me? Look.

Annie: Please answer me.
Annie: Come on, this is so not fair.
Annie: Look, I'm only asking for my cut from what I sold.
Annie: I can't believe you'd do this to me.

This was really doin me head in at this point, the manipulation, pure brazen manipulation. Some fuckin brass neck that lad, makin her spew shite like that.

Anyway, I neededta get through this. Wasn juss *my* money, neither, hadta get that wedge backta the Rat King sure. So I called Shamey fuckin Hughes, didn I? Sure who else would ye call? The most solid man in the six counties an the Free State combined, big Shamey, ar Shamey, the wee fuckin gem, that giantofa man. See I went through all th'options, which in fairness weren many. Risk it meself? No way. Muscle for hire? Yeah, maybe, but the fuckers might rob ye. Need someone ye can trust. There was always th'option'a callin on the Rat King's cousins over here, but then again, it'd feel too much like failure or somethin. An like, the trust wouldn be the same. I tell ye, I was never so happyta see someone as I was when I saw big Shamey walk through the security in Heathrow, the big conspiracy head on him. It's a wonder he wasn deep cavity searched or somethin, ye could practically smell suspicion in the gangly gait'a him. Sure look it.

Gave me one'a them big Shamey hugs. The big hugs where ye disappear inside his arms an feel like nathin can get me here naw, not here, here even the brutality'a time itself seems far away an ye think *sure I'll never get auld here, never get sick, here I'll live forever.* Well, ye don't actually think that, ye'd be a bitofa spa if ye did, but ye feel it sure an that's more important.

"Right b'y," I saysta him.

He gives me this smile, the big Shamey smile, the big Shamey smile only he can do an I know, I juss know everythin's gonna be alright sure. Hasta now, now there's an extra set'a steady hands aboard.

On the night we show up good'n early for the meetin time. An sure wasn the fuckin gallery closed. Fuckin amateurs. I hate that sorta shite. The spas hadn paid their friggin insurance.

Ye can't be lettin people see an hear nathin without the right insurance sure. Some sign in the winda made it sound like that wasn their fault, the whole forgottinta pay craic. Bollix.

Next thing the Caterpillar shows up. But he only has two'a his team with him, snide Sue an Smithy. Th'other feen's gone missin, an the Caterpillar has a big worried head on him.

We duck inta a pub. No choice, had we? Quiet enough night for London meanin it was jammers. Over a pint'a warm piss the Caterpillar explains that they haven heard from the cunt all day. Didn like this. Not one fuckin bit. Fuck it though. I'm not waitin. Too much dealin with amateur problems that night sure there was. I sell them what they can afford an decide that's it. Caterpillar looks heartbroken, begs me to wait sure. Fuck that like. We'll take ar chances on the road. Now fuck off an thank ye very much.

I tell ye, I was gladta have Shamey with me then so I was. Still, I didn like this disappearin Billy bit. Was I meant to believe he juss got stuck at pilates or somethin? Fuck off. The greedy eyes on him sure. Naw. Naw, see I was more worried bowt the combination'a that, the Caterpillar's big mouth an yon cunt Hamish out stalkin round lookin for me. London's a big town, but five kilos'a coke is boundta make some noise all the same. An he was one prick I didn want findin out bowt this. Time to move.

MARY HAD A LITTLE LAMB

I still don't know what your handwriting looks like, she says t'me, an us in bed, back in the Town one time. Can y'imagine? Sure *I* don't know what me handwritin looks like. Sure it's all the same. Isn it? Writin. But she insisted, feckin brought me a pen an paper n'all an said I hadta write somethin. The fuck. The fuck do I know bowt writin? *Just write whatever comes to your mind.* That juss makes things worse sure, cause there I am sittin in the bed, starin at this fuckin blank piece'a paper. Whatever comesta me mind. The fuck is s'post to cometa yer mind starin at a bloody blank piece'a paper?

I took a gouge'a me tin, hopin she'd juss change the topic or get bored an go on her phone an leave me sittin there with the bloody paper or whatever. But she doesn. Blank page. Like pure white. Nathin's that white in real life. Nathin. They should make paper dirty, like, kinda grey, greasy brown maybe. Like real life. Somethin that tells a story, not like this fuckin white yoke that doesn say shit. Somethin messy so ye don't feel like a prick for dirtyin it with feckin scrawlin shite an that. Load'a bollix. Not to mention the dirt'a yer hands. Hands are always greasy. It's natural. But they don't, do they? Maybe jussta keep people thinkin writin's somethin special, important like, somethin normal people can't do.

People say *everyone's got a book in them*. The fuck they do. Plenty'a pricks I've come across, they've barely got a sentence in them with the words in the right places. If they had a bewk in them, it'd be a trip straight t'A&E to get it out sure. Or savin that, the toilet. In any way, I don't think it'd be worth readin whatever came out. What's so good bowt bewks, anyway?

Anyway, Annie's still starin at me, waitin like. I sit up in the bed. I don't know a damn what to write but I decide I better give this a go.

MARY HAD A LITTLE LAMB
MARY HAD A LITTLE LAMB
MARY HAD A LITTLE LAMB
MARY HAD A LITTLE LAMB
MARY HAD A LITTLE LAMB
MARY HAD A LITTLE LAMB
MARY HAD A LITTLE LAMB
MARY HAD A LITTLE LAMB
MARY HAD A LITTLE LAMB
MARY HAD A LITTLE LAMB
MARY HAD A LITTLE LAMB
MARY HAD A LITTLE LAMB
MARY HAD A LITTLE LAMB
MARY HAD A LITTLE LAMB
MARY HAD A LITTLE LAMB

I handed it to her. It was all I could come up with, an I'm expectin herta get annoyed, or maybe laugh, thinkin I wasn takin it serious. But that's the thing, I was takin it serious, I juss couldn think'a anythin elseta write so I couldn. Fuckin shite. Sure everyone knows Mary had a little lamb.

But she doesn get annoyed. She juss looks it up an down. A couple'a times like, lookin real close n'all, at the shape'a me letters an that, to find some special meanin in there. But also the words an that. Maybe she thinks there's somethin real important hidden in there, but that's juss it. It doesn mean shite, does it? I juss didn know what elseta write.

She folded it up. Kept it in her purse. Still has it, probably.

ALL TEETH

On the way back from the meetin with them Caterpillar fools, this squirmin feelin comes inta me tummy. Squirmin away like a load'a fuckin live wires. Or worms even. Somethin that squirms like. Wrigglin insolence. Not a good feelin that, an it right down inside ye.

See I knew we were bein watched. A'course I knew sure. Followed. I'd clocked yon cunt just after we left the pub with the Caterpillar an that after the deal. The three-quarters deal. Billy Boy, the Caterpillar's pal, he'd been followin us since then. But sure he couldn do nathin, not in public. Shamey Hughes saw him too. I tauld himta keep an eye on him in case he made a move.

"Right ye be," he saysta me.

Gave me one'a them big Shamey smiles, earta ear like, an the squirmin juss plain stopped.

He shifted the weight'a the bag on his shoulder. Fierce heavy, all that money.

"No bother," he says.

But the cunt did, he juss followed us, brazen as ye like, on the bus n'all.

We're gettin closeta where I left the car. Haveta deal with this buck but. I tauld Shamey. Big serious head on him then. Not worried like, he juss doesn really love doin folk harm sure. But I had a big bag'a nice crisp twenty pound notes burnin away in me hand sure, an a kilo an a half'a coke. He knew the stakes. An I knew why I'd called him.

We turn round an start walkin right upta the cunt. This kindofa clarity like, in moments like them, these moments when everythin stops an I'm fit t'ate a cunt. Everythin calm now, everythin still.

Dead quiet in the street. Practically out in Heathrow so we were, where I'd parked Shamey's yoke.

"See you, d'ye?" Shamey shouts at him. "Fuck away off from followin us or I'll kill ye with a thump, ye humpy cunt."

Some man ar Shamey. Real proud I was. Real fuckin proudta have him by me side, I nearly swelt up three times me size with the warm'a it.

That fairly stopped the cunt in his tracks.

His mouth starts movin, like he wantsta talk or somethin. His tongue comes out an he tries wettin his lips. Looks fit to wet himself mind. An sure who could fuckin blame the wee cub with big Shamey starin him down. He hadn bargained on this. Then I see him smile. That's not good. Not good when cunts start smilin.

I turn around. See them comin. What the fuck like? An there was I thought this feen naught but a wee skitterofa smalltime shite. But here I see two sharks comin straight at us, swimmin full speed, proper London sharks all teeth an nasty an vicious. Fuck me.

It happened so fast. Folk always say that, but it did like, even though I didn want it to. I wanted. To. Slow. But. No it didn it was all boom-boom-boom an me fuckin chest heavin an boomin an that an I think bowt sayin somethinta Shamey but it's juss the startofa thought cause I don't even needta say it sure, naw he knows, we're juss go-go-go.

Hands real tight. Still. Ready. Knife in. Billy Boy an his eyes an oh an oh that squeal'a him an him nathin t'all. Sure it's quare'n real now isn it, Billy Boy, now ye've got yer cheeks cut open like a bitch like a pig now squeal away off home would ye? Cunt. Didn even know howta bleed like a grown-up. Probably his first time. Fuck him. An off he goes, gave him a kick in the bollix to seal the deal sure.

I turns round an them two're circlin him. Like a pair'a. Fuckin tigers or somethin. Like lions. An big Shamey standin firm. I'm not worried, not then. Cause it's Shamey, like. Big Shamey. Fuckin Shamey Hughes. But both'a them have blades in their hands like, like, like the war or somethin. Fuckin teeth.

Shamey jabs, real quick. Gets one. He falls but th'other, he sees it, he sees his chance. He takes it an Shamey's bleedin. The teeth. An I can't, I can't see. Too many teeth. Not clear, no wayta see. But I see him smile, an he goes again, he jabs an then Shamey's in this slow fall. A thousand teeth then it's all stab an I still can't I can't it's too fast an it's stab again an the blood it's too much now, an fuck I can now I can cause Shamey's down. An I do. I do, I pull an bang it goes it goes in me hands, the gun, the gun I took off Stripes Maguire.

An th'other shark's down. He's down. But Shamey's still bleedin sure, an I'm screamin. I'm tryinta get the car open, I can feel eyes on me, an blood on me, an the cops called on me for the fifth time I get it open an get him in. Him an the bag. Fuckin heavy.

Where's help though? Where *is* help? An me drivin up some motorway don't know where I'm goin juss goin knowin Shamey needs help an the blood, the blood an the bleedin everywhere. An those ragged breaths an that an still hardly not ableta talk but tryin an juss. Fuck! Shamey shush, would ye? Fuck!

Where's help? Is there? An him gurglin away an I know nathin bowt fuckin first fuckin aid an I know oh I know but I know.

The worst sound? Oh fuck me. The worst sound I ever heard ever was when he stopped makin any noise, any t'all, an fuck me it's all I heard since.

IN BITS

DISAPPEARIN DWARVES

Did y'ever hear the story bowt the disappearin midget, did ye? That was mad craic. We were havin a lock-in at McCormack's. Th'usual sortofa thing of a Saturday night. Some siegeofa session, too. The *craic*, the music, the drink. Pure class. Now, see, a lock-in at McCormack's is a fairly regular thing. Every Friday an Saturday like clockwork. But this night was different.

It was meself, Shamey Hughes an Tommy. Annie'd took off early, away up the Townta meet a crowd'a pill-heads. I wantedta stay there cause Shamey was playin songs with a few'a his trad-head pals. So I did stay. An Tommy too—like auld times it was.

Where was I? Ach aye, this wee dwarf fella. Fuckin mad, innit? Dwarfs, midgets, whatever it is that yer meant to call them. People of very short stature. I tauld Annie the story an she said it was badta call them midgets, but t'me dwarf seems juss as bad. Like, when I think dwarf, I think some *Lord'a the Rings* shite, I'd expect some beardy fella with an axe so I would, but this wee man that came inta McCormack's had a real friendly face. But the thing is, there's none'a them in

Dundalk so there's not. Not one, cause I'd know. There's not a lot gets by me haigh.

All the same, there he was! An he was mad drunk. Barged right in, an that's the first weird thing, I mean aside from him bein a dwarf in a town with no dwarfs an that. See, the key to a lock-in is that the door's fuckin locked—so ye shouldn be ableta juss barge in like that. That didn stop him but. An ye don't expect a midget could make such a mess so quickly like, but in he came roarin for drink, pullin down chairs an that. He even pulled ar Shamey off his chair so he did, but sure Shamey was three sheets to the wind by then, state'a him.

Now, Kevin's a lovely chap, treats everyone like they were a friend, but he wasn havin this. *No drunk dwarves after hours* I heard him roar, an out he comes from behind the bar with a hurley stick. Ar Kevin's a big softie really but the wee man got a fright so he did. He can't'a been a local sure. Figured Kevin meant business an bolted.

Here's where it gets weird haigh. Now, I don't believe in fairy tales an ghosts an goblins an that. Load'a bollix sure. But Kevin's dead careful bowt his lock-ins, otherwise he couldn be doin them every weekend. He has these double doors, saloon doors that swing closed behind ye, then a wee passage bit an a big sturdy door out onta the street that locks when ye close it.

The wee drunk dwarf man ran out the saloon doors, an Kevin went after him. Coupl'a us went too, jussta see what'd happen. Knowin Kevin, he'd probably juss spank him with the hurley an put him out. But sure the wee dwarf lad wasnta know that.

We got to the door, juss in timeta see the hurley slip out'a Kevin's hand, his face like the sea on a rough day. The wee bastard was gone. Vanished like. No door opened or closed, we'd'a heard it. The wee midget lad juss pure disappeared.

I later found out that the nearest dwarf was from Termonfeckin, but that he'd gone missin round the same time'a the lock-in incident so he did. Now, people from Termonfeckin are well knownta be quare, but a teleportin midget? I've seen it all now.

We were all a bit spooked after that, an the lock-in wound itself down fierce fast. Folk cleared off, an we helpt Kevin clear up the mess. Shamey was balubas but. I needed help gettin him home, lucky Tommy was there. He's a big lad sure, ar Shamey. I needed help with the weight. The weight, the big heavy size'a him.

But now Tommy won't talkta me anymore. Not after what happened over the water.

But I still need it, I need help with the weight.

WHAT ARE YE LIKE?

The trip home. The blood. The burnt car. Me brother's car. Shamey inside it. The fuck else could I do but? Bury him? Burnin was the only safe way.

I even denied she was gone. Juss on one'a her turns I saidta meself. Upset an that. Cause'a what happened. But she'll be back. She's blocked me now n'all that, but she'll be back, I thought. Backta the Town. Back to *me*. I even tauld that to meself, even when I knew like, I heard a voice inside me that didn sound like me t'all, that's the worst'a it, a voice that sounded like her. Her sayin, full'a ice violence, *she's never coming back*. The torment.

Everyone asked questions. I made up stories. An when they weren askin, they were lookin, lookin with their little dagger-eyes eyes that said *that's yer fault*. Everyone cept the Rat King. We never talked bowt it much but I got more comfort from him than anyone else. He understood. He juss did. That it was not. My. Fault. All mine. Them lads. There I was, scared bowt Hamish an all an one'a the cunts even looked like Hamish in fairness but I forgot to watch out for them. Them. The sharks. Pure London sharks. All blood an bone an tooth. An blood.

One time I was around at the Rat King's. Torture even goin out, but he insisted. Near four months after I came back like. He was handlin the gin an vodka with Joško for me fair playta him. Didn even take a cut so he didn, juss bounced it onta me. He was in bits bowt Shamey too, I knew he was, in his own way. He didn say nathin—didn needta, it was the sayin nathin thing that said everythin. The look. The sad-eyed look he kept with him. I'd often seen it in him but now it was there all the time. Was only after I realised it was mostly for me he was sad.

But bowt Annie? He acted like it was the most normal thing in the world, her not comin back. An the whole Hamish craic. Was like he saw it comin like. An I hated that, I hated that he had. At least he didn rub me face in it.

Anyway, I went round. He opened a bottlc'a whiskey. Nice stuff it was too. From America somewhere, right sweet but good too. Where'd he get the taste for good whiskey? Maybe it wasn even whiskey. But it was somethin like that. The caravan seemed, well, bigger somehow. I think it was cause it was tidy, like, someone had put the mess away.

The rat was still there though. An now the fuckin stinkin thing had babies.

"Rats don't live that long," he saysta me. "I have t'ensure the succession."

"So y'invited me overta meet the family, is it?"

Turns out he was worried bowt me, me stayin in all the time an that. I laughed, y'know, cause what d'ye do if someone ye love tells ye they're worried bowt ye? Ye try t'act like everythin's grand sure. Can't juss keep them worryin, cause that'd juss make the worry worse, an then *you* would start worryin bowt them worryin bowt ye an they'd be ableta see that. So it's better jussta make it look like yer alright if ye can.

We had a few drams, deep ones, but I didn wanna get drunk like. Had stuffta do. Before I left though, he took hauld'a me wrist. Not in a forcin kindofa way, juss held it like, real soft the way ye'd take a child's hand sure.

"C'mereta me," he says, an stands up. Gives me a hug. It's a bit strange, cause I've known him ages, but it's juss not somethin I'd expect himta do. Felt good though. I cried a bit, a fair bit.

"Look, ye did everythin ye could. Ye did yer best."

"Isn it funny though?"

"Wha?"

"No-one cares. Bowt the money I mean."

"What d'ye mean?"

"No-one cares that it's all covered in blood. In *his* blood. It still spends the same."

"Look. What're we meant to do?"

"I thought bowt throwin it in. Inta the fire with him, with him an the car."

He hugged me again. Tighter this time. Real tight an for a long time. A good long time tight.

"Never mind that. It's done. There's nathin ye can do to change it. I'm juss glad ye made it. Ye'll . . . sure look it. You'll be OK."

The lad took a raggedy breath.

"Juss be yerself. Everythin'll be alright. It'll take time. Juss be yerself."

I made meself smile an left. Squeaks offered me a lift home

but I decidedta walk. Had some messagesta do. I couldn get that out'a me head though, what he said. *Be yourself*. Now, I know he meant it in a good way, but fuck me, it terrified me.

I know he didn mean it like that, but *be yourself*, what the hell is that, some kindofa challenge? An who the fuck actually even does that? I don't mean that in a funny kindofa way, not some sorta hippie shite like. I'm not sayin that yer true self is somethin really hardta find an ye haveta do lotsa yoga an eat gluten freeta get there. I'm sayin it doesn fuckin exist. The self like. It's a big lie. Pure fiction. It's even a hideous idea, the thought'a havin th'one self. I'm not sayin people are bad or nathin, juss that people are people, not persons, an definitely not selves. We're juss a mad mix'a forces, all fightin their wayta the surface. Most'a the time, that's all we see, juss surface, juss this kindofa flat thing called a self. I spent a year with Annie, an I only ever saw bowt sixty shades'a her. Sure, that was enough like, enough t'overpowcr me, to surprise me, fuckin annoy the livin hell out'a me, an make me love her. Entirely. But the thing bowt seein these different things in her, the thing bowt that was juss realisin how many more there were in there, thrashin bowt beneath the surface. There were thousands down there, thousands'a sidesta her I never even saw. Maybe even she didn, surely she didn. But I could feel them. An even this thing, this self she showed me, it kept changin. Usually, we're juss caught tellin a story t'each other that we're the same person like. It's juss a big charade though. Sure is it any wonder we're all mad. Fuck me like, I think it's juss a natural reactionta the world like that, madness or at least a bit'a it. Annie, she's different. She lives with the changin madness'a her self, from one dayta the next. An I'm left wonderin who's the wiser one'a the pair'a us.

That's what spooked me with the Rat King tellin me to be meself. Cause so much'a meself was mixed up with her, there were still bits'a her in there, an I was afraid'a them. Her words, but her feelins, her thoughts too. It was like I kept all the nasty bits an she got away with the good bits.

Naw. Naw, a person, a bein—that's not a self. It's a collection'a selves, these forces an things pullin ye this way an that. The battle goin on behind the scenes, it's vicious, an we liketa think there's a great hero in there, someone who knows what's goin on, but that's juss bollix sure. That's what I learned bein with Annie anyway. *Be yerself?* Fuck that.

I was goin through all this when I got to Tesco's for me messages. Goin round on a fuckin loop-the-loop so I was, this goin round in me head an me too tangled upta the thought'a her. I was thinkin all this, stood there in front'a the frozen fish section, in front'a a fuckin box'a prawns. Caught me like a hook so it did. Brought me back, like some kindofa spell, backta this one time when we went for a nice meal. Yeah. That was lovely that one time. *She* suggested it, the dinner, juss the two'a us, jussta take time for each other. Seems like a funny thingta suggest when ye work with someone an live with them an ride them too, but it was dead nice'a her actually. I was dead happy that th'idea came from her, y'know? Showed proper love an that.

Of a Sunday it was. We went to this fancy gaff in town, Italian food. Real good too, proper noble peck. We decidedta go the whole hog, three courses, wine n'all that craic. Lovely.

Eatin with Annie was always a bitofa pain in the hole. She was dead picky, an she had loads'a these pretend allergies too cause she was real special an that an yer real special if ye've loads'a allergies. Like she said she was allergicta wheat. Cept she could stomach the stuff if it'd been cooked in a pizza oven, or brewed in beer. Juss normal bread she couldn hack. Same goes for dairy, cause at home we hadta drink this fake watery milk made from nuts cause she couldn even have it in the fridge, proper milk an that, but mozzarella was grand. In fact anythin on pizza was OK. Well, almost anythin.

Annie was goin off on one'a her politics spiels, talkin bowt how Irish politicians were *fundamentally insincere in their progressivist credentials*, whatever the fuck that hasta do with pizza. An I mean a'course politicians are insincere. That's part'a their game.

Anyway, she reaches over an grabs a bit'a me pizza an scoffs it down lookin dead happy an that. I'm juss goin along with all this politics stuff so I am cause Annie lovesta give out bowt the state'a the world so she does. Makes her feel clean I think, as if somehow we were separate from yon shite. I tried not to tell her too much that naw, we're not. She didn like hearin that.

Then she starts coughin an splutterin. She downs a glass'a wine but it's no help. She can't talk. Pretty soon she's. Blue. In. The. Face. Fuck. Some feen behind-grabs her, tryinta do that thing ye see on telly an ah! me hands are burnin up an the heavin'a me chest sure I can't breathe or nathin cause I can't do nathin an that TV thing yon buck's doin's not helpin. I look at the plate. *My* plate. An I realise. An allergy. But a real one. See, I'm eatin a seafood pizza. How did she not know?

Then in th'ambulance. All the way downta Drogheda we were goin. There's an actual hospital there, not like that kip in the Town. Yeah, it was an allergy. Anafafuckoff shock or somethin. Me talkin, juss tryinta keep her with me.

"I don't like Drogheda either, but maybe we can stop

inta Tí Chairbre after. Great wee pub that. Almost redeems the place. Almost. Remember we went there the week'a the Fleadh? You liked that. Great dingy wee place with the best singers in the world. Big Shamey Hughes with wind in his lungs all week sure. Some craic."

They gave her some medicine on the way down an that. I was juss sittin there, hauldin her handsta keep from tearin at mine, hauldin them real tight sure when it came through a whisper.

"What I was trying to say was that in my view, the political classes used the issue of marriage equality quite cynically just to score a victory. To be on the right side of history for once. The whole thing was just a carnival. You think they really care about us?"

I'm breakin me shite laughin listeninta her croak away. Juss happyta hear her sure. Happy she's OK. I point out that the Taoiseach *was* gay like, but she juss waves me words away like a bad smell or somethin, sayin he wasn the Taoiseach at the time, then I remembered the blueshirt before him, the most forgettable man in history whatever his name was, but he did though, he did stick around, for years an years, like a pile'a shite in the corner.

"Mickey D. seems pretty sound but."

"A powerless figurehead. Nothing but some scraps thrown to the ghost of social justice."

"So ye really do have allergies."

"I told you!"

"I thought ye were juss talkin shite like."

She stares at me proper hard like, pretend annoyed an that.

"Then why the fuck did y'eat me pizza?"

"Oh. I didn't know I was allergic to seafood."

"Ha?"

"Yeah. I just thought I didn't like it that much."

"Yer messin."

"No, no. I just have this vague memory of not liking it. From childhood. I guess I know why now. I just wanted a slice of yours because it was yours."

I'm bowt to kiss her but th'ambulance man stops me. No no. *You might have it on your lips.* It's not an anti-gay thing apparently, it's a health an safety thing. Sure isn that what they usedta say bowt the gays? Bowt stonin them or burnin them or whatever they usedta do twenty year ago?

Anyway I kiss her hand, an she kisses mine. We were dead happy then.

I must'a been starin at them prawns for ages an ages so I must'a cause some troglodyte from Tesco's came waddlin upta me askin if I'm alright an that or if I needed any help. Fuck off. I'm grand sure. Juss thinkin. Can't I juss think?

TIMES

Then there were times, long times'a worthless wanderin on th'insides'a meself, tracin backwards, stumblin forwards in the shadowy dark'a me room, dim-lit by day, brighter at night. An me lookin like a fright, sinkin away, sinkin inta somewhere I'd never been before.

I played things over a thousand times. Was like tryinta iron out a mountain with a rollin pin, the rocks, the rivers, the trees growin willy-nilly around me as I went, me feet gettin mouldy with wear from stalkin th'edges'a the night waitin, places full'a hungry teeth, there, waitin for me to finally falter. Dark flyin overhead, its eyes on mine, rollin, rollin, the sweet disaster, a trilogy'a pain. Them faces.

His face. Hers. Mine. Clawin at them, as ifta get backta them, to get backta that time when things could'a been, juss been, y'know. To when we couldn'a not gone on the road say, or dealt with things different.

But no matter which way I'd roll it, at th'end'a the day he'd still be gone. An she'd still be there. There, tauntin me, her face, her words, her hands, hands like no-one else's, as though no-one else's had ever touched me, the wriggly thought'a her, still on me, movin on me, a touch, a stroke, a look, an her fuckin off, her always fuckin off, the silence juss swallowin her up.

Cause that's how it happened. One day, after all was said an done, she juss blocked me. Bridges, burnt. Can't even look for her, no idea where she is or when she'll be back or if, an I don't want her but I do, I do, *I do*.

There in the swelterin dim, I see a thousand things. Things ye'd never spot when the world's well lit. Shiftin, shapin, they say thingsta me, an me hereta listenta them. The dark unbuttonin me. I juss move in the same place a hundred times an wait for herta be back. Cause she'll be back—*oh yes*—she'll be back.

An I don't know if I'll fogive her, if I'm fit to hug her or strangle the cunt or what. I haveta wait an think. To plan. Cause this is part'a her plan. Ye don't juss block someone an be done with it. Not after all we've been through. No fuckin way. These words. Them things. An I want her back. An I never, *ever*, wanna see her again.

I've tamed them in a way, the shadows, though ye can never really do that, not really, not properly like. Naw. Naw, ye needta be at ease with the wild'a them. That's where I got. I always was, really. Ye can't tame them but ye can learnta live with them an I live with mine.

They teach me. Everythin, they learn me. It's juss hard goin on me hands sometimes, all that shadow work. All the. The thinkin. An that. An if. An what. Now. All that scratchin sure. But I've wrapped them up right thick, an when I think bowt it I can stop, I can still stop.

See I've seen in there, a thousand times a thousand different ways things could'a gone. An what we don't reckon bowt things like that is that they actually *did*. The way we lived them is juss th'one way. But there're others too, out there, somewhere.

Scratched me hands halfta death by now so I have. Thinkin bowt it. Would'a took me brain out an gave that a good scratch jussta give me hands a rest if I could'a.

Things could'a gone different. So in a way they did, somewhere they did. Y'know? Now, I don't mean all happy-clappy fuckin rainbows an *la-la-la*. Naw. *I'm* a realist. I believe in *this* world, this here world. But this is a world as fucked as me head sometimes, as me hands. Things keep changin, comin undone, all over—juss you watch. An, I don't mean a happy endin or that, juss one enough different so, so that Shamey Hughes is still here. Juss enough that he's still breathin. An singin. An smilin. An the two'a us still wheelin dealin an havin the craic. The craic, awah, the craic'll kill ye but that's how he wantedta go anyway. Not like *that*. Not cause'a that. Not. Cause'a. Me. We'd be out there, Shamey an me, an we are somewhere, I can see it sometimes, there in the shadows.

Me big man, me good man, me one good fella an *fuck me!* me true blue the wee gem big Shamey Hughes. A'course it was him I called. A'course. Why didn I juss get a hape'a the Rat King's cousins? They could'a took them, they could took all'a them. Fuck. But naw. Naw, it hadta be him. But it could'a *still* gone different, *still*, it could. Not with. That knife. There. Fuck. It did. It's different, I seen it so I did, it didn happen not juss the same it didn an I seen it an he's OK.

But the knife. That fuckin blade, it cut worlds in half, worlds'a then an now an possible an still, an still he's gotta be out there, somewhere, juss like she is, somewhere.

AWAH HERE

THE RAPP

There it is.

Again.

Fuck it. It'll stop.

It's not stoppin.

Someone's at the door.

Gettin louder. Fuckin hammerin haigh.

But they'll go away sure. If I don't get up, they'll go away.

They'll haveta.

They'll fuckin haveta.

WE ARE FUCK

"Fuck me!"

"Yer not me type."

"The fuck're ye doin here?" I saysta him, an him there standin above me, that big toothy grin'a his.

"Ha?"

"How'd ye get in sure?"

"Awah. That. What, ye think it's Fort-fuckin-Knox here d'ye? Fuck off. I've cometa get ye."

"Wha?"

"Yeah. We're goin on a wee trip."

"We are fuck!"

I get up in the bed a bit, an shite, there's fire all down me sides so there is. Fuck it. The Rat King's lookin at me, kinda sad smilin. I feel dead bleary, like cloudy, like I'm stuffed with cotton or somethin, an I haven even had a drink in weeks so I haven.

The Rat King starts goin through me stuff, packin shit inta a bag, clothes an that.

"The fuck're ye doin, man?"

"The fuck'm I doin? The fuck're *you* doin? How many weeks is it yer in here, not leavin yer room, not doin nothin? I'm gettin you out'a here, that's what I'm doin."

"Y'are fuck."

"I fuckin am."

He haulds up me passport, smiles again an stuffs it in me bag.

"Fuck off, would ye? Juss leave me be. I haveta be here when she gets back so I haveta."

He juss looks at me, a puss on him fit to turn milk sour.

"Ye don't understand."

"I fuckin do, that's the point."

In comes Squeaks. "Right, love," he says, real soft. Not even squeakin sure he's not. "Ye'll be grand so ye will, don't worry."

The two'a them haul me out'a the bed. Fuck. The reek off'a me. Risin, in waves. It's nearly enoughta knock me out but the two'a them don't let on that they notice, they don't say a word. But they can't not've noticed sure.

If they hadn'a been hauldin me, I'd'a collapsed on the ground, cryin. So the tears, they juss fell on the floor. The lads say nathin, but Squeaks wipes me cheeks an juss shushes me, like he'd be tryinta comfort a baby.

They bring me to the bathroom an close the door on me.

"Clean yerself up. Yer not comin in me van like that."

"I'm not goin in yer van t'all so I'm not."

"Ye fuckin are. Now wash, or I'll do it for ye an trust me, neither'a us want that."

The water feels. Well it feels. I feel it. It's somethin. Wet an somethin, somethin good. I'm in there a long long time I don't know how long, them lads say nathin, though I can hear them chattin an that. But the water goes cold, so I must be in a fair long bit so I must.

The fuck does he want, hoofin me out'a it like that?

I'm standin at the mirror long enough for the fog to clear, but I can't actually look at meself like. Can't lock gaze with that cunt. Don't know how I dressed meself.

Tryinta steady me hands an look stern but they're rebels juss then, all shake n'all. Fuck it. I'm gonna give him a bollickin so I am. Gonna learn him not to break inta *my* house. Who does he think he is, anyway?

But when I step out the two'a them big lumps'a men juss grab me. This time I'm roarin an kickin an screamin. The works. But it's like they don't notice.

In the van then, squeezed in beside them. Fuck.

"This is kidnappin, y'know," I says, an us flyin up toward the motorway.

Rat King hacks a gob'a phlegm out the winda.

"Is it? Deadly. I'll add that to the list so."

"Always wantedta kidnap someone," says Squeaks. "Class."

I elbow him in the ribs, but it's pretty hardta be mad at Squeaks. Somethin bowt him juss not bein ableta be a proper prick an that.

We're flyin down the road. Music blarin. Fuckin Van fuckin Morrison. A CD if ye don't mind. Old-school. Pretty soon we're south'a Dublin. An I'm still fuckin pisst off but y'know it's lovely down there, the hills an that an I've never been south'a Dublin. An lookin at this through the blear in me head.

Squeaks cracks a can an hands it t'me. I take it sure. The fuck else'm I meant to do?

It's good. God it's good.

"Where're ye takin me?"

"Away."

"Away where?"

"To a weddin."

"Ye wha?"

"Yeah. Squeaks here's gettin married sure."

"Yer jokin."

I looks acrossta Squeaks an he nods his head in this kind-ofa half-mournful way. Half happy but with sadness in there for the mix too.

"Squeaks, lad, I'm delighted for ye. Promise. But I can't be goin. I'm in no state. An besides, I gotta be there. I gotta be home."

"For what?" asks the Rat King.

"For when she comes, for when she comes home."

Now, juss then we're barrelin down the motorway bowt a hundred mile an hour so we are. An he juss starts swervin, mad jagged like, an screamin, that pure noise screamin when nathin's a word at first an then, then *SHE'S NOT COMIN BACK SHE'S NEVER COMIN BACK AN SHAMEY NEITHER. THEY'RE GONE THEY'RE BOTH GONE. They're juss gone so th'are.*

As he screamed it, see, he startedta speak an the swervin an that, sure everythin slows an that's juss. That's. Juss. It. All thick voices an that each word hard an then *an that's that. It juss is.* An then *we are all we have.* Then nathin. A long time nathin.

We slow down so much some prick starts beepin from behind. Rat King slams the brakes an then takes off again. Fuck him sure.

We're drivin slow. A long time slow. An I'm juss cryin an I don't care an he is too but *he* cares, an Squeaks looks dead sad too, though he didn even really know them all that well, but he's a daecent skin so he is ar Squeaks so he feels sad. Cause. It. Is. So it is, it is sad.

I don't know. I think I cried until night. At least I felt it, all ah-ah-ah fuck get out'a me chest an that.

Somethin was different but. Different from other times. Like. Like somethin broke. Broke inside'a me. I felt it break n'all, like a proper big crack. Down deep inside. In th'insides'a me bones. Like a dead branch fallin off the tree.

An the Rat King thereta catch it.

I'm in bits like, totally in bits. Like on the first day, all covered in blood an hidin when I hadta go to his cousin for helpta burn everythin. Bits. But different bits.

CROSSIN

We spent the night outside Cork, in some patchofa field that felt known to the two lads. Was a thingta see all the same, the pair'a them gettin ready for the night, burstin inta action. An not in a *look what I can do, sure I'm only class* kindofa way but in a *this needs done* kindofa way. In no time t'all they'd a fire on the go an peck cookin too. Rat King was sortin out beds for us, an Squeaks cracks a can an passes it t'me, that same look in his eyes.

Says nathin. Sure what can ye say? Weddins like.

From where we're camped, ye can see the lights'a Cork. An I'm there wonderin what life is like down there, what the people are thinkin or doin or if they're daecent t'all. There's all these wee trees round us, all bent over like, as if they're apologisinta the sky for th'intrusion. Brisk winds the masters'a them.

The pair'a lads drift off inta their own buzz, talkin low bowt the weddin an the beor an that. I'm away in me own world suppin on the few cans, but I can see the Rat King checkin on me now an again. I sit up past them like that, past embers an all, juss watchin the lights an listeninta the noises an the trees.

Next mornin we're on the move again. We don't even go to Cork city—an I was kinda lookin forwardta that. Naw, we bypass the whole town. An I kinda liked the look'a Cork, looked like a big Dundalk, an I mean that in a good way. Like a place sound people might live, not a bunch'a pricks with big notions'a themselves. A daecent kindofa place.

We end up in this wee ditchofa place by the sea. *Ringaskiddy*. Quare name. An I'm wonderin what the fuck's all this bowt, an then I see it. A boat. A big one.

"The fuck're ye thinkin, ye header?"

"We're goin on a wee trip, I tauld ye."

"Yeah I can see that. I'm not fuckin goin back over there. I won't. Ye can't make me sure. Ye juss can't. I'm fit to jump overboard so I am."

"Ye can't swim, ye spa."

"Ye think I wanna swim? I'll juss jump."

"Relax," he says t'me, all big toothy grinnin. "It's not goin t'England."

"Ha? Then where?"

He juss drives the yoke on up onta the boat, casual as ye like. Squeaks is silent the whole way, a heavy, sinkin silence like.

He does all this so quick, the Rat, an I'm juss left disarmed by the whole thing, demented, in a fright'a energy, but it all rushin round me with nowhereta go. Like, I could get out'a the van, I could clamber over Squeaks an get out, he'd hardly stop me an the gards an the customs men starin drills inta the sides'a the van like. But I don't, an it's not for fear'a the caustic eyes we're gettin—I don't give a fuck. It's like this energy's come inta me out'a the unknown, an us ones headin there, at least I am.

"The fuck're we goin, then, if not there?"

"Ha? Ah that. France."

France? The fuck? Who goesta France? What quare notion is this he's gone an took, marryin poor Squeaks to the Frenchies? Fuckin hell.

An I'm there thinkin, I'm thinkin, these ones have gone an lost it. I haveta see this.

Up on deck, I'm stood with the two lads watchin the coast clear off inta the distance, drain away there until it becomes horizon an then disappears entirely. It's beautiful. I'm full'a questions, that mad energy's wakin all the bits'a me back up it feels like.

Squeaks cracks a couple'a cans an hands them around. Them thousand questions, they'll wait, I'll watch this unfold an fill itself up.

Rat King leans inta me an whispers somethin. Don't know why he's whisperin, there's no-one round, an the wind is pickin up.

"Smokey's out," he says, an I snap me head round, eye-ballin every inch'a the feen, every speck, the watery stillness'a his eyes.

"Good behaviour I heard. But I'd say there's somethin more there."

Me hands flash hot, then cold, then warm.

I don't stay long on deck, but go to the cabin the lads

booked me, an fall inta me bed, inta sleep, long an deep. I'm not bothered by the waves t'all haigh, an this a much deeper sea.

Pretty soon we're out again an rollin through the French countryside, an it's lovely, real lovely like. Not a thousand miles from home, but different, y'know. Loads'a lovely wee villages an that, auld churches an all. Can't make head nor tale'a what the folk're sayin, an they don't seemta get me neither, but the Rat King, he's like some special diplomat, see. It's true what he said, he does speak French n'all. Fuckin mental like.

Some craic. But I'm at peace, somehow quieted by it. By not knowin what's comin, but knowin we're rollin, rollin towards somethin. Somehow the silence of it fills me up.

The lads are quiet too. The Rat's on his phone a lot, an Squeaks seems less nervous, more excited now. Like this change'a place has reassured him.

I juss wish. I wish, y'know, I wish he was here. He'd'a fuckin loved this craic, he'd'a lapped this up.

SO I AM

A TINKER'S WEDDIN

Awah now c'mere til I tell ye, the music an the craic an the food n'all! Pure siegeofa session, Squeaks's weddin. The fuckin food, pure noble peck sure. Like bein at a fancy restaurant cept no-one was even bein a snotty prick, everyone was juss enjoyin, juss pure enjoyin so they were. An it was better than a restaurant too, realer, cause real folk cooked it an ye didn needta pretend like ye liked it if ye didn or ye knew what it was or that. Juss good for th'atin sure, meat an fish an hapes'a bread an cakes an fruits an fuckin barrels'a wine an beer an different spirits I didn know a fuck what they were. But they were all dead good too haigh. Three sunny days in a row like that we had, the clouds juss like lazy cats moochin far off up high in the sky an away. Them French travellers know howta have a hooley I'll tell ye that much.

Even the flowers smelt more . . . flowery. Y'know, what flowers smell like, but more. An there were loads'a them. Real simple way'a decoration, I liked it, juss flowers an big wooden tables full'a peck an drink an flowers out in a field right out in the country somewhere. Th'air. Th'air an the sun an the flowers an the food an the swill. Nathin like that air in the Town sure, all light an good an, fuck me, if I could only juss bring this backta the Town I remember thinkin, sure the world'd be perfect.

Feelin daecent like. That's a feelin I'd haveta take back. Feelin daecent for the first time in a long auld time now. No fears. Pain. But that I can manage. Still, th'auld shakin in the hands, that was all gone, they'd all steadied up. An I knew part'a that was juss bein back on the drink an that doin me a power'a good an that, an th'air n'all, but all the same it felt fuckin glorious, pure daecent like. An I looked at them then an saw the scars, all lines an still a bit red an raw, an I didn even feel like goin at them, an me knowin everythin, rememberin *every-fuckin-thing* but not doin it, juss leavin them be. It was a heavy kinda knowin, deep in the chest an the throat an heavy everywhere.

It was me an the Rat King an the Rat King an Squeaks an sure he was a happy man with that beauty. Like a fuckin cat that fell inta a bucket'a cream, the head on him. Jaysis, it was juss, well, good, for the first time in ages. That kindofa good. For once not a kindofa good full'a torment at th'end, remindin me, remindin me, remindin me as if I'd ever forget. I mean that was still there, I don't think that's goin nowhere. The knowin it, the heavy knowin of it. But I can deal with that. Knowin without drownin in it. Naw. Naw, now was juss good. Juss good bein here an bein with the Rat King an seein Squeaks an him all happy sure. Even scored one'a Squeaks's new sisters-in-law. A beauty, lovely wee slipofa thing with a tongue like silk. Hardly spoke no English, but who cares sure, sure it was juss a one-time thing.

An the music. Decades'a it. Centuries sure. Good music,

an even me singin. Me! Singin! Fuckin tears all in me eyes
n'all over me sure an down me an in me an hot an streamin
until there's no more. But I thought no more was ages ago so I
did, there's always more. A'that there's always more. This time
they're streamin, but in a good way. An I'm singin an singin an
not even carin that I'm no good at singin cause someone else is
singin through me sure. Someone good. They were his songs,
see, his own ones, that's how I know them, my friend, my good
friend gone. He'd'a been there but. But he couldn, could he?
So I sung, I sung, I sung for him, to feel him with me when I
did. An I did so I did. He was there with me, I mean I know
he wasn but I felt him all thick an oh, an oh, Shamey, ye b'y ye,
big Shamey Hughes.

I'm screamin singin an screamin cryin too an I look at
them ones all them French ones an ar ones too, all the Rat
King an Squeaks's cousins like, the big throng'a them an me
voice all ragged an the last words comin out'a me juss nathin,
juss nathin t'all, a pure whisper but they all heard sure. An
them all clappin, them roarin, them pure happy cause they
know well they juss know. I mean they don't know, how
could they know sure? But they *feel*. They do. So they do. So
now they know. Pure magic haigh. We're magic then, we're all
magic. An I look at the Rat King an the hug. The hug, the hug,
the big Shamey hug. A big Shamey hug, a pure Shamey hug
like Shamey himself'd be huggin me. An he is y'know. He
is. Not in some fuckin idiot yoga Jaysis way juss the way he
always'd hug me an I'd feel OK, like he juss knew, he knew
when an how an he'd do it an I'd feel OK an I do *I do*. I do
feel OK. Finally. An I look at the Rat King an he's cryin too
sure. Pure happy then the two'a us huggin Shamey, huggin ar
friend Shamey, ar good friend gone. An I look at Squeaks an

he's cryin a bit too but mostly laughin, he's *laughin*, an I feel happy like dead happy for him, I do so I do, him an his wife cause she's lovely so she is an she even looks dead lovely too.

An the Rat King looks at me, big serious head on him.

"Will you be alright, Aoife?" he says t'me. "There somethin comin. Somethin big. I need you with me. I fuckin need ye. Will ye be alright?"

An I looks at him an us still huggin, Shamey still with us n'all, real tight an close an still ragged but proper clear then.

An I saysta him, I says, "I will. I will so I will. I fuckin will."

ACKNOWLEDGEMENTS

I used to be very uncouth. Not by choice, but just not cut of the right cloth to know, really, the point of the bit at the back of a book where you say thanks. But now I do. Now that I know that people are actually going to sit and read this shit, that they're going to have this book in their hands, to hold it, and let this rowdy band of rascals into their lives, at least for a while. That they'll make them that bit more real, thicker, more vibrant through their reading. I'm talking about you, reader. Thank *you*, for accompanying me—them—through this. Because I love them, Aoife, Shamey Hughes, Detective Kelleher, the Rat King, Smokey Quigley, the whole bunch— and I want them to live. Thanks for taking them in. It's quite incredible, what you've done.

Aside from that, I'll limit myself to thanking people who have had a direct role in shaping the book, supporting it from start to finish, because to thank everyone who has been a friend to me would take too much space, and nobody would read it. Besides, you know who you are and I hope you know I love you.

Alina! First and foremost, is the person who helped me most at the actual time of writing. It's impossible for me to express how important your many, many readings of this book were, for the voice, for authenticity, for emotional depth and for all the things that I might have missed otherwise.

To Brian Langan, at Storyline Literary Agency, Ireland, who took me under his wing, thanks for your unwavering decency, patience, and belief—even when things looked grim. And for your friendship. Thanks equally for the same to Ryan Harbage of the Fischer-Harbage Agency, New York, and for injecting new hope into the project at a crucial moment. Thanks to Emily Rapp Black for your positivity and every piece of buoyant support. To Niall Griffiths for your early encouragement—it took time, but the horse is run. Thanks to Niamh Campbell for helping me feel less alienated from the word *literature*.

Thanks to Paul Baggaley at Bloomsbury for being the first to take a leap of faith and for following through, and for your patience. Thanks to Charlotte Geig for your deep editorial insight, to Ian Critchley for your diligence, and Greg Heinimann for your vision. At Vintage Books I'd like to thank Edward Kastenmeier for letting this particular dream come true. Caitlin Landuyt, there isn't really a proper way to thank you for justifying my faith that the perfect reader for this strange book would be out there—somewhere. It's massive. Thanks also to Ella Sackville Adjei, Emma Luffingham, and Jake Lushington at World Productions for starting an exciting new journey together.

To Mark and Gary, thanks for keeping me right, and to everyone from the Town for moments of mental insight and messy nights together. Thanks particularly to Seán B. and Tiff, to Spud and Fahey, to Dom, to Annie, to Áine and Cow, to Willy, and to Charles, Andrew, and Seán McK. You all helped me somehow discover and rediscover the strange sense of place the book spins around. C'mon the Town.